MW00744710

The Painting

Enjoy

GEOFFREY R. TIGG

The Painting
Copyright ©2013 Geoffrey R Tigg

ISBN: 978-1-939288-13-4
Library of Congress Control Number: 2013936442

All rights reserved. Except for use in any review, the reproduction or utilization of this work in whole or in part in any form by an electronic, mechanical or other means, now known or hereafter invented, including xerography, photocopying, and recording, or in any information storage or retrieval system, is forbidden without the written permission of the author.

This is a work of fiction. Names, characters, places, and incidents are either the product of the author's imagination or are used fictionally, and any resemblance to actual persons, living or dead, business establishments, events, or locales is entirely coincidental.

A special thanks to my fine editor Karen Kibler whose dedicated work has been invaluable in the production of this book.

Published by Rushing Tide Media, Imprint of Wyatt-MacKenzie
Contact: grtigg@rushingtidemedia.com

Dedication

To my wife Diana and my daughter Danica for their support and encouragement.

A special thanks to Diane Stickney and Stephanie Kurenov.

Chapter One

The explosion of a forty-three-foot Bayliner interrupted the Canada Day celebrations of the Bowen Bay residents. It was July 1st and another spectacular summer day on the West Coast. The rising plume of white smoke funneled up like a nuclear cloud and marked the location of the burning yacht a kilometer or so from the westerly shoreline of Bowen Island.

People stood in horror, eyes glued to the tragic event that sent smoke swirling into the clear blue sky over the Strait of Georgia. Nothing like this had happened before. The curiosity gave way to concern, triggering screaming cell phone calls to the Coast Guard and local police. The ongoing image of the explosion aftermath imprinted itself in the minds of the onlooking residents.

Bowen Island is five kilometers west of the Horseshoe Bay ferry terminal, a twenty-minute drive west of Vancouver. The island offers a unique lifestyle, populated by artisans and business executives wanting both easy access to Vancouver and the serene charms of an island. Bowen Bay's residents live on the southwestern shoreline, on the opposite side of the small island from the bustling Snug Cove ferry terminal that connects the island to the mainland in less than twenty minutes.

No one knew what had happened, but the majority of the island residents heard about the explosion long before the Coast Guard arrived on scene. The yacht's burning fiberglass shell was partially submerged by the time the rescue team had arrived and there appeared to be no survivors. It was unknown how many had been aboard.

The explosion's white cloud had dissipated and was being swept away with the prevailing south-easterly breeze, erasing the evidence of the disaster. The stench of gasoline and charred fiberglass resin had impregnated the ocean air and the odor was strong as the Coast Guard vessel drew close to the listing hull of the yacht.

"We can't see any signs of the boaters! Send a salvage crew out here and tow the wreckage to Snug Cove so we can figure out what happened," a strapping tall young man instructed into the radio mike. "Have the guys note the registration number from the bow so we can check out the owner." The marine radio squawked its message to the base attendant on the mainland.

"We'll establish a search grid and begin combing the waters and shoreline. There must've been someone navigating this thing; it's over forty feet long and these luxury boats don't leave their berths on their own! It looks like a typical Canada Day party where the drinking got out of hand," the Coast Guard officer commented as he continued to peer through his field glasses searching for survivors.

They had been through this routine many times before and the crew knew drinking and boating didn't mix, often leading to avoidable accidents causing injury or death, like this one appeared to have done.

Within the hour the Coast Guard had found a body bobbing on the surface of the calm ocean; the body was being carried northward by the current up the Collingwood Channel. The corpse was badly mangled and severely burned by the explosion; only major parts of the torso, one arm and the head were recovered.

"Okay, let's see who we've got," the tall uniformed man muttered as he placed each of the three fingers of the hand onto his iPhone® and transmitted the fingerprints to the West Vancouver RCMP, the precinct responsible for Bowen Island and area.

The Coast Guard continued to search for additional victims until dusk. No one else was found.

♓

Kelly O'Brian had spent the last two Canada Day holidays visiting with her father. She always came to see him after his lunch on the days she visited. It was early afternoon when her gray Taurus turned into the parking lot at the *Westview Center* in Burnaby. The seniors' home specialized in caring for people with dementia and Alzheimer's. She had admitted her father two years prior when he was unable to care for himself and had become easily disoriented.

Kelly was a tall attractive twenty-eight-year-old Caucasian woman with shoulder-length brunette hair, a well-toned figure, high cheekbones and an alluring smile. When she was fifteen, her father's computer animation company *DigiCast Software* was bankrupted. His partner had been embezzling money from the company for more than two years and her father lost everything in the end. His wife Rosalyn had become accustomed to the high-end lifestyle of Kerrisdale, and following the disgraceful social fallout, had filed for divorce and moved back to Toronto.

Patrick O'Brian had been a good and well-intentioned man and was devastated when his employees lost their jobs and when he couldn't pay his bills. He was forced to withdraw Kelly from her Croften House private school and he agonized over her difficult teenage transition. She lost her friends; as a family they had to struggle to make ends meet, so they moved to Marpole and rented a small two-bedroom basement suite. She transferred to a public high school that was a half-hour bus ride away and learned the difficulties of being a teenager without money.

Kelly often wondered if her father's affliction was his mental attempt to escape and forget the tragic past or was just another cruel and unfortunate circumstance of life.

She sighed, put on a happy face and found her father sitting in a community room with others.

"Hey, Dad! How're ya doing today?" She approached the 59-year-old gray-haired man sitting watching the large flat-screen TV.

The man turned to see the visitor, but he didn't recognize his daughter.

She took a seat next to him on the sofa. "What are you watching?"

He smiled with an Irish twinkle in his eye at the tall slim brunette. "It's Canada Day and there's a parade on TV." His ingrained charm still carried through his voice.

Kelly just smiled as they both turned toward the television and watched the celebrations. She was just pleased to be able to spend some time with him. It made her feel better somehow.

After a short while, Kelly got out of her seat and kissed him on the forehead. "See ya later Dad, love ya!"

She walked to the front reception desk, eyeing the day nurse reviewing some charts. "How's my dad doing, Carman?" Kelly asked, knowing the answer.

"Good afternoon, Ms. O'Brian. He's doing well and hasn't been any problem. He gets on well with everyone here and he's a real charmer with the ladies. He's getting good care."

"That's great. I'll stop by again soon," Kelly said with a smile, turned and left the building.

Kelly found it difficult to not be able to carry on a conversation with her father and spend quality time with him. She remembered that he had always been there when she needed him, and she made sure that she was there for him now.

"I'll figure out what happened and get that bastard who robbed us of our happy lives!" she promised herself. It was time to restart her quest for the truth.

It was late afternoon when Kelly returned to her apartment in Kitsilano. She had moved into her one-bedroom Maple Street condo a few years ago and loved the energy of the singles scene in the English Bay area. Her place was one block from the beach front and she jogged the adjacent Hadden and Vanier Parks each morning to stay in shape.

She unlocked the door and was greeted by Hunter, who was wagging his tail and begging for a walk. He was a smart Australian Shepherd that had steely blue wolf-like eyes and a likable personality. Hunter had lived with her for six months.

He had belonged to Ricardo Sanchez, who was killed in a case that she and her partner Simon Chung had been involved in last December. She had known Ricardo and thought that it would be the right thing to look after his dog.

Hunter was being trained as a police dog and had completed half of the program. He loved his new companion Kelly, and loved the long walks along the downtown beaches and boardwalks that they took together each day.

Kelly changed into her casual summer light-weight gray jogging outfit, slipped on her Adidas runners and grabbed Hunter's leash. She stuffed some cash and a doggie bag into her pocket, locked the door and added the keys to her stash.

"Okay Hunter, let's see what Canada Day things are going on down here."

English Bay was busy with sailboats, surfboarders, Sea-Doos® and motor boaters taking advantage of the calm and warm Vancouver summer day. The beaches were cluttered with umbrellas, picnic chairs, coolers, and sun worshippers soaking up the sun and the party atmosphere. It was a typical family day as children and adults played in the sand and swam in the warm ocean. Dogs were not permitted on the beaches and waters of English Bay in the summer months so Kelly had to be content to walk Hunter at the fringe of the activity and, from a distance, watch the people having a good time.

She found a street-side café and decided to eat out, embrace the day and celebrate all that her native west coast Canada had to offer. Doing it in Vancouver was a bonus, at least to her.

She found that visiting her father gave her mixed emotions, as she wanted to see him, but really not the way that he was. The visits had become stressful; the time with Hunter helped her to relax and put her father's condition into the back of her mind.

"Come Hunter, let's go home. It's your dinner time and I'm not in the mood for celebrating anymore," she commanded as she changed her mind about dining out.

Kelly's apartment had comfortable furnishings and the painted yellow walls uplifted the room and were calming. Her kitchen was efficient and the white kitchen cabinets and stainless steel appliances brightened the room. She enjoyed making meals and spending time with Hunter. His companionship was calming and relaxing.

The young woman poured dog kibbles into the empty bowl and refreshed the dog's water.

"Here ya go, Hunter," she mumbled to the dog.

She reached into the kitchen cabinet and pulled a wine glass from the shelf. She poured a glass of white Okanagan Chardonnay. She only bought Canadian wines and believed supporting the local economy was the proper thing to do.

"Hey Hunter, I think I'm going to restart unraveling my mysterious past. I think it's time to find out who I am and what really happened to Dad."

When Kelly was very young she had overheard her mother talking to her father, in one of those fights that parents sometimes have. They had thought that she was asleep in bed, but the raised voices woke her and some of the conversation drifted up the stairs to her room.

"She's not my daughter. I wanted you to give me my own child," her mother's voice rang in Kelly's ears. Neither of her parents had ever told her that she was not their natural biological daughter and she never asked. The words haunted her and she had never been able to confront her father after her mother abandoned both of them following the divorce.

Kelly had been very cautious about having a relationship with anyone. Her father's experience showed her that no one could be trusted, even your closest partner. With her promotion to detective last December, she began to feel that her life was getting better and she had agreed to date Ricardo Sanchez. She had been attracted to the man and she thought they had similar goals and values, as he had been in the Royal Canadian Mounted Police like she was. She wanted the relationship with Ricardo but it turned out that he had used her for his own personal gain and the relationship had been a con all along.

She felt betrayed by Ricardo Sanchez and her distrust of people started all over again. Following the disastrous end of the relationship she couldn't find the strength to pursue her quest and her personal project remained untouched. She realized that it now was time to move on.

"Hmm … let's see, where was I with all this?" From a kitchen drawer, she grabbed a notebook where she had made notes and entries on her prior findings.

"Yes. I was working on finding that deceitful partner of Dad's who embezzled all the money!" she muttered to Hunter as she opened the notebook and sat at her dining room table. Hunter settled in, lying beneath the table, as Kelly spoke as though the dog understood the one-sided conversation.

♓

The *West Coast Casino and Suites* high-rise sat on the Coal Harbour shoreline. The hot new destination towered over Burrard Inlet, a short distance west from the Vancouver harbour and convention centre. It was a new glass-faced building at the foot of Jervis Street. It had a breathtaking view of Stanley Park and the Sea Bus travelling between Lonsdale Key in North Vancouver and the terminus by Gas Town.

It was the newest casino in Vancouver. Besides the casino and the gambling room full of slots and horserace betting, nine executive suites were available for the wealthy clients. The casino was packed and the exclusive restaurant and lounge expected a full house to watch the Canada Day fireworks planned for eleven that night.

Marcel Bessier was seated with five others playing poker. He was a regular patron from the time the casino opened and he could always be found at the poker table. His luck was spotty and he had racked up a sizable debt. Jako Palma, the executive partner of the casino, knew Marcel well and allowed Bessier's line of credit to grow. Palma owned other gambling operations in the lower mainland and it had been necessary to pressure Marcel to pay a substantial debt seven years before and Marcel had found a way to make the payment. Marcel had been able to stay within his casino limits since then, but Jako was becoming concerned again with the growing size of Marcel's casino debt. It was time to remind the West Vancouver lawyer that it was time to pay down some of his line.

Sandra Vaughn was one of the casino's high stakes poker dealers. Marcel Bessier always sat and played at Sandra's table, captivated by her alluring smile and inviting painted lips. She was a full-figured attractive six-foot-two tall redhead with a toned slim body and sensual tanned skin. She worked from five in the afternoon until closing at one in the morning. She took Wednesdays and Saturdays off, and she only ran the high stakes poker games. She knew every player by name. She knew some of the men players better than others.

The club was busy and very noisy and Sandra sat wearing a braless wrap-around blue short-skirted dress, long dangling diamond earrings and had her arm-length hair pulled back into an elegant pony tail. A small gold chain necklace dangled around her neck, supporting a large diamond that teased her open cleavage each time that she leaned over the table to dispense the cards to the players.

"Okay boys. Anti-up!" Sandra waited for the $1,000 burgundy chips to be tossed into the pot before she dispensed the cards, sliding them from the card tray.

She studied the players as the evening progressed and she had become very familiar with each player's expressions and body language as they each executed their individual strategies. The house didn't care which player won the game, as the casino took a share of each pot. Sandra didn't care which player won either, as she was only interested in the men.

Sandra was tapped on the shoulder as her hourly ten-minute break had arrived. Her replacement took the dealer's chair and continued the poker game.

Marcel watched as Sandra worked her way toward the woman's washroom at the back of the casino. "Excuse me. Deal me out of this hand. I'll be back shortly." Marcel vacated his place at the table, leaving his chips and scotch and headed for the washroom following the route Sandra had taken.

"Hi Sandra, good to see you tonight." Marcel spoke to her in a low voice as she exited the woman's washroom. "Are you available at your 11 o'clock break?" he asked with a grin, knowing that Sandra took an hour break at eleven each night.

She smiled as Marcel had asked her this question many times before. "Sure, your nickel Mr. Bessier!"

Marcel smiled back, "I've room E09 tonight. See you then," he said, still in a low voice, and then entered the men's washroom.

Sandra returned to her poker table and resumed her place.

Marcel was a large-boned stocky, average height, fifty-seven-year-old wealthy lawyer with black thinning hair and black-framed wire-rimmed glasses that wrapped around his round face. He lived an extravagant lifestyle and worked long hours at his practice. The poker game was one of his vices, and Sandra Vaughn was the other. He regularly requested one of the executive suites on evenings when his luck was running better than usual. He loved celebrating his success in the company of his favorite poker dealer. His successful card-playing nights were becoming less frequent and he knew he was getting further into debt with the casino, but tonight he was going to put all that aside and enjoy an hour in room E09 with Sandra.

Sandra had spent many an hourly break with Marcel and she restricted her attentions to the wealthy men who frequented the casino. The club paid minimum wage to the majority of the staff, as the tips and other opportunities substantially compensated for the poor base paycheck.

Jako Palma selected his girls very carefully as he understood that they were an important and key attraction for his business. His waterfront operation catered to many desires of the wealthy and the addition of the executive suites was just another specialty service that generated large cash flows. Jako didn't publically acknowledge the girls' activities, but did monitor the room-booking details. All the staff working the high end tables were given an hourly break each shift and the regular clients knew this policy.

The eleven o'clock break came faster than Marcel had expected. He was having a very good night and wasn't sure that he wanted to break his winning streak. He was almost forty-five thousand dollars ahead when Sandra's relief appeared.

"Okay guys, I'll take my hourly break now. My luck's with Sandra tonight and I want to wait until she returns. I'll be back at midnight." Marcel gathered his chips and slid them into a silver bucket. He got up and walked toward the cash window, sorted through the tokens, stuffed a few into his pocket and deposited the remainder into his account.

The high-speed elevator stopped on the eighteenth floor. All nine executive suites had panoramic views of the Vancouver harbour. The *Lions Gate Bridge* was lit up and could be seen over the Stanley Park cedar trees to the northwest. The night was clear and there was a perfect sky for the planned Canada Day fireworks display.

Marcel reached into his pocket and pulled out the key for room E09. He was glad that he had booked the room early, as there had been only two suites available for the eleven o'clock break period. Many rooms had been reserved for the entire night, but Marcel was satisfied with the hourly slot.

He entered the room, and placed three burgundy tokens on the dresser. He went to the mini-bar, grabbed two glasses, selected a bottle of Australian Cabernet and uncorked the bottle. He removed his shoes and placed them underneath a large sitting chair.

A soft knock on the door announced that his visitor had arrived and he rushed to open the door.

Sandra entered the room and gave Marcel a passionate kiss as he closed the door. He returned to the mini-bar and poured the wine into the two glasses. She eyed the three tokens, slipped them into her clutch purse, and joined Marcel at the bar.

The exploding sounds of the fireworks signaled the beginning of the light show celebration at Canada Place. Sandra strolled to the large hotel room window and watched the bright lights illuminate the sky and inlet. Marcel followed her, kissed her on the back of her neck and placed his wine glass on the side table by the window.

"Mmm … I've been thinking about you all day!" he whispered, beginning to slowly unzip her blue sleek dress and kissing her bare shoulder as he guided her dress zipper down to her buttocks. She placed her empty wine glass next to his on the table by the window and let her dress slide from her body and drop to the floor, as she continued to stare out the large glass window at the fireworks display.

"You have, eh?" She stepped out of her shoes and she freed her hair from its ponytail band and shook her head to untangle the strands. "Having a good night at the table tonight I see, huh?" Sandra asked provocatively, turned from the window and helped the man unbutton his short-sleeved shirt as he stared at her firm large bare breasts. "I'll help you with that!" She smiled and pulled off his shirt and pitched it across the room.

"The good night's just starting!" he said softly as he drew her closer, pressing her breasts into his hairy chest. "Oh, nice!" he muttered as ran his hands down her bare back and then kissed her passionately on her soft lips.

"Hmm … I noticed that you liked my dress tonight, eh Marcel?" she asked, her dark brown eyes studying his face as her hand found his pants button and zipper.

He moved back from her as he eyed her seductive figure, removed his trousers and placed them on the sitting chair. "Dress … I loved it!" Marcel replied; he turned to the king-sized bed and pulled the bedcover back, exposing the silk sheets underneath.

She came behind him, caressed his groin then ran her hands up his hairy chest and pressed her breasts against his back. "You were very generous tonight, Marcel!" She brought her face to the back of his neck and exhaled, her hot breath tantalizing his senses as she kissed his neck. "Mmm …." Sandra ran the tips of her painted fingernails slowly down his body, pulling Marcel's shorts down to the floor and following her hands with her tongue and hot lips.

"Slide that hot butt under those sheets, lover." She placed her hands on his thighs and lifted herself off her knees.

He turned toward her, sat on the bed, removed his socks and placed his excited body between the silk sheets.

"You won't need these!" she teased, taking his wire-rimmed glasses and placing them on the side table and then slipping her body alongside his. She caressed him under the sheet and she felt him slide his hand under her wet panties and begin to work his own magic, arousing her through her pubic hair. The foreplay increased their breathing and she allowed him to stimulate her without distraction as she encouraged his erection, knowing how he liked to be touched.

"Oh … Sandra … ah!" Marcel exclaimed, fondling her breast and teasing the nipple to stiffen.

"Ah ….!" she exclaimed as he slipped a few fingers inside of her, pushing the pubic hair aside. "Ah … okay … ah!" she sharply exhaled, pulled herself on top of the man, pulled aside her thong panties and inserted his penis. "Oh … ah!" she gasped as she lowered herself onto his thick organ.

The sexual encounter climaxed before the fireworks show had completed outside. Both sat in the bed finishing their wine and watching the light display light up the private waterside room.

"Wow, you're really pumped tonight, Marcel! Winning is a great aphrodisiac, huh," Sandra remarked with a grin as Marcel traced the dark skin that encircled her right breast nipple with his forefinger.

"It's just you, honey, it's just you. Winning at the table's just the bonus!"

"I've got to be back at the poker table in twenty." She slipped out of bed and Marcel watched her tight behind head for the shower. Sandra smiled at Marcel as she closed the glass shower door and Marcel got up from the bed and poured another glass of wine.

After showering, she finished dressing and left the room, leaving Marcel to dress by himself.

Marcel played poker and stared at Sandra until the casino closed at one. He broke even for the remainder of the night and was ahead for a change. He exited the building, waving to the parking attendant, indicating it was time to retrieve his vehicle. Valet service was complementary for the regular customers and the attendant knew exactly which vehicle belonged to the wealthy lawyer.

As Marcel waited for the valet to bring his ride, he was joined by another man. The husky large figure stood close to Marcel. "Hey Marcel. I bring a message from Jako!" The gruff whispering voice was cold.

Marcel turned and stared at the muscular blond-haired man. "A message?"

"Yea. It's time to settle down and bring your debt in line. You've one week to bring your loan below the one hundred K threshold as agreed when you got your line. My next visit will be less friendly, otherwise."

The candy-red BMW Z4 roadster appeared and the valet vacated the seat. "Nice ride, man!"

Marcel gave the valet a twenty, and pointed the car toward West Vancouver.

Chapter Two

The buzz was all over Bowen Island. The local newspaper's front page headline, "Boat Explosion Kills Local Man," was the talk of the day.

Elizabeth Richardson heard the customers talking about the boating tragedy as she restocked the shelves at the *Cocoa West Chocolate Boutique.* Elizabeth had been working for the chocolate company since it had opened seven years before and the owners made their own chocolate products on-site. They added two bed-and-breakfast overnight rooms a few years ago as the tourist popularity of Bowen Island demanded nightly accommodation; the boutique and B&B was only a fifteen-minute walk from the Snug Cove marina. It was a picturesque stroll during the summer and the B&B was within the walking range of most tourists.

The small town of Snug Cove was always alive with the comings and goings of cars and pedestrians taking the ferry to the mainland. The quaint destination had upgraded its historic landmarks and was the commerce center for the island. All goods and many services were supplied from the mainland and the ferry was the only link unless one had a private boat.

Elizabeth lived alone, and stayed mostly to herself. The news of the boating accident was a surprise to her since she didn't receive the local newspaper, and therefore could not have read the newspaper article while still at home. Her working day started at seven and she was the only employee other than the owners, who focused on making the chocolates and running the business. Elizabeth did everything else. The summer tourist activity left her exhausted by the time she finished at two in the afternoon.

She was a very attractive woman, now in her mid-forties, had jet-black curly hair and wide hazel eyes. She had retained her youthful figure, likely from all the physical work demanded by her job. Elizabeth was very appreciative of her employers, as they had offered her the work without references when she desperately needed a job. She had absolutely no knowledge of the chocolate business when she started but had quickly learned the intricacies of the small business.

That morning, Elizabeth took one of her few coffee breaks, sat in the small boutique café, and picked up a newspaper left by one of the customers.

Upon seeing the headline, her heart pounded and her eyes stared in shock as she discovered that Charles Whitford was the unfortunate victim of the Canada Day boating accident at Bowen Bay. Tears began to well up in her eyes and she rushed to the bathroom down the hall.

♓

Sandra Vaughn got out of bed early every morning. She lived less than ten blocks from the casino and was usually in bed before one thirty in the morning. Her West Georgia Street condo was exclusive and sat at the entrance to Devonian Harbour Park, a fifteen-minute walk to the Vancouver Rowing Club in Stanley Park.

She was an avid sailor and belonged to a number of rowing and sailing clubs in the city. Each morning she walked along the causeway to the rowing club and checked out her single-seat shell from her security locker. She could be seen pumping her way around Coal Harbour and rowing to Canada Place and back. The workout was better than any gym and she savored the outdoor sport and took every opportunity to enter any competitive rowing contest. Sculling improved her stamina and upper body strength, which she needed to race her Sabot sailboat in competitions at the Kitsilano Yacht club.

Wednesdays and Saturdays were Sabot sailing competitive days at the exclusive Kitsilano Club. The hours of the summer competitions conflicted with her casino job and she booked those days off so she could be ready to compete.

She was tired this morning, as the casino had been busy with regular patrons and Canada Day party goers. Her sexual encounter with Marcel Bessier had drained her as well. She disliked making money servicing men who didn't really attract her but that was the business she was in. Forsythe Harrison was something entirely different. He was hot, attractive, and they shared the love of sailing.

♓

Kelly O'Brian's sleep was shattered by her alarm. Hunter's ears perked up and his steely eyes watched her navigate into the bathroom. She quickly brushed her teeth, pulled on her summer jogging outfit, and laced up her sneakers.

Grabbing Hunter's leash and her door keys they both began their daily route around Hadden and Vanier Parks that skirted English Bay. It promised to be another banner Vancouver morning and the blue sky was void of any cloud. The easterly glow of the sun could be seen reflecting in the windows of the condos that were strung along Beach Avenue that faced her as she worked her way around the public parks. The jogging trip was Hunter's only exercise and it would not likely be repeated until Kelly returned from work, typically about twelve hours later.

The situation wasn't ideal. She had arranged for a walking service that could take Hunter out in the early afternoon, but she felt uneasy giving her key and apartment access to someone who she didn't know well. It was a compromise that she uneasily accepted for the moment.

Vancouverites love the outdoors and many were out early getting a start on their workday or favorite activity and could be seen making their rounds through the jogging trails. Her circuit around the parks and along the Burrard corridor was frequently interrupted with passersby wanting to visit with Hunter. He loved the attention and took every opportunity to visit.

Her morning routine had become cramped after her detective's promotion. Kelly's RCMP detachment office was in West Vancouver and she usually picked her partner up at the Burrard Street bus station. Today she was running late, as she had offered to pick him up at his place in Chinatown. She had to have her butt out the door before seven.

Kelly was an attractive woman, five-feet-eight and her shapely figure drew the attention of many men. The typical summer weather pattern had parked itself and the strong high-pressure conditions dictated cool outfits and short hair styles. It was too hot for long pants and Kelly chose a short cream skirt and cotton blouse. She put on a light cream short-sleeved shoulder jacket that concealed her service weapon placed in the back of her belt. She grabbed her sunglasses on the way out.

"See ya later, Hunter," she said, closing the condo door behind her.

Kelly had been partnered with Simon Chung since last November. He was a seasoned detective and was chosen by their Captain, Samuel Hollingsworth, to join the West Vancouver precinct when Kelly had been promoted to detective. She was promoted from within Hollingsworth's precinct as soon as she passed her detective program and was the first to be promoted from the officer ranks in Hollingsworth's precinct. She had been a rookie detective but a seasoned, competent, and tough street cop. Simon's job was to help her become a topnotch detective. Sam Hollingsworth knew she had the stuff that it took and Simon had the track record in building quality detectives. They made ideal partners.

Simon was the quiet one of the pair and was five-and-a-half feet tall, had a rounded face, black hair, and had a small goatee on his chin. He had been on the force for twenty years and was in his mid-forties. He was a second generation Canadian and his grandparents had immigrated to Vancouver because it was the second largest Chinese community in North America. They didn't want to be US citizens, so they came to Canada instead.

The stealth-gray Taurus SHO had stopped at 123 East Pender Street and Simon jumped into the passenger seat. "Great outfit, KO! Looks like you've dressed for a hot Vancouver summer day."

"I wouldn't want the guys thinking you were slumming!" she retorted and grinned as she pointed the unmarked RCMP car toward West Vancouver.

Kelly O'Brian was nicknamed "KO" by her friends and co-workers. It worked for her and it was less of a mouthful.

"I heard on the radio this morning that there was a yacht that exploded off Bowen Island yesterday. That's our jurisdiction. I wonder if we'll be given that investigation." Simon brought Kelly up to date with the latest news that he'd heard on the TV newscast that morning.

Kelly knew that Simon listened to the morning news every day and that he didn't have the distraction of a dog in the morning and she was happy to get her regular update from Simon during their ride to work each morning.

"Bowen Island's a nice place to go in the summer and the ferry ride's fun, too," Kelly replied, concentrating on the traffic that streamed over the *Lions Gate Bridge.*

The summer Vancouver traffic was lighter than usual and the drive to the precinct was quicker in the summer months. The two-story concrete RCMP building was on Marine Drive and the employees' parking lot was at the back of the building off Bellevue Avenue. The large steel door rose when Kelly activated the controller placed in the visor of the car that allowed her to park in a private space assigned to the detectives on the second floor.

The detectives' room looked like any open concept office workplace. Desks were placed in pairs and shared a small cubicle-type barrier that rose about a foot above the desk surfaces. The south wall was encased by a full bank of large windows that overlooked the Burrard Inlet and Ambleside Park to the east. Small thin metal blinds were installed to keep the bright glare of the late afternoon sunshine from overheating the room. The large Captain's office was at the end and placed in the corner sharing the south wall; the back of the office and the rear west wall was filled with filing and storage cabinets. Small interview rooms were placed on the north side of the room; their windows, facing Marine Drive, could be seen strung along the concrete wall at the back of each room. Each interview room housed a table and a pair of chairs, and had a door and a window facing into the centre of the workspace. The hard floor was designed for heavy traffic and a light gray speckled tile was placed throughout. Kelly and Simon sat at a pair of desks at the back of the room by the window.

"Hey you two, come into my office and take a seat!" Captain Hollingsworth called out as he saw the two exit the elevator on the second floor.

The fit and trim five-foot-six gentleman had reddish brown hair parted on the left side. He had narrow eyebrows, an oval-shaped head, fair skin, and had a well-groomed reddish mustache. He had a light-weight blue summer short-sleeved shirt and a tie, and looked up as the two detectives entered his office.

"I suspect that you've already heard about the boating accident off Bowen yesterday. The information file's on your desk, Detectives, and we received the victim's prints from the Coast Guard and identified the body as Charles Whitford. The press has his name already and it was front-page news in the local Bowen paper. See if this was an accident or homicide," he said glancing at the two standing by his office door.

"Hmm … the forty-three-foot Bayliner that exploded was registered to our vic." Simon thumbed through the thin file. "The registration has his address on Bowen. We don't have much else, so let's look and see what's out there. We've got the search warrant KO, so let's go."

The Bowen Island ferry ran every hour. The Horseshoe Bay ferry terminal serviced Bowen Island, central Vancouver Island, and Gibsons on the other side of Howe Sound. The ferry service was very busy in the summer and travelers often had to wait at least one sailing before being loaded onto the boat. It was late morning and the majority of the Bowen traffic was Vancouver-bound and there was no additional wait to cross to Snug Cove from the Vancouver side.

"We should grab something to eat before we head out to the Whitford place," Simon suggested. "The GPS shows the address is on the opposite side of the island," he told his partner as he punched in the Bowen Bay road address.

The pair spotted *Doc Morgan's Pub* and headed in that direction. The pub overlooked Snug Cove and patrons inside could see boaters tying up at the busy marina dock.

"You know, owning a forty-three-foot Bayliner's quite expensive. This guy must've had some bucks! He would've known how to run that thing, too, so I doubt this was an accident. No other bodies were found either, so we've some work to do." Kelly contemplated the facts.

They ordered a light lunch and enjoyed the surroundings while they watched the activity of the busy terminal. Bowen Island's not very large, and the detectives found the Whitford property on the west side of the island within a half-hour drive. The island was quiet, had a calm mood and it was surprising that the bustle of Vancouver was less than an hour away.

The Whitford home was secluded and a long driveway wound down the embankment servicing a large spread on the waterfront.

"See, I told ya this guy had bucks!" Kelly smiled and pointed to the estate ahead as the pair drove down the cobblestone drive.

A private dock was visible from the driveway. The home was a large rancher built into the bedrock hillside. The view was stunning in the early afternoon light and the rugged mountains on the northern mainland toward Gibsons could be seen running up the coast, contrasting with the calm sea water below.

"No wonder people love living here! The tranquility and spectacular views are breathtaking. Let's see what's inside," Kelly said as she exited the car.

"Hey, KO. There's been a B&E here; the front door's been forced open! I wonder what they were looking for," Simon commented before he pushed the door open.

The home looked like it was out of a magazine. It was clear that it was owned by a man and that it was very nautical in theme. A feminine touch wasn't evident, but the furnishings were sophisticated and tasteful. The house was tidy and not cluttered.

"I see no sign of a toss or anything, the intruder must've easily found what they wanted and split. Funny though, lots of expensive stuff's still here. The perp must've wanted something specific," Simon remarked, taking a quick look about.

Kelly entered the study. "Eh, Simon, come look in here!" she called out, holding a photograph of a man and boy standing by a boat. "I'd bet this is Whitford's son. I wonder where and who he is?"

The open room had a large wooden desk and executive leather chair pushed underneath. There were framed charts and photographs of old boats and fishing trips placed on the desktop.

"There're internet cables here and power bars. Hmm … no computer though! You know Simon, I bet the perp got the computer!"

"Yea, well, I suspect there's a safe in here somewhere, too. These wealthy guys always have cash and papers stuffed somewhere in their house," Simon remarked, looking at framed awards and documents on the walls. "Hey, this guy's a Canadian CA, his certificates and association memberships are on the wall. Look!"

They continued going through the house of the boating victim.

"Hmm … I don't see anything else here and if there's a safe I can't find it either, so let's check out the dock and see what's out there. Boaters likely leave some emergency keys and other things, just in case they lose their stuff overboard," Kelly said as she headed toward a pair of glass French doors that lead to an outside patio.

"Good thinking, KO. Let's see."

A small shack was at the end of the walkway by a private wooden dock; it was one of those shed kits that could be purchased from a lumber yard. Simon kicked in the locked door, fished about and found the light switch. The small shed was full of boating gear, spare red fuel containers, flares, life jackets, and garden tools.

"I got keys here in the fishing tackle box," Simon yelled out, grinning and holding a door key. "One of these looks like a spare boat key and the other a house key. Ah … nothing else though." He pulled the shed door closed and joined Kelly by the dock.

The two started back to the main house to close up and a young man appeared at the back door.

"Hold it right there!" Simon called out. "RCMP!" The two detectives ran toward the young man, who looked to be in his early twenties, and was about to enter through the open French doors. "Who are you?"

"I'm Tyler Whitford, but people just call me Ty. This is my dad's place. I heard on the radio that he was found dead after a boating accident. I came to check it out for myself," the man said, standing stiffly by the doors.

The young male was of medium build, had light brown dirty hair pulled back into a ponytail and had a pierced-steel nose ring and his jeans and t-shirt looked like they hadn't been washed in weeks.

"Okay, Tyler. We're sorry you found out that way, but we didn't know that Mr. Whitford had a son until we arrived today. Let's go inside," Simon said in a consoling tone.

The man in his late twenties nodded his head and the three entered the house and found a seat in the large family room. The young man stared at the floor. "I can't believe my father's dead. I feel so sad. Do you know what happened?"

"We're just trying to put the pieces together. You're father's boat has been taken to Vancouver and we've a team going through the remains now. They may be able to find the cause of the explosion if we're lucky." Simon spoke in a somber voice, watching the man facing the floor. "Where's your mother, Tyler?"

"Ah … Mom took off when I was twelve and I don't know where she went and I don't give a shit. I don't know much about what happened to make her leave. Dad said that she was a selfish bitch and had some drug habit or somethin'. She left when I was very young and I don't know much else."

Tyler looked up. "Do you think that bitch had something to do with all this?"

"We don't know, but that was a long time ago! Do you have anything that can help us find her?"

"I don't think so. Dad burned all her shit when she left. I would've done the same thing if a bitch like that fucked me around, suckin' me for cash to feed some fuckin' habit!" he growled.

"Tyler, do you know anyone who would want to hurt your dad? Business associates, girl friends, ya know!"

"No, I don't know very much about what he did and we didn't speak much. I rarely saw him. He was always alone when I was around and I never saw any women around here either. Dad always kept to himself but I know that he did some freelance finance stuff. He said he hated bosses and wanted to control his own life." Tyler sighed.

"Is there a safe in the house, Tyler?" Kelly asked, peering at the young man.

"Ah … I never saw one. Don't know. Dad preferred to pay cash for most things, but I haven't any idea where the cash stash may be. As I said, I was rarely here," Tyler replied looking out the window toward the dock.

"We didn't find a computer here either. Does he keep that equipment somewhere else?"

"It's always been on his desk." Tyler inhaled. "Look, are we done now? I'd like to spend some time by myself. This is very hard, ya know."

"Yes, of course. Where can we reach you, Tyler? We may need to talk to you some more," Kelly requested with a smile.

"Yea … uh … my cell's 604, 555, 7123."

"Thanks, Tyler. We'll let ourselves out." Kelly smiled and jotted down the number in a small black notebook.

Simon and Kelly returned to their car.

"Nice wheels!" Kelly noticed the new yellow Porsche in the driveway. "It looks like the kid seems to be doing okay for himself, eh Simon?"

"Yea. I wonder if he's telling us the entire story. I think he knows more than he is saying," Simon replied as he jumped into the passenger seat of the gray Taurus.

Kelly started the car. "My impression exactly!" she muttered as she backed out of the driveway and headed for the Snug Cove ferry terminal.

Chapter Three

Tyler heard the police car leave the property. He went into the washroom, took a pee and splashed water on his face. "Fuckin' cops! I'm not telling them anything. Dad must've stashed his stuff here somewhere. I just have to find it!" he said, looking at himself in the bathroom mirror.

Tyler came to Bowen to look for his father's papers and money. "I didn't think that the cops would get here before me. They didn't have anything, though, and that's good!" Tyler muttered; he really knew that there was a safe in the house, but he had never seen his dad access it, even when he pressed his father for some cash.

"Humph! Knowing dad, the stuff's likely in the bedroom or in the study. The study's the most likely place, so I'll start there." Thinking about his dad's habits, he returned to the study. "Hmm, the cops didn't find it, so it isn't that obvious, or is it?"

Tyler remembered that his father had often said that the obvious was often the most overlooked and that thieves and robbers usually looked for safes and physical hiding places behind books, pictures, or in desk drawers. He looked around and walked over to a large old sea chest sitting under the window. "Hmm!" He peered at the chest, moved the telescope straddling the box, pulled the chest forward away from the wall and lifted the heavy lid.

The smell was musty and it apparently hadn't been opened for some time. There was a woman's fancy black evening dress, black pump shoes and a small purse inside. Tyler stood puzzled. "This is weird. That old fart was up to something!"

Tyler pulled the stuff out of the chest, one article at a time. There was nothing else. He knew that the old sea chests were used by people immigrating to Canada years ago and the old travel chests had compartments, like this one did. These were empty, too.

"Shit," he growled, frustrated, and got up and went to the bar on the other side of the room. Tyler poured a brandy from a cut glass decanter and sat in the office chair behind the desk. "Hmm …." he muttered as he looked at the woman's things on the floor. He took a sip of the brandy and became curious as to what the clothing and woman's things were all about.

"Dad was a cagy old bugger!" Tyler mumbled, thinking about his past experiences with his dad.

Tyler placed the brandy glass on the desk, and returned to the open chest. He leaned over, grabbed the stiff hardboard sides of the compartment separators, and yanked upward. The entire compartment base easily pulled out, and Tyler placed it on the floor and looked inside.

He discovered what he'd been looking for. "Holy shit! Look at all this stuff!"

He found a package of cash. "Must be five grand in here!" Tyler exclaimed, checking the plastic wrap that encased the cash, then placed the package on the floor. Next he took out an old wooden box and removed the lid. A 9mm Glock handgun was placed inside with a dozen rounds. "Interesting place to keep this thing. I wonder what's so special about this gun and why it's hidden in here," he asked himself, then placed the lid back onto the box and put it next to the package of cash on the floor.

There was another zip plastic bag that was jammed with old photographs and papers. He pulled the bag from the chest, squatted on the floor and opened the bag. He briefly thumbed through the contents. "Old photos of Dad with some group of people dressed in office clothing, a couple of old faded newspaper articles and a birth certificate." He spread the stuff around him on the floor after looking at each item.

The photographs didn't have anything written on the back side, and Tyler only recognized his father in the photos. He picked up one of the news articles that had obviously been torn from a newspaper page. The article was a story about a scandalous failure of *DigiCast Software*, a prominent company owned by a Patrick O'Brian and Mark Rawlings. There were allegations that his father, Charles Whitford, and Mark Rawlings were involved in an embezzlement scheme, but the crown couldn't prove their case. The second article was about the murder of Mark Rawlings and how his body had been found on Galiano Island just after the *DigiCast* company had become bankrupt. The Rawlings' case detective was Arthur Fleming. Fleming had fingered a Terence Weiss for the murder of Rawlings and the news piece indicated that the trial for the accused man hadn't been set at the time the article had been printed.

"Humph!" he muttered, as he pulled a CD disk from the old chest that was unlabeled and had been inserted into a plain white paper CD cover. Tyler pulled the last plastic zipped bag from the chest and there were only a few items stuffed inside. The bag contained a driver's license for someone named Joy Bessier and some of her credit cards.

"Wow, Dad had lots of secrets, I see. I didn't know anything about this stuff! I wonder what all this has to do with Dad's death, if anything!" Tyler mused, as he collected all the papers spread around him and placed them back into their original zip plastic bags. He stopped and took a second look at the birth certificate. "I don't get this document. Why did Dad have this?" he wondered, as he carefully read the information. The date was March 19th, 1980. The certificate was for a Marriam Tremblay, daughter of Joy Tremblay and Mark Rawlings. "So what's this shit got to do with Dad?"

Tyler went into the kitchen, found a plastic shopping bag and stuffed in all of his findings from the chest. "I'll go through all this crap again at home and figure out what to do with it. I need a computer," he said, then replaced all the clothing, closed the trunk lid and returned the chest to its original place under the window.

"Time to split and think," Tyler thought, heading for the glass of brandy on the desk.

It was late in the afternoon by the time Tyler had reached his False Creek condo. The bright sun was streaming into his eighteenth floor living room and the air conditioning was having a struggle keeping the room temperature below twenty-one Celsius. The large glass windows faced north, overlooking the million-dollar view of the Vancouver downtown core and the mountains on the north shore.

Tyler dropped the bag full of his dad's stuff on the sofa, grabbed a beer from the refrigerator and checked his phone for messages. His Sony laptop had been left running, and he picked it up from the glass table by the sofa.

"I'll return those phone messages later," he promised. "I need to see what I can find out about Dad and that embezzling thing."

He opened the bag and spread out the contents on the glass table. He stacked the cash on top of the wooden box. "I'm sure I can use both of those things, no problem." He smiled to himself, pleased with his good fortune. Sorting through the bagged papers he found the one that contained the newspaper articles.

"Let's see," he muttered, running his finger down the column of the article about *DigiCast*, looking for the names that he had read earlier. "The article's about Dad and Rawlings, but Rawlings was murdered, so I can't find anything about the reported embezzled money there. Hmm."

He placed the news clippings aside and took a drink from the bottle of beer. He looked at the other things spread on the table. "What's the story on this Bessier woman and her license and credit cards? Strange that Dad would have those with all the other stuff. I'd better start with her stuff and see what I can find."

Tyler grabbed the running computer from the table, placed it on his lap and loaded Google®. He keyed "Joy Bessier," and pressed enter.

The Internet search produced pages of results, and a lengthy list of links appeared on the screen. Tyler scanned the results looking for things that could possibly be related to the mystery woman. "Ah, here we go!" He made a selection partly down the list. It was a Vancouver Sun newspaper article from 2001.

"**Wealthy West Vancouver woman assumed drowned**."

The article read: *The accomplished artist Joy Bessier, wife of a prominent West Vancouver lawyer, was assumed to have drowned off the western coast of Bowen Island yesterday. Her husband, Marcel Bessier, said that they were having an argument after they had returned from some friends' party. He said that she had been drinking heavily and during their heated argument had run off in their yacht that had been moored at their waterside estate dock. He further reported to the police that she had taken the Bayliner and didn't return.*

The following morning, the Coast Guard found the yacht adrift on the west side of Bowen Island by Bowen Bay. It was reported that no one was aboard, and it is assumed that Mrs. Bessier had fallen overboard and drowned. Her body has not been recovered.

Tyler pondered the story. "Funny she went missing in the area around Dad's place. He has her stuff and it's unlikely it washed up on shore, and there's the dress and shoes! Yea, I'd bet the fancy dress and stuff belonged to her." Tyler took another drink from the beer bottle and pondered the facts.

"If that woman knew Dad, and he stole the money from *DigiCast*, maybe she knew all about it! Hmm … partners or something, maybe." Tyler sat for a while, turning the story around in his mind.

"I wonder what the story is on the husband, Marcel Bessier. Things sound fishy to me, maybe he knew about the money and that was what they were fighting about. Dad's stolen money!"

Tyler keyed into Google® "Marcel Bessier," and pressed enter.

The standard Google® list of article links displayed on the screen; among them was:

"**Bessier Pilot House Motor Yacht for Sale**."

The advertisement read, *"Rare chance to own this exclusive luxury 45-foot 1989 Bayliner, only $169,900. For viewing appointments contact Fisherman's Cove Marine Sales, West Vancouver. (604) 555-boat."*

"I need to meet and talk to this guy," Tyler mumbled, reaching for the phone. He dialed the sales office.

"Fisherman's Cove Marine Sales. Can I help you?"

"Good evening. I'm looking for a Bayliner just like the Bessier Pilot House you've advertised. I've a pending business opportunity and I need that type of yacht. Can I see it today?"

"That's an exclusive listing, Sir. The owner wishes to attend all showings and outings with potential buyers. I'll need to call him to see if he's available later today. Is that okay with you, Sir?"

"Ah yea, sure. Please call when you know when Mr. Bessier can show his yacht. My cell number's 604, 555, 7123."

"Who shall I say the appointment is with, Sir?"

"Mr. Tyler Whitford."

"Thank you Mr. Whitford. I'll get back to you after I reach Mr. Bessier."

Tyler hung up the phone and smiled.

An hour later the cell phone rang. Tyler recognized the number and answered the call. "Good evening, Mr. Whitford here."

"It's Fisherman's Cove Marine Sales. Mr. Bessier can meet you tonight at eight. Will that work for you, Mr. Whitford?"

"That's perfect," Tyler replied with a grin.

"That's great, Mr. Whitford! See me at my sales office then, and you'll be able to view the yacht and meet Mr. Bessier. Thank you for your patience."

Tyler sat back into his sofa, thinking about the scheduled meeting that he had arranged with Marcel Bessier. "How am I going to play this? I've got to find out if he knows anything about Dad's money. Shit!" Tyler paused and looked over at the wooden box on the table. "I'd better take Dad's Glock with me, just for insurance."

He took the firearm from the box and loaded the six shells into the empty clip. "I don't need all these," he said as he took a deep breath and left the rest of the bullets in the box. He closed the lid, picked up his cell, ordered a pizza, and extracted another beer from the fridge.

"Hmm, I haven't looked at that CD yet!" He reached over the table, pulled the disk from the sleeve and inserted it into his computer. A list of files appeared on the monitor. "Cool. Let's see what these are all about!" he thought, took a drink from his beer can and selected the first file on the list.

"Please enter your password," flashed in the center of the screen with the curser in the password box.

"Damn! I should've known." Tyler closed the dialogue box and selected the next file. He received the same result, as he did with the rest of the files. "I'm not going to get anything from this shit today! I'll have to get this to Marcus tomorrow so he can crack this password thing. God damn it, I wonder what that'll cost me." Tyler extracted the disk and placed it back into the paper sleeve.

He waited for his pizza to arrive, staring out the window and watching the late afternoon melt away, thinking about his day and his scheduled meeting to find out what Bessier had to say.

♓

Marcel Bessier was still at his law office downtown. He felt good that he had an interested buyer for his Bayliner. He needed the cash to pay Jako, and Dobson wasn't going to cut him much slack for too much longer. He knew time was running out!

"If I can get, say one hundred and fifty grand for the boat, it'll be enough to get Dobson off my ass and restore my line with Jako," he thought, relieved that there might be a quick fix to his debt problem with the casino boss.

Marcel recalled the last run-in with Jako, seven years before. His wife's death, as tragic as it was, gave him the insurance money and also transferred her half of the house ownership to him. He'd promptly mortgaged that half and got enough cash to pay his debts and continue his extravagant lifestyle.

"I don't know what happened to that bitch, but her drowning was certainly a timely blessing!" Marcel mumbled to himself as he considered the unexpected event that had allowed him to pay off Jako Palma last time.

Marcel hadn't eaten yet and he had to change into his casual marine outfit before he met Mr. Whitford. He closed up his office and headed for his waterfront home, hoping for the best.

♓

Kelly O'Brian shook her head as she hung up the telephone. She had just finished talking to the forensics detective who had completed his investigation on the destroyed Bayliner that exploded on Canada Day across from Bowen Bay.

"Simon, the boys found an explosive timer in the burned wreckage of the Whitford Bayliner. That explosion was no accident and we've a homicide, no question!" She paused, took a deep breath and then continued, "With the size of the explosion and the fire, there was nothing else left that the boys could tell us. Not much to go on, I'm afraid!"

Simon scratched his head. "We'd better check into this Tyler Whitford joker in the morning then. I got this vibe about that guy. Let's go home."

Chapter Four

"Look you stupid prick; I needed you to find out where that Charles Whitford diverted those funds! My forensic accountant told me that Whitford had stripped more money than I thought. He hadn't accounted for numerous donations and there appears to be expenses that can't be substantiated." Raj Jattan was furious and Lothar Zoric got the message through the phone loud and clear. "I paid that bastard big bucks for years, and he pays me back by ripping me off!"

"Boss, I got you his computer like you asked," Lothar tried to explain respectfully. "I didn't know there were passwords. You know I don't do computers!" The young man spoke on his cell while lying with his feet up on his sofa.

"Well everyone knows about computers these days! Shit man, you blow this guy up and I'm no further ahead in finding the missing cash!" Raj took a breath and then continued yelling angrily into his BlackBerry® cell phone. "You'd better go back to his place and pray you can find something that'll fix this mess. That asshole screwed me out of three-quarters of a mil; I'll take it out of your hide if you come up empty. Get your ass in gear!"

"Yea, okay. On it, Boss."

♓

Tyler Whitford pulled his yellow Porsche into a "members only" parking space at the *Fisherman's Cove Marina.* He wasn't a member, but they had the best parking. "No one gets twisted about parking this time of night anyway!" he justified his breach of courtesy to himself.

The sun had gone down behind the mountains and the parking lot and marina were now in shadow. The marina served the *West Vancouver Yacht Club* and many wealthy marine enthusiasts who paid hefty fees for moorage at the prestigious location. It was the largest and best of its type in West Vancouver, situated a short distance south of the Horseshoe Bay ferry terminal.

Tyler walked to the front of the marina and found the sales office.

"Good evening, I'm Tyler Whitford and I'm here to view the Bessier yacht. I believe that you've made an appointment for me at eight."

"Ah yes, Mr. Whitford. I'm pleased that you're interested in one of our best buys of the season. Mr. Bessier's waiting for you, but you need to complete some paperwork before I can grant you access to the marina." The young man in the sales office passed Tyler a sales form that had already been partially completed.

"What's this paperwork all about?" Tyler asked as he grabbed the document from the counter.

"We need to register all viewings of boats we've for sale. The completed and signed document also covers our liability should you have any injury during your visit or if you damage the boat during any test outing. It's a requirement of our sales office and insurance company. Is that all right with you, Mr. Whitford?"

"Humph! Insurance seems to be in everyone's face these days," Tyler grumbled as he completed the form, which included his home address and contact phone number. He signed and dated the bottom of the document and slid it back over the counter to the young man.

"Thank you, Mr. Whitford. I'm required to wait here until you've completed your visit with Mr. Bessier and your inspection of the vessel. I'll see you later." The salesman pointed toward the door. "I'll open the security gate for you. Come with me, please."

The salesman unlocked the chain link gate. "Proceed down this ramp; turn right and go to the far end of the dock. You'll find Mr. Bessier in the boathouse second from the end."

Tyler smiled and proceeded toward the boathouses lined together on the far dock. The tide was out and the ramp from the wire security gate to the boat dock was very steep. Tyler walked carefully down the metal aluminum walkway grid, holding onto the handrail ensuring that he didn't lose his footing.

He came to the metal-clad boathouse and opened the small man-door. The stern of the boat faced the doorway and the name *Four Aces* was printed in bold black letters on the shiny white hull. "Mr. Bessier, its Tyler Whitford. Are you in here?" he called out, standing on the wooden dock.

"I'm in the galley! I'll be there in a moment," Marcel yelled from within the cabin.

A stocky round-faced man appeared on the rear deck of the yacht. "Yes, I'm Marcel Bessier. Sorry for the late appointment. I worked late at the office today, and I wanted to change before I came down here," he said peering though his wire-rimmed glasses at Tyler.

"I appreciate you seeing me on such a short notice. I'm Tyler Whitford." The young man climbed aboard the boat and shook the outreached hand.

"Hmm … you look a bit young to be able to afford a boat like this, Mr. Whitford," Marcel commented with concern.

"Ah … no problem. Don't let my looks fool ya. You can check out my yellow Porsche in the parking lot if you wish," Tyler grinned. "I'm prepared to pay cash if I like your boat, Mr. Bessier."

"Well then, I'm sure that you'll love this beautiful boat. There were only about three hundred and fifty of these produced and it's recognized as one of the best big-boat buys in the industry. Shall I give you a tour?"

"Great! The boat looks like it's in wonderful shape for its age. How long have you owned it?"

"Well, I think it's been about ten years or so, I'd say. The marina here has done all the maintenance. They likely have all the records if you need to see them."

"It's fully outfitted and it has three staterooms, two heads, a shower and a tub. I use the third stateroom for my office. The technology today makes living or working from this type of boat very easy."

"Can we take her out for a little spin? I'd like to see how she handles. My dad had a forty-three-footer, but every boat has its own personality."

"You're right about that! Why don't we go around Passage Island southwest from here? It's not very far but the short trip should provide you a feel as to how she handles. I'll get her started and you cast off the lines," Bessier instructed.

The inboard 220 horsepower engine's throaty sound echoed in the shell of the boathouse. The cruiser's full service galley and salon lights had been turned on and Marcel guided the yacht through the northern small marina channel that protected the marina, passing Eagle Island. The summer evening was turning dark and the lighthouse at Point Atkinson appeared as a large beacon, announcing the entrance to Burrard Inlet. The ocean was calm and void of any running lights of other craft as Bessier navigated the boat from the marina.

The electronics in the pilothouse cast a blue glow and dimly lit the face of Marcel at the helm. The Garmin GPS showed the vessel's position but Marcel knew the waters well and the navigation markers were all he needed, as he pointed the bow past the Horseshoe Bay harbour limit.

Marcel gave a full description of the technical details of the Pilot House Bayliner as the yacht plowed a wake toward Passage Island, now barely visible in the darkness.

"I assume you know how to handle one of these things at night. Am I right, Mr. Whitford?" Marcel asked, concerned with his decision to take the test trip so late in the day.

"You bet!" Tyler replied confidently, even though it had been quite some time since he had skippered his dad's boat.

The helm was handed over to Tyler and Marcel pointed out the controls and electronic hardware. They were the only boat in sight. It was dark. The Vancouver shore lights twinkled and the lights of a couple of anchored freighters in the Inlet could be seen off in the distance.

The GPS indicated that Passage Island was just off their port bow and that it would be time to alter the course southward along the backside of the island and begin the trip back to the marina.

Tyler pulled the engine throttle back. "This boat handles like a dream. Let's talk."

"Okay, good idea," Bessier replied. "The list price of the boat includes the boathouse and mooring that is paid until September. As you know I'm asking one hundred sixty-nine, nine. It's a good deal and I've to pay a commission out of that."

"Well, it does come down to the money in the end, doesn't it, Mr. Bessier?" Tyler paused, looking directly into Marcel's eyes. "I wanted to ask you about what you know about my dad's money! He was the man killed in the boat explosion on the weekend around Bowen Bay. I believe that my father and your wife knew each other."

"I don't know anything about your dad's money, and don't know about my wife's connection to him either, if there was one. None of that has anything to do with me!" Marcel's voice became angry. "Besides, she drowned over seven years ago."

"Yea, well, I'm not so sure about that and I wouldn't bet on it either. I went through some of Dad's stuff earlier today and I found a number of interesting things. One, there seems to be a large stash of money somewhere and two, I think your wife knew where it was!" Tyler peered at Bessier with a determined look.

"You're crazy! What money are you talking about? I think we need to return to the marina!" Marcel pushed Tyler away from the helm and pushed the throttle forward to full speed. The yacht lurched ahead, knocking Tyler off balance. He fell away and struck the back wall of the small cabin. Marcel yanked the steering wheel sharply to port noticing that Passage Island had passed behind the boat and there was a clear route back to Eagle Island and the marina.

Tyler pulled the Glock handgun from his windbreaker as he struggled to regain his balance. "Cut the power!" he yelled and pointed the muzzle directly at Marcel's head.

The boat lurched in the backwash and then drifted in the open channel. Tyler got to his feet.

"Look, I found all the papers my dad had hidden regarding an embezzlement scheme fifteen years ago. I figure that he must've been involved and somehow your wife was connected. Anyway, I figure she must've told you something or you've got something that can lead to the money," Tyler sneered in a raised voice.

"How do you figure my wife was connected?" Marcel asked, confused with the story.

"I found her driver's license and credit cards in the stash of papers at my dad's place. I also found a fancy dress and shoes that I think must've been hers, too." Tyler's heart was pounding and he yelled, "Tell me what you know about your wife and my father!"

Marcel lunged at Tyler, knocking the engine throttle full ahead as he grabbed Tyler's hand holding the pistol. They both hit the floor and struggled, squirming on the wooden deck of the yacht. Tyler punched the stocky man in the face, knocking Marcel's glasses off his face, but both men's hands remained locked onto the gun.

Bang! A shot rang out, shattering a side window. Tyler pounded the older heavier man again and hit Marcel's ear, shifting the big man's weight. *Bang!* A second round fired and the bullet whizzed past Tyler's head and struck the roof of the Pilot House cabin.

Tyler rolled on top of Marcel, eyes glaring and neither man had control of the firearm. Marcel, who was the stronger man, pushed the gun into Tyler's face and the barrel hit Tyler's cheek. *Bang!* The gun exploded again and the third bullet pierced Tyler's eye, exited out the back of his skull, lodging into the captain's leather seat. The blood pool ran down Marcel's shirt and the blood splatter had projected onto the front window and navigation instruments.

Marcel pushed Tyler's body aside and struggled to his feet; his ears were ringing with the three close range shots as the yacht was moving at fifteen knots directly toward a flashing red beacon. Marcel reached the helm, squinted his eyes so he could focus better, and turned the wheel sharply starboard. The wide beam of the boat listed and the bow swung sharply toward Atkinson Point. The bright concentrated beam of the lighthouse momentarily illuminated the speeding yacht in the blackness of the night, and then moved away.

Marcel's heart pounded as the panicking sailor regained control of the speeding hull. He pulled the power levers back and the Bayliner bobbed in the backwash of its rushing wake. "Where the hell are my glasses?" he screamed out, squinting his eyes as he searched the floor of the cabin.

His brain raced as it tried to process what had happened and Marcel turned on the cabin light to get a better look at the situation. "There!" he growled and stepped over Tyler's body to grasp his wire-rimmed glasses and then put them in place.

The cabin was covered in blood and the dead young man's face was burned and shredded by the passing 9mm bullet. The Glock lay on the floor and Marcel could hear the rolling shells on the floor as the boat continued to slowly roll on the surface of the calm sea.

"I need time to think!" Marcel looked about. He was alone. The lighthouse flash reminded him that his yacht was visible every sixty seconds. He pushed the throttle forward to half speed and headed for the backside of Passage Island.

Marcel turned on the autopilot, reduced the yacht's speed and took a deep breath. He looked at the young man. "Christ, I'd better call the cops. This was self-defense! Better not touch the gun either!" He turned to the VHF radio. His hands were shaking as he reached for the microphone.

"Mayday, mayday, this is the yacht *Four Aces.* Come in please, over." A crackle came over the intercom as Marcel waited for a response.

"Yes *Four Aces*, what's your emergency, over?"

"I've been attacked by a man and I shot him. He's dead, over."

"Are you all right sir, over?"

"Yes. I'm okay. I'm just off Passage Island and am returning to Fisherman's Cove, over."

"Roger that, *Four Aces*. To whom am I speaking, over?"

"Marcel Bessier. I'm the owner of the *Four Aces*, over."

"I'll arrange for the RCMP to meet you when you arrive at the marina, over."

"Thank you, over and out!"

Marcel decided that he shouldn't be in a hurry to return to the marina and that he needed to get his thoughts together before talking to the police. He took a deep breath to calm himself, then looked about the cabin. "What a mess. I can't sell this thing like this. It'll take longer to get Jako his money now. Damn son of a bitch!"

His attention turned to the conversation with Tyler. "Interesting story that kid was telling," he mused. "I wonder if I can figure out the secret of the missing cash he was fussing about. Hmm … and then what's that bullshit about Joy?" Marcel asked himself as he glanced at his course, and then back to the dead young man.

Marcel noticed Tyler's back pocket bulging with a partially exposed wallet. "I'll take a look at that, and then throw it on the floor. The cops'll think it came out during the struggle," he planned, reaching and pulling the wallet free.

Thumbing through, he extracted all the cash, except for one twenty and stuffed the bills into his own wallet. "He won't need that!" Marcel exclaimed out loud as he pulled the driver's license out and peered at the name and address. "Tyler said that he had his dad's papers and some stuff about Joy! They must be at his place at this Moberly Road address. I'd better get to those before the cops and see what he was yakking about." Marcel turned his attention to his course again as the lighthouse flashed through the cabin again.

"I'll have to take his keys to get into the condo. That'll be a problem for the cops though, when they can't find this kid's keys on the body! Damn. Hmm," Marcel mumbled as he realized that the autopilot was still taking the boat northwesterly and Passage Island was showing on the radar. "If

I were to dump the body overboard on the backside of the island, the missing keys wouldn't be a problem." He turned the option around in his head. "Nope, the large blood pool in here and his shot-out face would generate questions for sure! Huh … I could take his keys and say they likely fell out of his windbreaker during the struggle." He took a deep breath and sighed. "I'll have to take them and figure out some story later." Marcel pitched the wallet onto the floor. "One step at a time, and if I keep my head straight I'll be okay."

He turned off the autopilot, headed for Fisherman's Cove, and got himself ready to face the police on his arrival.

♓

The flashing lights of a RCMP squad car and another vehicle could be seen as Marcel navigated the yacht through the small channel toward his boathouse. The marina salesman had opened the gate for a pair of uniformed officers and a pair of detectives, and had told them how to find the Bessier boathouse. The Tyler Whitford visit was longer than the young salesman had expected and he realized that the RCMP visit had something to do with the late arrival of the yacht.

Kelly O'Brian was curled up on her sofa watching TV. A glass of red wine was on the side table and Hunter was sprawled out at her feet. The phone interrupted the commercial on the screen.

"Hey, KO. I just got a call from Burrows. He and Jensen were called to a homicide at Fisherman's Cove. They say a Marcel Bessier shot a kid in self-defense. The kid's name was Tyler Whitford, and they thought that the case might be connected to our open Charles Whitford case. You want to check it out?"

"Man, that's bazaar, you bet Simon! Call Burrows and tell him that we're coming and that we'll handle the file. I'll get ya in fifteen."

John Burrows placed his cell phone in his pocket. "Hey Frank, KO and Simon agree that the coincidence of two Whitford people being killed the same week is strange. They're on their way, so we should secure the scene and wait for them."

The two uniformed officers and the detectives watched as the Bayliner was backed into the covered boathouse slip. Marcel, still covered in blood, jumped from the boat and secured the lines.

"Mr. Bessier, we're Detectives Burrows and Jensen from the West Vancouver precinct and we'll take your initial statement. The assigned detectives for your case will be here shortly but we need to board and view the scene right now if we can," Detective Jensen explained as Marcel finished mooring the large boat.

"Yes, I called you. It was self-defense!" Marcel blurted out nervously as he and the two detectives climbed aboard the yacht.

Burrows spotted the galley and salon. "Could you please sit over there? It looks like a comfortable place to talk." He pointed to a sofa and stood as Marcel took a seat. "We were told by the young marine salesman that you were out showing the boat to a potential buyer, a Mr. Tyler Whitford."

"Yes, that's correct. He said that he was interested in buying the boat and wanted to take it out for a short test run. He pulled a gun on me and asked me to hand over any cash and demanded that I take him to my house and give him any cash that he thought I had there! I really don't think he wanted to purchase this yacht. The sales thing must have been a scam or something," Marcel rambled.

"What would ever make this Tyler Whitford believe that there was enough cash on this boat and in your house to risk demanding it using a gun?" Detective Jensen asked taking notes. "Sounds very strange to me, eh Mr. Bessier?"

"I've no damn idea. He must've found out my address and decided that I had lots of money, I guess. I've a house down here on the waterfront and maybe he scoped me out earlier."

"Okay. Where's the body?"

"It's up in the Pilot House; up those stairs."

Detective Burrows entered the cabin and took a quick look at the scene. "Okay. We need to wait for Detectives O'Brian and Chung to join us. They're expected shortly."

"Okay detective. That sales kid doesn't need to stay around, does he?" Marcel asked, knowing the young man must still be waiting to close the sales call. "Someone should let him go home and later I'll thank him for waiting around here."

"Eh Frank, go see that kid up top, get his statement and let him go home."

"Can I go and clean up now? All this blood's stressing me out," Marcel asked looking exhausted.

"Sorry Mr. Bessier, you need to wait for the other detectives and our forensics team. They'll want to take photos and document you as you are, I'm afraid," Detective Burrows replied, studying the man.

"Can I get a scotch then?" Marcel asked looking frustrated.

"I think we need a blood sample to check alcohol and all that medical stuff first. It won't be long. Hang tight."

The medical examiner and the forensics team appeared at the stern of the yacht.

"Hey boys, I hear we've a customer in here."

"Yup, come in. He's up front in the nav cabin," Burrows replied.

The forensics team unloaded their gear on the rear deck of the luxury boat and started taking photos and documentation of the crime scene. Once completed, the ME was able to begin his examination of Tyler Whitford. "The cause of death is obvious looking at the damage caused by the bullet to the head," the examiner remarked as he knelt down to take a closer look at the victim. "Mr. Bessier, we'll need to seize your boat pending a thorough study of this event. Please provide keys to the yacht and we'll advise you when you can regain access to the boat."

Marcel started to comment when he was interrupted by a voice from the dock.

"It's Detectives O'Brian and Chung. Can we come aboard?" Simon called out, watching CSI Richard Sommers place some gear in the back deck of the yacht.

"It's about time you guys! The forensics team has taken their photos and gathered what evidence they need at this point. The crime scene's yours." John Burrows flashed a big smile at Kelly. "Enjoy your night!" he smiled as he and his partner climbed off the boat.

"Good evening, we're detectives O'Brian and Chung. We'll be working this case." Kelly handed Marcel her card.

"Yes, I'm Marcel Bessier, and I was attacked by Tyler Whitford, and I have already told the other detective here!" he said, annoyed to repeat the story again.

The pair of detectives looked at the blood-covered man sitting inside the boat. "I see that our team's finishing up here." Kelly watched the forensics team prepare to leave. "Hey Sommers, ya got everything ya need?"

"Hey KO … nice night to be out, eh? We're going to take custody of this boat for a few days and I've processed Mr. Bessier, too. I didn't find any keys on the vic and couldn't find them in the cabin either so I'll take another look in the morning. I'll advise ya what we find," he replied, and grinned as he prepared to leave the yacht.

"You can wash yourself up," Detective O'Brian advised, as she turned to face Marcel who was still sitting on the sofa in the back lounge.

"Great. The guys have taken my blood sample as well. Can I get a scotch now?" Marcel glared, looking for something to calm his attitude.

"Sure. We'll take a seat here," Simon replied. He sat down as Marcel quickly got up from his seat.

Marcel opened the liqueur cabinet, poured a stiff scotch and took the drink into the yacht's toilet. The head was the only place for Marcel to get some time away from all the questions; he took a long drink of his scotch and looked at himself in the mirror. He took a deep breath, placed the glass of scotch on the lid of the toilet and began to wash his face.

Simon took the opportunity to take a quick peek at the crime scene. The coroner was still completing his report, talking into a cell phone, recording his findings.

The Glock and three bullet casings had been collected, documented, and placed into a plastic zip-lock bag that lay on the floor. "Looks like the weapon, detective," the coroner said, seeing Simon from the corner of his eye. "It was found on the floor a few feet from the victim and some slugs are still in the cabin. There were three shots and we've three casings. The forensic guys will extract the two slugs from the boat in the morning."

Marcel exited the head and poured another scotch.

"Mr. Bessier, I hear that we're going to impound your boat until we've completed processing all the evidence. So tell us what happened here," Kelly said as she pulled a notepad from her pocket.

"As I told the other detectives, that young kid pretended that he was interested in purchasing this boat and he wanted to take an evaluation trip around Passage Island. Once we started to return, he pulled a gun and demanded money. I said I didn't have much cash on the boat. He told me that there must be a lot at my house and to head for there."

"Your house! How was that to work?"

"He must've looked me up on the Internet or something, as he knew I live a very short distance from here on the waterfront. I'll bet he even went to my place. Anyway, I grabbed the gun and we fell on the floor struggling. The gun went off a couple of times and he got hit. You can see the rest! I called right away." Marcel's heart began to race as he recalled the event.

"Anything else?"

"No. Can I go now? This has been quite an ordeal and I'm tired of telling this story!" Marcel asked looking toward the floor. "He tried to kill me and I shot him, the little bastard. That's it!"

"Yes, of course. We'll call you if we need to talk some more. The lab will call when you can pick up your boat keys."

While giving the instructions, Simon watched the man's body language.

Marcel put his empty scotch glass onto the bar and turned to leave, "By the way, this kid was mumbling something about his dad was the man in the boat explosion on Canada Day and that was why he needed a boat right away. I don't really get the connection!"

"Thank you Mr. Bessier, we'll look into that possibility. They both had the same last name but we aren't sure yet either if there's a connection. Good night, Sir." And with that, Kelly put her note pad away.

"Things look like they're buttoned up for tonight, why don't we go back home, eh Kelly?" Simon suggested as he watched Marcel climb off the yacht. "You know, I didn't want to say anything in front of Mr. Bessier, but Tyler Whitford is the young man we met this morning at the Charles Whitford place at Bowen Bay!"

"Yea I know! The question here is, what's the connection between Whitford and Bessier? This certainly wasn't a random attempt at a robbery!" Kelly remarked. "Maybe Bessier was involved in Charles Whitford's death and Tyler came after Bessier!"

Marcel had no intention of going home when he climbed off the stern of his yacht. He jumped into his BMW roadster and headed for False Creek. "This kid must have information on the stash of money he talked about. Likely his dad was killed for it, too; if I can find it, that stash might get me out of my jam with Palma!"

It was almost midnight by the time Marcel reached Moberly Road. Most lights were out in the high-rise and no one noticed Marcel enter the building.

The 18th floor condo was certainly exclusive. "This is quite something for a young guy like Tyler Whitford! He certainly must've been up to no good himself, I'll bet!" Marcel thought. With a last glance around, he opened the door with Tyler's key.

The apartment was well furnished and there were framed posters of expensive cars on the walls. The living room table was just as Tyler had left it. The cash placed by the empty revolver box was scooped up and stuffed into Marcel's pocket. "Wow, a windfall of cash. What a bonus." Marcel noticed a CD envelope and number of plastic bags containing papers and documents. He gathered everything together and put them into a plastic shopping bag lying at the end of the sofa.

Marcel eyed the computer by the table. "I'd better leave that. I don't want the cops to suspect that someone's been in here." He took a quick look around the bedroom to see if he could find any more cash. Satisfied with his discovery, he left the condo and locked the door.

♓

Sandra was glad that her shift was finished. One of her regular clients had booked a room for the remainder of the night. She felt better about having sex with a man when it didn't have to be concluded in an hour and she would be able to romanticize the experience because she knew that she didn't have to watch the time. The extra cash didn't hurt either!

She knocked on E07. The door opened. "Good evening, Sandra. Come on in. I've the wine chilled."

Sandra smiled, "Hi Harry. I've been looking forward to being with you all night!"

Chapter Five

"Good morning you two, I understand that Burrows and Jensen called you out to the homicide at Fisherman's Cove last night." Captain Hollingsworth's English accent usually had a cheerful tone, and this morning was no different. He stood by the detectives' desks, looking down at the pair as he stood there.

"Morning, Cap. Yea, Burrows recognized the last name of the marina victim and thought that it was unusual to have two different homicides with the same last name; Whitford isn't that common of a last name. He was right and our vic last night, a Tyler Whitford, was the son of Charles Whitford. We met Tyler yesterday morning at Charles' house on Bowen," Kelly said, looking up at her boss. "We believe that there's some connection between the two Whitford deaths and Bessier."

"Okay then, give me a briefing later today. I'm sure the press will be all over this one when they find out the name of the dead victim and I'll need some answers." Hollingsworth turned to head back toward his office, with the words drifting over his shoulder.

"You know, Bessier's a prominent high-end and wealthy lawyer in West Van," Simon said, as he was going through the notes he had taken the night before. "I'll bet that the press will have this story out before breakfast."

"Yea, well, Bessier's story seems a little off to me. Why would Tyler Whitford go to all the trouble to lure Marcel Bessier out on that yacht just to get into Bessier's house? Bessier's hiding something!" Kelly was replaying the facts in her head.

"Well, I think Bessier definitely left something out in his story. Let's start with the victim and see what we've got on Tyler Whitford." Simon pulled the computer keyboard forward and keyed his inquiry into the RCMP database. "Ah … here we go. Tyler has a rap sheet, what a surprise! This guy likes jacking expensive cars. We've arrested him at a high-end chop shop once and have booked him twice on boosting expensive wheels within the last 12 months. We've nothing on robbery or extortion, so he must've been up to something else on the Bessier yacht."

"We need to get a warrant to enter Tyler Whitford's apartment and see what's there. The lab boys in Vancouver should've pulled the slugs from the boat and the body by now, too."

"Okay, let's get downtown and check on the ballistics results and pick up our crime scene photos from Richard Sommers."

♓

Marcel Bessier didn't sleep at all after he had returned from Tyler Whitford's apartment. The thoughts of his struggle, the piercing sound of the gun shots, combined with the realization that he could've been killed, haunted him and dominated his consciousness. He worried about Peter Dobson and knew there was little time to find the one hundred and fifty grand that he owed Jako Palma.

Another perfect summer morning was forming over Vancouver. The sky was clear and Marcel sat drinking his coffee, staring out over his dock at Passage Island in the distance. His home was the envy of his friends and he recalled how close he'd come to losing it all seven years before. "I'm not going to have that happen again! I got lucky then, and I'm going to get lucky now!" he thought.

He got out of his easy chair and wandered into the spacious living area that sat behind large glass picture windows showing the sprawling secluded waterfront landscape. The shopping bag that had been taken the night before from Tyler Whitford's apartment lay on a glass side table. Marcel placed his unfinished coffee on the table, sat in a cream-colored leather sofa and picked up the plastic bag.

"The clue to the money that kid talked about must be in here somewhere!" he muttered as he began thumbing though the contents of the bag. "Hmm!" he mused as he read through the news clippings that confirmed the young man's story of the embezzlement and the murder of Mark Rawlings, who was one of the men suspected in the theft of funds from *DigiCast Software*.

He grabbed the birth certificate and peered at the names imprinted on the paper.

"Hmm … Rawlings and Tremblay. That's interesting. Tremblay was Joy's maiden name!" He looked about for the other plastic Ziplock® bag. "The kid said something about Joy's stuff at his dad's and that he thought she might've been involved in the scandal! Hmm … that doesn't sound like Joy!"

Marcel finished his coffee and returned to the kitchen for another cup, rolling the facts in his head. "So, if Joy faked her drowning and was involved in the money scheme, where the hell is she, and where's the money?"

He returned to the living room sofa and sat back down. The facts ran through his brain, over and over again. "Where's Joy hiding, then? The money in that embezzlement went missing some eight years before she disappeared off that yacht! Shit, it doesn't make any sense," he muttered as he grasped the news article again. "Hmm … where does Whitford fit into all this and why did he keep this stuff?"

"These news clippings say that the Rawlings body was found off Twiss Point on Galiano Island. It also says that the cops thought that he had been murdered at his house and his body was likely dumped and carried by the tide. So where's the house?"

Marcel sat processing the clues for a moment and then he picked up the phone and dialed his office.

"Good morning, Margaret. Would you please check out a property title for me? The property's on Galiano Island, and I need a listing of all properties that are owned by either a Rawlings or Tremblay."

"Oh, good morning, Mr. Bessier! Sure, call back in an hour and I'll see what I can find. Will you be in later this morning? Remember you've a one o'clock appointment this afternoon."

"Oh … ah, you're right! I forgot all about that meeting," he sighed. "Something urgent has come up that I must attend to today. Can you reschedule that meeting please, say, next Monday?"

"Sure, I'll talk to you later when I've got something on those properties. Bye!"

Marcel hung up and continued to work the facts around in his head. He couldn't believe that Joy could still be alive!

♓

It was late morning by the time Sandra had reached the Rowing Club and she was glad that it was her day off. Between the sex and the numerous bottles of wine, she was tired and had a hangover. She had her Sabot sailing race with Forsythe later in the afternoon at the *Kitsilano Yacht Club*. She needed to be sharp and ready, as the competition was intense and demanding.

The day was becoming hot and the fresh ocean water always brought a relief from the intense heat. She pulled her sleek rowing shell into the inlet waterway, slipped on a cap, climbed into the rower's seat and headed up the Burrard Inlet for Canada Place.

Sandra thought about how far she had come in gaining control of her life. Her mother, a Native Canadian, had been drug-dependant and had abused her before Sandra's fifth birthday. Her father was white and Sandra's white complexion hid her native heritage. She left her parents when she was thirteen and lived in the streets and learned from the other runaways how to survive. Oppenheimer Park became her neighborhood and she promised herself that she would never live like that again.

The intense competitive training and the physical demands of her passion drove the pain of her youth into submission. Sailing and money was all that had mattered, until Forsythe. She wanted to tell him all about her life and her attraction to him, but he was becoming a successful associate lawyer and she was convinced that her past and current profession would ruin everything. She held her tongue and her feelings, focused on the competition and trained hard. She hoped that one day it would all work out, but didn't really expect that it would.

♓

Kelly and Simon entered the RCMP downtown lab building.

"Please let CSI Richard Sommers know Detectives O'Brian and Chung are here concerning the Whitford case. He's expecting us," Kelly told the young woman at the front desk.

The receptionist picked up her phone and called the lab. "Yes, it's reception. A couple of detectives are here about the Whitford case. They say you're expecting them."

The receptionist acknowledged the instruction, pointed across the room, and buzzed the locked door.

The laboratories were secured rooms, and the detectives walked down the hall, entered a glassed-in waiting room and found a seat. A serious-looking young man appeared and joined the duo.

"Hey guys! It's always a pleasure." He smiled at Kelly and opened a file folder that he had brought. "The DNA test confirms that Mr. Tyler Whitford is the son of the Charles Whitford, victim of the Canada Day boat explosion. The ballistics test was very curious, though."

"Curious?" Kelly interrupted.

"Yes, the slugs taken from the body and the boat did come from the Glock that was found at the scene but the curious thing is that they matched a cold case from fifteen years ago," the CSI reported and flipped to another sheet in the folder. "The records show that a matching bullet had been extracted from a murder victim at Galiano Island, a Mark Rawlings, in 1993. A Terence Weiss was convicted for that shooting on circumstantial evidence, but the weapon was never recovered."

The two detectives looked at each other.

"So the gun that killed Tyler Whitford was the weapon that killed Mark Rawlings fifteen years ago, and that means it's highly unlikely that Terence Weiss shot Rawlings," Kelly remarked, looking at Sommers. "Humph! What was young Tyler doing with the weapon then?"

"There's nothing to tie Charles Whitford and Terence Weiss together, either, from what we can tell," the CSI said and handed the file to Simon. "The crime scene photos from the yacht are included in this file. That's all we've got right now, and oh … we didn't find Tyler Whitford's keys either!"

"Thanks, Richard. This case's is becoming more interesting by the day!" Kelly replied smiling at the CSI.

Everyone vacated the briefing room and Simon called Captain Hollingsworth on his cell.

"Hey, Cap. We got interesting news here. It looks like a Terence Weiss may have been convicted of murder in error fifteen years ago." Simon filled in the new information. "Can you pull all the information on that case and advise the DA? We'll be back in half an hour." Simon listened to the captain's response and hung up the call.

"KO, the captain says that our warrant for Tyler Whitford's apartment access is at the office and he'll leave it on our desk."

"So Simon, what does a fifteen-year-old murder case got to do with our two Whitford deaths? Maybe Tyler's place will tell us something," Kelly commented as she fished for her car keys.

♓

Marcel Bessier realized that the ordeal with Tyler Whitford was more traumatic than he had first thought. He was unable to concentrate and tried not to think about how close to death he had been the night before. He paced around the house thinking about the events that had led up to Joy's disappearance seven years earlier.

"I can't believe that she staged that evening," shaking his head in disbelief. "She was a recognized competent artist! What made her give all that up? I don't get it!"

The phone rang, breaking his concentration and he walked to his desk in his study and grabbed the phone.

"Marcel, it's Margaret."

"Hold on a moment." Marcel walked to the front of the desk to grab some notepaper and a pen.

"Okay, what've you found?"

"Well, there aren't any properties registered to a Rawlings, but there is one to a Marriam Tremblay on Galiano Island. The address is 3691 Cain Point Road," she replied as he wrote down the information.

"Great work, Margaret!"

"I've rescheduled your appointment for ten Monday morning. Is that okay?"

"Yes thanks, Margaret. I'll talk to you later. Bye"

Marcel sat down at his desk and pulled out the keyboard from under his computer monitor and loaded *MapQuest*®.

"Let's see, 3691 Cain Road, Galiano Island." The detailed map location appeared. "Hmm, okay. I wonder where this Twiss Point is." He keyed the new search.

"Ah ... I see that Whaler Bay's in the area and there's a marina. I'd better go and look about. Humph, maybe Joy's living there! I'd better call the cops and see when I can get the *Four Aces* back!" Marcel muttered and picked up the phone again. "Detective Chung, this is Marcel Bessier."

"Oh yes, Mr. Bessier. How're you feeling today?" Simon asked curtly.

"Still somewhat shaken up I'm afraid and I thought a little cruise would help. When can I expect my boat to be released?"

"I've been told that you can take it tomorrow morning. We'll be done with it by then, Mr. Bessier. You may want to clean the blood up first, though."

"Yea, I forgot about the mess and looking at that sure won't help me relax. I'll have the marina do it first thing. Will you advise the marina when they can have access?"

"Sure thing, Mr. Bessier, I can arrange that. Is there anything else?"

"No thank you, Detective." Marcel hung up the call, got up from the desk and started to think about what he would need to be ready for his trip to Galiano.

♓

Kelly and Simon found the Tyler Whitford apartment just off West Sixth Street. The high-rise was on the False Creek waterfront and was considered one of the prime living locations in the downtown core. The detectives had been able to get in touch with the building manager and he had agreed to open the 18th floor condo when they arrived.

"Thank you. We'll let you know when you can lock up," Simon told the building manager and closed the door as the pair of detectives pulled on some rubber gloves.

"Nice digs for a young guy. I guess carjacking really pays off these days!" Kelly remarked as she spotted the Sony laptop sitting beside the sofa. She lifted the lid and pressed a key.

"Hey Simon, this thing's still running, but I need a password. We'll take this and see what the IT guys can do." She turned off the machine, gathered the power cable and set it aside.

"Hey KO, find a bag. This old wooden box is about the size of the Glock and there're still some good rounds in here. Let's see if Sommers can lift some prints."

The detectives poked around for a while.

"Nothing else here but the view!" Kelly exclaimed as she stood by the living room window.

Simon noticed that the answering machine had read messages, but they hadn't been erased. He played the messages and took notes of the recordings and the phone display numbers. "We can check these out later. The numbers may give our guys who're working on carjacking cases some info to chase."

Kelly called the building manager and advised him to come back and lock the apartment. "Hopefully the Captain should have our info on the Rawlings cold case by the time we get back."

Chapter Six

The lunch hour patrons at *Cocoa West Chocolate Boutique* had thinned out and Elizabeth Richardson had her first break of the day. The Snug Cove chocolatier was busy with tourists and the bed and breakfast suite had been fully booked since Canada Day. Everyone at Cocoa West was run off their feet and the lull in customers was a welcome relief.

Elizabeth cleaned up a table and sat with a hot coffee. She closed her eyes and could still hear the hum of machines grinding out chocolate treats in the back room. She smiled and took a deep breath of the chocolate aroma engulfing the café. She turned her attention to the newspaper that had been left open, partially un-read, sitting on the table beside her. She turned to the front page.

"**Whitford Son Shot to Death**," the headline screamed at her.

Elizabeth snatched the paper and read the story on the tragic shooting at Fisherman's Cove. She was shocked to learn that the prominent West Vancouver lawyer Marcel Bessier was attacked and then shot the young assailant in self-defense. She sat frozen in her chair with her eyes glued to the article.

"Tragic. First one of our own Bowen citizens, then his son! It makes you think that even Bowen Island is becoming an unsafe place. You're not safe anywhere anymore!" an elderly woman remarked as she left the café shaking her head, and started her walk back down the hill to Snug Cove.

Elizabeth felt her heart race and she began to worry. She remembered how Charles Whitford had helped her those many years before. She owed him because he had helped her escape! He had gotten her a new identity, for a fee of course, but it was worth every penny. "He didn't deserve this!" she muttered; she remembered the young Tyler boy and recalled how she had felt saddened when his mother skipped out and left the boy devastated. "It certainly is tragic!" Elizabeth replied to the old lady who had already left the store.

"That bastard Marcel's getting involved," Elizabeth growled. "I don't know how he found out about the Whitfords but he'd better not find me!" She thought about the plan to leave Marcel those seven years earlier. She remembered the verbal abuse and the constant pressure for her to pay off his gambling debts. She had to leave him. Giving up her successful life was a small price to pay for safety and freedom.

"I'd better get my old stuff back from Charles' place." Her heart pounded as she remembered that Charles insisted on keeping her old ID and credit cards for security. "I'd better go there tonight!"

She knew that when her work shift ended in a few hours she would be able to go home and work out a plan.

♓

The Terence Weiss file was on Kelly's desk when the two detectives returned from False Creek. The two partners got settled at their desks and Kelly placed the CSI lab file on Tyler Whitford beside the Weiss folder.

"The Glock pistol and slugs from the Tyler Whitford killing matching Mark Rawlings' case definitely places reasonable doubt on the Weiss conviction," Captain Hollingsworth commented as he joined the two detectives getting settled into their places. "The DA thinks that Weiss should be released now. His sentence was going to be completed in two months anyway. He's going to be pissed and the RCMP's going to take a lot of public heat when they find out the wrong guy was convicted all those years ago."

"It looks like an elaborate set-up at this point, Captain. The Charles Whitford killing certainly triggered something," Kelly said, looking up at Hollingsworth.

"Hey, KO, pull that Weiss file and find out who the detective was on the Rawlings case. We need some firsthand information," Simon instructed. "There're often things in a case that don't get recorded."

"Let's see … it was a Detective Arthur Fleming. I'll get records to find out where he is, if he's still alive."

"Good. Get records to pull the old Rawlings case file, too."

♓

Lothar Zoric had arrived on the late morning Bowen Island ferry and he hadn't worried about getting something to eat before he left. He had a mission and he focused on that. Raj Jattan had made it clear that there was no more room for error. This was his chance to prove that he could fix the Charles Whitford problem and find the computer passwords or other paper records that he had forgotten on Canada Day.

It was important that no one notice him, so he left his car a few blocks down the street from the Bowen Bay Road house. He remembered breaking into the house and expected the front door to still be open just as he had left it. It was, and he entered the house.

He began to trash the place, looking everywhere for something that would please his demanding employer. He noticed the old sea trunk in the study, pulled the heavy lid and yanked the woman's clothing and shoes, dumping them on the floor.

"What's with the woman's shit? This guy must've been weird! Damn, nothing here either!" he growled and headed for another room in the house.

The executive home looked like a disaster zone by the time Lothar realized that he wouldn't find anything inside to help him satisfy his boss. He sat and stared out the large back window, struggling to think of his next move. The boat shed by the dock caught his eye.

"Hmm … maybe I'll find something out there!" He unlocked the rear glass French door, rushed out of the house and headed directly toward the shed, leaving the back door wide open as he marched toward the dock.

Lothar noticed that the shed door had been kicked in and he pulled back the damaged door. "Humph! Someone's been here already!" he muttered as he fumbled around and located the light switch.

Minutes later all the contents had been pitched onto the lawn. There was nothing of interest.

"Ah … what a mess I'm in!" Lothar sighed, and decided that he would return to the pub he had seen in Snug Cove and think about what to do next.

♓

Kelly O'Brian was reviewing the lab reports and photographs from the Tyler Whitford scene.

"Hey Simon, so why weren't Tyler Whitford's keys found at the scene? That's very strange. I can't believe the guys missed them, so where did they go?"

"Hmm … did there seem to be anything missing from the wallet?" Simon asked while continuing to check all the photos. "If there was a struggle, as indicated from the blood impressions and Mr. Bessier's story, then the keys may've ended up somewhere else besides the pilot cabin."

"The lab reports don't indicate anything unusual was missing in the wallet and Sommers is pretty good, besides having a second shot at looking around this morning."

"Hey, you two. Retired Detective Arthur Fleming's alive and living on Pender Island. His address and phone number are on this sheet," Captain Hollingsworth said as he handed the printed report to Simon, "and the Rawlings file will be here within the hour."

Simon picked up the phone and dialed the long distance number on the printed report. "There's no answer. I'll have to call again, maybe later in the day."

"The lab boys say they covered the boat top to bottom and didn't find any keys. They didn't check the wallet for prints though, to see if Bessier was routing through Tyler's stuff after the shooting. They're going to dust the wallet and advise what they find," Kelly continued reading from the Bessier report.

Simon listened and quickly thumbed through the Terence Weiss file. "We should go and talk to this guy before he gets out! I'm sure his side of the story will be interesting." Simon picked up the phone and dialed the *Fraser Regional Correctional Center* in Maple Ridge.

"Hello. I'm Detective Chung. Can you direct me to someone who can arrange a visit with one of your inmates, please?" The phone went silent and Simon thought that the receptionist had forgotten his call as he sat on hold for quite a while. He put the phone on the speaker setting so everyone could hear the conversation.

"Sorry for the long wait, Detective, but I can put you through to Warden Drew Fisher now," the woman said and the line went dead again for a moment; Simon rolled his eyes and sighed.

Finally a voice came on the phone and asked, "Detective?"

"Yes sir, this is Detective Chung. We have new evidence on an old case involving your inmate Terence Weiss, and my partner and I would like to talk to him this afternoon. Can you arrange a meeting for us right away, please?"

"I'll ask him if he wants a lawyer in attendance. You know he's scheduled for release in two months, don't you, Detective?"

"Yes sir, but he may have some pertinent information on a current homicide that may involve his case. Can you ask him? Call me on this number when you have spoken with him."

"Sure, Detective. I wouldn't expect his cooperation, but I'll ask."

"Thank you, Warden."

Simon hung up the call and redialed Arthur Fleming's number, leaving the phone on speaker. "Hello, is this retired Detective Arthur Fleming?"

"Yes it is, what can I do for you?"

"I'm Detective Chung, and my partner and I would like to come and see you to talk about the Rawlings case."

"That case was fifteen years ago, Detective. Why do you wish to talk about that old case now? A Terence Weiss was convicted for the murder of Rawlings, so what's up?"

"Yes Detective, but some new facts have come to light and we've a current case that we think is related. Can we see you tomorrow to fill in some blanks?"

"Well all right, but all the information's in the case file, Detective."

"I've reviewed the file and think there are a few things that you may be able to tell us that will help with our current investigation," Simon pressed, hearing a little reluctance in the man's voice.

"Okay, it's your time, Detective. The BC Ferrys are very busy this time of year so you better book a passage if you plan on getting here for tomorrow."

"Thanks. Where can we meet you and what time would be convenient?" Simon smiled.

"Ah … how about *Poets Cove* on Pender Island at twelve-thirty for lunch? I'll be in the lounge on the water side of the resort."

"See you then," Simon replied, then hung up the phone and looked up at his partner. "Hey, book a ferry for Pender Island for early tomorrow. Bring your dog, Hunter; he'll like a ride and a chance to get out of your apartment. Oh and ah, book the last return boat, too. That should give us enough time to find out what we need and get back."

Simon's phone rang again. "Detective Chung."

"Detective Chung, this is the warden at the *Fraser Regional Correctional Center*. Terence Weiss has agreed to talk to you and your partner without a lawyer. He says that a lawyer for two more months is a waste of time and money. He can see you at four this afternoon." The voice came through the phone speaker that Simon had forgotten to turn off.

"Great. Thanks, Warden, see you at four." Simon hung up and turned off the conference call feature on the phone.

"Hey KO. Get on your horse. We've an appointment with Weiss and have to get to Maple Ridge before four. The rush hour will be on our tail, so let's hustle!"

"I've got a ferry reservation out of Tsawwassen at ten ten tomorrow morning, returning at eight forty tomorrow night.

It'll be tight but we should make the twelve thirty lunch. Let's go and see Weiss!"

Simon thumbed through the jacket on the Rawlings case as Kelly drove to Maple Ridge.

"The background information here says that Mark Rawlings and Charles Whitford were alleged to have been in a scheme to embezzle a large amount of money from their company fifteen years ago. It says that Rawlings was one of the owners. Ah … the evidence collected by Detective Arthur Fleming implicated Terence Weiss for killing Rawlings in an attempt to locate the missing cash. The conviction was circumstantial but Weiss got fifteen years for the murder anyway."

"I would've thought that Weiss would be out by now," Kelly remarked as she concentrated on the road and the heavy traffic.

"This case jacket doesn't cover that. We'll have to find out when we see the warden why Weiss did a full term," Simon remarked, looking over at Kelly. "Weiss has served his time and is due to be released in September. I wonder what his reaction will be when we tell him about the Whitford Glock!"

"You know, Simon, my father had to declare bankruptcy for the same type of thing!" Kelly said as she glanced over at her partner. "Our lives were turned upside down and it was a living hell. My mother couldn't handle the social disgrace and left my dad and me. They divorced two years later. I was about fifteen and thought my world had come to an end. No one gets killed in those embezzlement things, but people's lives are destroyed just the same!"

Nothing else was said during the rest of the trip, each detective lost in their own thoughts about past family events and how those events had shaped their lives.

"Okay, we're here. Let's see what Weiss has to say," Kelly said, drawing the gray Taurus into the entranceway.

The large brick building appeared like a fortress. It sat back from the roadway and didn't look like an inviting place to visit or spend time for that matter. A huge expanse of lawn spread from the street to the building. A winding roadway, lined with large old alder trees in full foliage of summer, led to the parking lot.

The detectives parked and found the reception area.

"We've an appointment to see Warden Drew Fisher, please. It is Detectives Chung and O'Brian." Simon flashed his gold shield at the receptionist.

"I'll inform the warden that you're here. Please take a seat over there," the middle-aged woman replied stiffly and pointed to a set of old chairs to her left.

The building felt cold, even on the hot summer afternoon. The barred windows allowed the sunlight into the waiting room that had an old, worn, gray granite stone floor.

"Warden Fisher can see you now. Please come this way." The receptionist got out of her chair, led the party down a wide hallway and stopped outside a large wooden door that appeared to be almost eight feet high.

The receptionist lightly knocked on the door. The sound was almost unnoticeable, and she opened the large door.

A short medium-built man, about fifty-five years old with gray thinning hair, stood up from his chair behind an old large wooden desk.

"Good afternoon, Detectives, I'm Warden Drew Fisher. I understand that you wish to see Terence Weiss," he said as the receptionist closed the door.

"Warden Fisher, I'm Detective Chung and this is my partner Detective O'Brian. We've come across some new evidence concerning Mr. Weiss and wish to talk to him about his case."

"I'd say he hasn't been a model resident here! He's been quite problematic and is a very angry man. He has had his request for early release denied twice due to his uncooperative attitude," the warden said as he sat back down.

"We noticed his sentence will be completed in September," Kelly remarked, looking around the large office.

"Well, he's done his time but he's still angry with the world. He has always said that he was framed, but many inmates here say they've been falsely accused. The DA has been in contact with me about the plan to revoke his sentence due to your new evidence and the discovery of the murder weapon in his case. That evidence and associated facts cast reasonable doubt that Weiss was guilty of his charges and are adequate cause for his release."

"Have you told Weiss yet, Warden?"

"No, I'm waiting for direction from the DA to see if Weiss can be released without a hearing. I'll call the DA before you see Weiss. I'm sure that you'd like to tell him if he gets to be released early!"

"That would be helpful, Warden. Ah … can you direct us to the washrooms? The drive from West Vancouver's quite a trip," Kelly requested.

"Yes, of course. Turn left and you both will find the washrooms down the hall. I'll make that call while you're gone."

The two detectives returned to the Warden's office as the phone was being hung up.

"Good news! The DA has issued the order to release Weiss. The paperwork will be completed by tomorrow morning and he'll be released then. Come, he's waiting in the visitors' block."

The Warden led the group down the stone-faced hallway to the end. The warden pressed a security code into the keypad box mounted by the steel-faced door that had a large Plexiglas window inserted into the centre and metal bars strung across the frame.

Buzz. The security lock echoed down the stone, dimly lit, corridor and the warden pulled the door open, allowing the three to access to the visitors' room. Terence Weiss was seated in a small cubicle facing the detectives as they passed through the doorway.

"Press this button when you wish to leave. A guard will come and get you," Warden Fisher said and then left the two detectives, shutting the door behind him.

A concrete block wall was placed between the visitors and the inmates. Heavy thick Plexiglas windows were positioned every six feet and were separated by small block walls creating an illusion of a private meeting space. A pair of metal chairs was placed on the visitors' side of the wall. A phone receiver hung on either side of the cubicle.

Terence Weiss sat stone-faced peering at his two detective visitors. He looked almost six feet tall, his head was shaven and a single stud earring was pressed into an earlobe. Weiss was muscular and his body appeared well toned.

Simon selected a seat, sat down and picked up the receiver. Weiss followed and placed the handle to his ear, stared blankly, not changing his expression.

"We're Detectives Chung and O'Brian and wish to clear up a few things about your case," he said as Kelly sat down next to her partner.

Weiss eyed Kelly for a moment and then answered, "It's a bit fuckin' late don't you think! I've been rottin' in this stinking hole for fifteen years and I'll be out in two months. Why should I talk to you two cops now?"

"We've been working on a case that has led us back to you. We found the weapon that killed Rawlings, which casts doubt on your conviction. We want to hear your version firsthand on what happened," Simon said, staring directly into Weiss's eyes.

"I've been saying from the beginin' that I was framed by that bastard Detective Fleming!" Terence growled and his eyes bulged as he uttered Fleming's name. His face remained without expression. "Yea I was there at Rawlings' place. I had come over that day to talk to him about some money that he owed me. He said that the cash wasn't in the house and that he would get what he owed me in a few days. I roughed him up a little to ensure that weasel didn't get any ideas about jerking me about. I gave him three days to pay up, and said that I would be back!"

"So how did Fleming frame you then?"

"That bastard was trying to make a name for himself and he needed to stick someone with the Rawlings murder. He found out that I stayed overnight on Pender Island and that I ate at the pub in Port Browning the night Rawlings was killed. Rawlings' place had my fingerprints around and Fleming built a circumstantial case I shot Rawlings. That fuck Fleming didn't have the gun, but I had a record with the cops so I became the easy suspect."

"A heavy sentence for a circumstantial case, huh?" Simon pressed for a reaction.

"Yea, well I had a shit public lawyer. I don't look like a model citizen, either!" Weiss sneered.

"The discovery of the Rawlings murder weapon now sheds enough doubt on your case that the DA has agreed to revoke the remainder of your sentence, Mr. Weiss. We believe that you'll be released tomorrow morning, once all the paperwork's been processed."

"Well as I said, I was innocent. Pretty fuckin' late if ya ask me!" Terence growled, hung up the phone and remained stone-faced, still staring straight ahead.

The two detectives turned and looked at each other. The conversation was over and they got out of their seats and left Weiss who remained motionless in his chair.

Kelly buzzed the guard. "Not too joyful to hear that he's getting out, I'd say!"

"Well, if I had served fifteen years with two months remaining for a crime I didn't do, happiness wouldn't be my first emotion, either!" Simon remarked. "It's rush hour and time for you to navigate home, partner. We've an early morning to catch the ferry by ten."

"I'll pick ya up by seven. Remember they load those ferrys at least twenty minutes before they sail, so I'm thinkin' we need to be in line by nine-thirty."

♓

Lothar Zoric sat in *Doc Morgan's Pub* watching the Horseshoe Bay ferry arrive at the Snug Cove docks. His pint of beer was almost finished and his burger had been only partially eaten.

"I know I've to report in, but don't know what to say to RJ! I didn't find what he wanted and he will be really pissed," Lothar thought and continued to seek a plausible excuse or another solution. "I sure hate this type of work and RJ is such a miserable bastard, treating me like a kid or somethin'. I need to find a way to do somethin' else. I don't trust RJ and blowing up that Whitford guy was a little crazy. He goes nuts too easy," Lothar mumbled quietly to himself as he watched the busy terminal get ready to unload the latest deck-full of vehicles.

"Shit! I gotta go," Lothar muttered, gulped the rest of his beer and ran to find his car and get into the line for the next boat back to the mainland.

Chapter Seven

Elizabeth Richardson had been painting in her studio since she came home from work. Laying the paint on the canvas was soothing, and she found that the ocean vista out of her studio window was inspiring. She lived on the northern tip of Bowen Island in Smugglers Cove that looked across the channel directly at Halkett Bay on Gambier Island. Sailors frequented the channel and sailboats and powerboats frequently entertained the residents on both shorelines.

The northern part of Bowen Island was less busy and Elizabeth had selected the quiet locale based on the desire to keep her life as private as she could. She had been a renowned artist as Joy Bessier, and her oil works had been well received by collectors and national followers. She changed her medium to watercolor and altered her style and expression, trying to keep her other life in the past. That was the most difficult part of changing her life and moving away from the notoriety of her passion.

The calculated and planned escape from Marcel Bessier was a brazen and desperate move to take control of the other aspects of her life. The sensitive artist and abused-wife lifestyle didn't work for her and she had become desperate to find a safe way out. She knew that Charles Whitford was not a friend, but her early acquaintance with him had presented the opportunity to regain her independence and sense of security.

Her quaint house was modest and small but gave Elizabeth a feeling of tranquility and cozy calmness. She never appeared in public as an artist and only worked in her studio. She had selected a local agent to market her works and her biography had been designed to hide her true identity. Elizabeth lived in constant fear that one day Marcel would find her! The murder of Charles Whitford frightened her, and she had to ensure that there were no leads exposing her new life. It had been many years since she had been at Charles' house at Bowen Bay but she knew that there was little time to retrieve her belongings. The knowledge that her husband was involved in Tyler Whitford's death only made her situation more desperate, and the urgency to remove any possible connection to her old life paramount.

Elizabeth continued to layer the color on the artist's canvas and tried to calm her stressed mind. She knew that she shouldn't arrive at Bowen Bay until the darkness of the day could conceal her presence. The time seemed to drag as she became impatient with the waiting; her artistic efforts were not able to distract her from the tense mood so she decided to plan her evening adventure instead.

♓

Sandra Vaughn loved being a part of the *Kitsilano Yacht Club*. She enjoyed sailing until sunset followed by the club's evening three-course dinners on the patio. The sailing of her KYC5O5 model sabot sailboat was the best part, especially since she joined up with Forsythe Harrison. The sailboat was built for racing and required a two-person team. Sandra and Forsythe became an instant pair when he joined the sailing club following his appointment to a law firm downtown. It was hard to find attractive single young men over six feet who loved sailing as much as she did. Sandra hoped the attraction was mutual.

She kept her extracurricular income a personal secret from everyone at the club. She admitted to being a poker table dealer at the *West Coast Casino and Suites*, as that fact would've been difficult to hide. Sandra talked a good sailing story and she focused on that vein of discussion whenever possible.

Sandra always arrived at the club by four thirty. The club was alive by five and Sandra usually spotted Forsythe before then. Everyone at the club was pumped for the Sabot races and all the competitors had to be ready for the competitions that began at six.

"Hey Forsythe, over here!" Sandra called out as she caught her sailing partner entering the lobby and heading toward the lockers to change.

"How's my beautiful partner tonight? Ready to kick some butt?" Forsyth asked with a smile.

"Yours will be the only butt I'll kick if we don't win some heats tonight!" she grinned. "See ya down on the beach in ten."

There were close to thirty Sabot sailboats finding positions on the beach by the time that Sandra had pulled hers from the storage yard and was checking the rigging. She named her boat *Second Chance* and the sleek boat was painted a bright yellow. As Forsythe joined her, his face lit up with a large smile.

"I drew the second heat to start tonight," she flashed a smile back to him.

"The weather's perfect!" Forsythe looked out over English Bay toward Stanley Park. "The course is already marked and so far no unwanted traffic to sail around. Let's hope it stays that way!"

The first heat of boats was jockeying for position, waiting for the starting pistol to announce the beginning of the first race. The shot echoed in the ears of the boaters and the dash for the markers began.

The flurry of colored sails pulled the small boats with bullet-like speed through the water. The pairs of sailors could be seen ducking and weaving as they tacked and wove their way out into the bay. The screaming of the shore-bound audience was in contrast to the soundless breeze filling the sails of the maneuverable hulls flying across the ocean top. The race was mainly about sailing skill and calculated tactics as the pair of sailors had to operate as one body, communicating and reacting together in the small hull. Sailing failures usually resulted in overturned boats and wet bodies.

The first five boats that were able to reach the markers and return to the starting line won the right to continue in another race. Races ran through the evening until the last heat, where the winners for the day were celebrated.

It was just pure fun.

♓

Kelly O'Brian was glad to be home as the drive from Maple Ridge had been long and tiring. She took Hunter for a long walk and watched the Wednesday night Sabot races from Hadden Park. It was a sight to watch, and many spectators sat on the park benches and on blankets spread on the park lawns. The distinct odor of summer hibachis and barbeques saturated the air and reminded Kelly that it was time to get something to eat. She stopped at a pizzeria on the way back to her apartment.

"I need to work on research tonight, Hunter. Something's bugging me about this Rawlings case!"

The dog looked up at her as though to say, "I know."

Kelly opened the kitchen cabinet, pulled out a wine glass, opened the refrigerator door and found a half bottle of cold Kelowna Chardonnay. She refreshed Hunter's water bowl, poured new kibbles into his dinner tray, and poured a glass of wine.

"We can't work too long tonight, Hunter. We've to be at the Tsawwassen ferry terminal by nine thirty. I'm bringing you along on this trip, my friend. You'll like that and it'll be late before we get back."

Kelly put her wine glass on the dining room table next to the running computer. "Let's see, Mark Rawlings." She pulled the laptop closer and typed the name into the Google® search box using the small keyboard.

The list of results was too cluttered and unhelpful. "Hmm … maybe if I add Vancouver with Rawlings, that string may narrow things down a bit." She added the extra search criterion.

"Hmm … better! Let's try this one: 'Murdered man found at Twiss Point.'" She read the article to Hunter, who was lying at her feet under the table.

One of the suspected embezzlers of DigiCast Software was found shot to death today at Twiss Point. Detective Fleming said that the investigation was ongoing and that no suspects had been identified. Rawlings was one of two men accused of stealing large sums of cash and securities that resulted in bankrupting the Vancouver animation software company. There has been insufficient evidence to charge Mark Rawlings or Charles Whitford with the missing DigiCast assets, which have not been recovered.

Kelly couldn't believe what she had just read, and reread the 1993 newspaper article.

"Hunter, I think that was my dad's company. I don't believe it!" Kelly exclaimed; she jumped out of her chair and ran to the closet in her bedroom. She rummaged around for a moment, then pulled a box containing all her father's papers and photographs that she had stored when he had been admitted into *Westview Centre*.

She brought the box back into the dining room and spread all the materials on the table, putting the photographs in one pile and the loose papers into another. Kelly sat, took a long drink from the wine glass, and stared at the items from the box.

"I know I've seen that *DigiCast* name somewhere," she muttered and started to thumb through the few photographs on the table. "Hmm … only four photos! Strange so few. Dad must've destroyed all those with Mom in them I guess—too bad!"

She sat back down and began to look carefully at each photo. The first photograph was a black and white with a lighthouse in the background. Four people and a young five-year-old girl posed for the photo. The names were printed in pencil on the back, "Joy, Patrick, Charles, Mark, and Kelly." A second line in pencil read "*DigiCast* team at *Georgina's Lighthouse*."

At the bottom of the photograph the following inscription read,

Georgina's place of note to view,
Marriam's place the point you can see,
To plot by the legend of Fisher's 3462,
The captain's compass will be the key.

"There ya go, Hunter! I knew I had seen that *DigiCast* name somewhere. I haven't really looked at this stuff closely before! I wonder what the inscription means. Hmm … it's surely a strange poem, whoever wrote it!"

Two other photographs didn't have any inscriptions on their backs: one photograph was with the same adults raising a glass of wine in someone's house living room, and the other was of a baby girl. "The baby must be me, I suppose, Hunter. Wow, it's the only one I have!"

The last photograph was of a pair of golfers holding a trophy. The inscription on the back read, "*DigiCast* golf tournament winners 1986."

Kelly sorted through the few papers on the table. "Nothing new to tell me here, just stuff about the failed company, it looks like. Financial records and client lists, maybe." She placed them back into a pile, finished the glass of wine and went into the kitchen and poured another glass.

"Hmm … *Georgina's Lighthouse*. That seems familiar. Where have I seen that name before?"

Kelly entered the name into Google®. The picture and description appeared, "*Georgina Point Lighthouse* at the mouth of Active Pass, Mayne Island."

Kelly eyes widened! "Hunter, I've seen that place before!" She bolted out of her chair and ran into the bedroom. There it was, an oil painting of the lighthouse just like the internet photograph. She took the painting off the wall and returned to the dining room with the painting.

"Hunter, Dad gave this painting to me a number of years ago. He said it was a special piece of art, but didn't say why. Too bad I didn't ask him!" The artwork was signed "J. Tremblay." She placed the canvas on the table.

"So, what's so special about this painting?" Kelly's mind was in overload. "This is too much for me today. I'll have to tell Simon, first thing. This case is all about Dad's company! How bazaar is that, eh Hunter?"

♓

Lothar Zoric drove off the ferry at Horseshoe Bay. He hadn't figured out what to do or what to say to Raj Jattan. He turned off the Number One expressway and decided to wait for the rush hour to ease, so he found a bar in the small local town and parked.

The little village survived on traffic attracted by the ferry services and residents who lived up the Sea to Sky Highway. Lothar ordered a Bud® on tap and found a stool at the bar. "RJ's sure getting his shorts in a twist over this computer stuff. He works in a charity group or something, so what's the big deal anyway?" he muttered; there was a bowl of nuts on the bar counter and he grabbed a handful. "I don't get it!"

He twisted in his barstool and looked out at the passenger traffic scurrying toward the terminal. "I had nothin' as a kid and I went to work when I was fourteen and we didn't need any charity! I never hurt anyone until this Whitford thing, maybe a bump or bruise or somethin' but not what I was forced to do by RJ to that Whitford guy! Jesus Christ." Lothar's beer had disappeared and he twisted back around on his stool and ordered another as he continued to mumble to himself.

He fished out his cell phone and called Raj Jattan. "Hey Boss, it's Lothar."

"Hey asshole, I expected your call hours ago. What the hell are ya doin'?"

"I went to Whitford's place as you told me. I ripped the place apart but couldn't find anythin'; no safe, nothin'. I don't know what to do now, Boss." Lothar took a deep breath waiting for the string of foul words to pulsate through the phone.

"Okay, okay. Come back to the office in the morning and I'll figure something else out. The newspapers say Charles' son Tyler was killed by a Marcel Bessier yesterday, so maybe there's some connection for ya to follow-up."

Lothar hung up the cell, gulped his beer and ordered another; he was surprised that he hadn't gotten his ass chewed out.

♓

The beautiful summer day had surrendered to the night sky. Bowen Island was very dark and the roads were sparsely lit. Elizabeth drove to Bowen Bay that was on the western side of the island. There wasn't a direct route to the western side and Elizabeth had to wind around the entire length of the island to reach her destination. She usually considered this a good thing, but tonight it added to her stress. She knew that with the abundance of wildlife, an animal often darted across the roadway and drivers had to be extra cautious and alert at night. It added to her stress as she peered carefully into the darkness while she drove the deserted island road.

Charles Whitford's house sat in blackness of the night, as Elizabeth had expected. She grabbed her flashlight and a shopping bag from the passenger seat and headed out, down the unlit driveway toward the waterfront. A few lights could be seen on the shoreline of Keats and Pasley Islands, but nothing else was visible. The secluded estate was protected by large trees on both sides of the lot and the neighbors remained in darkness from her vantage point.

Elizabeth reached the front door, which was locked as she had expected, so she decided to go around to the back. The rear door was open and she saw RCMP yellow tape torn and lying on the ground as she stepped over the warning tape. She knew that she wasn't the first visitor to Whitford's house since his death and worried what she would find inside.

"This doesn't look good!" she told herself, carefully walking around the debris scattered around the floor as the thin beam of light illuminated her route and she headed directly for the study. "I know he kept my stuff in that old sea trunk under the window!"

The beam of light displayed the strewn articles lying beside the open trunk. She picked her way to her clothing and scooped the dress, shoes and evening bag into the bag she had brought with her. There was nothing else. She checked the inside of the trunk. It was empty. "Curses, my old ID, credit cards and Marriam's birth certificate—they're all missing!

That's not good!" She stood frozen on the floor wondering what to do next.

"Damn, nothing I can do now! Better get out of here before someone sees me." She turned and wandered back through the house the way that she'd come. She stopped at the front door and listened. There was nothing, not a sound. She opened the door and bolted up the drive to her car.

Her heart was pounding and her face was flushed by the time she reached the place where she had parked her car. She tossed the bag into the backseat and drove down to the neighbor's driveway, turned about and headed her vehicle back to Smugglers Cove. She hoped that Marcel hadn't been the one to find her stuff and she felt very uneasy. There were still loose ends and she didn't know where they were.

♓

Dusk had fallen and Sabot racing had concluded for another day. Sandra and Forsythe had placed third for their efforts and were celebrating their victory in the club's lounge.

The two had finished their meal with their boating friends and they both wanted to find some quiet time together so started a stroll along the sandy beach.

"You're a great sailing partner, Miss Vaughn!" Forsythe turned with a smile to face her in the moonlight.

Sandra blushed, but Forsythe couldn't tell in the filtered evening light. "Not so bad yourself, Mr. Harrison!"

They looked at each other in the glow of the moonlight; he moved close to her and they kissed.

"I'd like to be more than just sailing partners, Sandra," he whispered as he moved his face to her neck, placed his lips on her skin and gave her another kiss.

She knew that she wanted him, but wasn't sure he would accept her, all of her. She faced him, smiling. "I know Forsythe. I think we need more time together without the crowds around."

"I can do that!" he exclaimed, somewhat disappointed that their relationship was not going as fast as he wished.

She gave him a big wet kiss with her soft lips on his. "Good, I'd like that. Let's get back."

Chapter Eight

Marcel Bessier arrived at Fisherman's Cove at first light. He had been called by the marina and advised that they had been given permission to board and clean his boat late the prior day. The marina said the Bayliner would be ready for him early that morning.

He spent the night considering how he was going to find the Cain Point address, and decided to rent a car at Montague Harbour and drive to the house location that he had found on *MapQuest*®. The harbour was the largest on Galiano Island and the marina provided the best place for him to moor his yacht overnight.

He found that the marina's cleaning crew had done a superb job and there were no longer signs of young Tyler's blood in the pilot house cabin. The side window had not been repaired, and a makeshift plastic cover had been taped in place to keep any water from entering the cabin. The 9mm bullet that had pierced the cabin roof had been pried out by the RCMP lab team and a large hole still remained, reminding Marcel how close to death he'd come. The bloody bullet that exited Tyler's head had severely damaged the back of the Captain's leather seat and Marcel made a point of not looking at the damage and focused on his quest to find the hidden *DigiCast* cash.

Marcel estimated that it would be midafternoon by the time he would reach Montague Harbour. He started the yacht's engines and began to navigate out of the marina. It was another high pressure Vancouver summer morning and it was clear that it was going to be hot and clear all day.

♓

It was just before seven in the morning and Simon waited for Kelly at a crosswalk outside of his Chinatown apartment. The streets were already busy with locals preparing their small shops for their morning opening as many others were rushing to get to their offices.

Hunter sat in the backseat of the gray Taurus, happy to be going on a car trip; he stuck his head out the open rear window as Kelly navigated the car to a place where she could stop and pick up her partner.

"A day of adventure and my first trip to Pender Island!" Simon exclaimed as he jumped into the front passenger seat. "It's going to be a scorcher and I'm glad we're going to be on the water."

"I haven't been to the Gulf Islands since I was a kid! I remember that Dad used to take us out there before the business fiasco and divorce. Hey, you aren't going to believe what I discovered last night!" Kelly spoke quickly and the words could hardly come out fast enough. "Remember Weiss telling us yesterday that he was framed for the murder of Mark Rawlings? Well, I wanted to gather more information about that case before we talked to Fleming today."

"Yea, and Weiss thinks that Fleming was overzealous about the conviction. So what did you find out?" Simon asked, looking at Kelly's excited face.

"I found a newspaper article online about the Rawlings murder, and it turns out that Mark Rawlings and Charles Whitford worked for the same company, *DigiCast*, years back!"

"So if Rawlings was murdered, and the weapon was found in the possession of Charles Whitford, Charles was likely the gunman!" Simon followed the link. "Great work!"

"Yea, yea … but that's not the best part!" she exclaimed bursting with excitement. "My father was one of the owners of *DigiCast* and he lost everything when the embezzled cash and securities resulted in the company's bankruptcy. No one could prove who stole the money and it was never found!"

"So your father was a partner in *DigiCast* and was left holding the bag when the company went under and you think that Fleming's mixed up in all this?"

"I don't know Simon, but it's just something to keep in the back of our minds when we talk with him," she replied and watched the traffic as she pulled the car from the curb.

Tsawwassen is a small community on a unique isthmus that crosses the Canadian and US border isolating the small US town of Point Roberts on the southern tip. The BC Ferry's terminal is placed at the end of a long spit of land at Tsawwassen that terminates in the Strait of Georgia at the Canadian and US border line. The Provincial Highway 17 ends at the terminal and restarts in Saanich, north of Victoria. The ferry is the link that joins both ends of the highway that winds through the Gulf Islands. Large ferries run directly between Tsawwassen and Saanich and smaller ferries complete a milk run that stops at numerous Gulf Islands on its route between the two main terminals.

Kelly glanced up at the large digital display that stood on the approach to the mile-long Highway 17 spit. The display showed the occupancy rate of the ferries waiting to depart. "Wow, look! The next ferry to Victoria's already completely full and the next one is 82% full! You sure have to get out here early these days to avoid lengthy waits!"

"It looks like you made the right call to pay the advance fee and book our trip to Pender, Kelly. Our boat's already full!" Simon exclaimed as he watched the information change on the electronic board.

Kelly pulled into the single line designated for the smaller Gulf Islands ferry. The other four lines were for the larger boats that serviced Victoria and Nanaimo.

"Lane 26, over to your left, Madam," the ticket attendant took her payment and directed Kelly toward the correct numbered corridor.

Kelly parked the car in the lane as instructed. "We've forty five minutes before the boat leaves. I'll take Hunter for a stretch before we load."

"Okay. I see a large concession building over there." Simon pointed to the large new building in the centre of the huge parking lot. "I'll get some coffees and donuts." Simon needed a stretch, too, and the walk gave him something to do other than sit in the car and wait.

The cars in the front of the line began to move toward the loading berth just as Kelly and Simon got back to the car.

"My God! They're loading already, I forgot about the loading time. Lucky we got back early!" she exclaimed loudly to be heard above all the vehicles' engine noises as she opened the back door to let Hunter into the back seat. She and Simon jumped into the car and Kelly followed the stream of vehicles loading onto the boat deck.

The single deck ferry was a lot smaller than the others in the terminal. There was a small passenger lounge above the car deck, but most motorists stayed in their vehicles.

Kelly and Simon vacated their car and slowly worked their way between the parked vehicles to the port side of the boat and peered out at the view as the ferry pulled away from the berth.

"This is really neat! It's like going on vacation, eh Simon? This ride's quite an experience but I don't remember any of this from my childhood trips," Kelly grinned.

"I've never done this before. I don't know why I haven't, maybe just caught up in my own cultural environment in Chinatown and never thought about exploring beyond Vancouver. I've got to bring my mother on this trip."

The Gulf Islands became like large land masses as the ship pushed its way through the calm ocean waters of the Strait of Georgia. The ship's bow headed for a small pass between two large islands.

"Look, Simon, there it is!" Kelly almost tripped and fell as she walked down the deck and saw a lighthouse looming larger. "That's it. That's *Georgina's Lighthouse* so that must be Mayne Island!" she exclaimed, pointing at the landmark.

Simon stared at Kelly with curiosity, as he hadn't seen her so excited before. "So what's with the lighthouse? It's cool, I'll grant you that."

"Oh yea, uh … I forgot to tell you. I went through my dad's stuff when I discovered the *DigiCast* link with Rawlings. There were a few photographs in his box and one of them had this lighthouse in it. I was in it, too, and I must've been about five years old. Anyway, the picture reminded me of an oil painting my dad gave me when I graduated from RCMP training. The painting is of this lighthouse, and my dad told me that the painting was very special, but didn't say why," she blurted out quickly.

"Curious. There must be a reason that he gave the artwork to you. I wonder if the lighthouse has some special meaning to him, or to you!"

"Strange, huh?" Kelly asked and shrugged her shoulders as the ferry continued on its route past the lighthouse to enter the mouth of a narrow waterway.

The ferry turned toward the island on their right and headed for a small terminal. The boat turned to align with the dock and a large sign saying, "Welcome to Sturdies Bay, Galiano Island" was printed in bold black letters.

A few cars drove off the deck of the ferry and one truck replaced their spot. The ferry blew its whistle, reversed and started the next leg of the trip. The ferry blew its horn as it wound through the narrow passes between the islands and minutes later one of the large ferries appeared travelling toward Tsawwassen on the starboard side.

"Wow, that thing looks huge close up! Must be 300 cars or more and there must be at least three passenger decks. I've got to try that one, too."

Their small ferry exited the narrow pass and turned toward the island on the left. The next unloading ramp appeared and another greeting, "Welcome to Village Bay, Mayne Island."

"I guess this would be your stop when you go to investigate your lighthouse!" Simon poked his partner, laughing.

The visit wasn't very long and the ferry continued on its southern trek and with another short trip the next small terminal came into sight. The sign confirmed that they had reached their destination. "Welcome to Otter Bay, Pender Island."

"We'd better join Hunter. The adventure is about to begin!" Kelly said excitedly as she headed for the car parked in the centre lane of the ferry deck.

♓

Terence Weiss heard the loud sliding slam of the cell doors as he vacated his assigned cramped room. He had no expression on his face as he heard the cheering and applause from his cellmates. He wasn't popular and most of the inmates had left him alone. They cheered because he was getting out, not because they liked him. He didn't care. He was just getting out, finally!

Two guards accompanied him to the Warden's office, then one guard knocked on the door.

"Come in and close the door," the gruff voice commanded.

Both guards remained outside the office and Terence entered the office, closed the door, and took a seat in front of the warden's large desk.

"Looks like your day has finally arrived, eh Weiss?"

Terence said nothing and sat without expression, staring directly at the round face of the man.

"Sign here and you're released. You can pick up your personal effects at the reception on your way out. The government gives you some cash to start, and it'll be in an envelope with the rest of your stuff," the warden said coldly.

The big man leaned over the desk, signed the documents in the marked places, and sat back without saying a word.

"Okay good. Stay out of trouble. Good luck, Weiss." The warden stood and looked directly at Terence.

Terence Weiss faced the warden, eyed him with a narrowing stare and stuck his right index finger in the air at eye level but remained silent. He turned and headed for the receptionist.

♓

All the vehicles filed off the ferry at Otter Bay. A parking lot was full of travelers who were waiting to have their turn to load and take the return voyage back to the lower mainland.

"An hour and a half, that's not too long of a trip I'd say, eh Simon? I'll drive up this road for a little way and find a place where Hunter can have a short walk."

The stream of vehicles exiting the ferry wound up the hillside and each selected a route at the main road stop sign.

"We're on North Pender and *Poets Cove* is on South Pender, at Bedwell Harbour," Simon instructed, looking at a map that he picked up at the Tsawwassen ferry terminal. "Kelly, you have to turn right at this intersection and follow the road down that looks like it runs down the centre of the island."

The island was heavily forested and a few areas had been cleared for farming. The narrow roadway was not busy and the bulk of the ferry traffic soon dissipated. The occasional home could be seen perched overlooking the water's edge, watching the peaceful day and ocean tides. The contrast to the bustling city was evident as the detectives followed the winding island road toward their agreed meeting place with Arthur Fleming.

The *Poets Cove Resort* sat on the crest of a hillside and overlooked the protected Bay. The sprawling resort was sophisticated and it looked like it deserved its five-star rating. The back of the property was skirted by exclusive condos surrounding an outdoor pool that overlooked the bay and distant islands. Each of the hotel's guest rooms had a view of the busy marina and the comings and goings of boats and float planes. The marina housed the Canadian border reporting station for all boaters crossing the international line that was less than a mile south in Boundary Pass.

Kelly parked the car in a visitor's slot. The day was getting warm.

"Okay Hunter, let's go," Kelly called as she opened the back door so the dog could get out. She clipped on his leash. "Simon, we'll be back in time for the meeting; why don't you check out the lobby and I'll meet you there in ten."

Kelly and Hunter went down to the waterfront promenade and the dog had fun checking out the new surroundings. They found a dog bowl with fresh water and Kelly watched the visitors mingling on the small beach.

The pair returned to the car and Kelly rolled down the car rear windows, returned Hunter to the back seat and headed toward the front of the hotel to find Simon. The relaxing atmosphere of the lobby provided a warm setting for the display of local artists' work; the lobby opened onto a deck that faced the marina. Simon saw Kelly as she entered the lobby.

"We're to meet Arthur at *Syrens Bistro*. It's on the lower level down these stairs," Simon said as he walked toward the wide staircase.

The pair entered the casually elegant lounge. The room was empty and all the patrons were seated on the outside patio. A trim medium-built man rose and waved his hand as the pair of detectives appeared at the entrance to the outside courtyard.

"Good afternoon, I'm retired Detective Arthur Fleming." The man gestured for the pair to take a seat at his table. "Enjoy your trip from the big city?"

"It was spectacular! This type of resort was unexpected, though; it's sure inviting," Kelly remarked with a smile. The bistro waiter took their drink orders and left menus on the tableside.

"It's a very popular destination. It's only a short distance from Vancouver Island and the hotel's complete makeover about five years ago has made it very attractive for the tourists." The man spoke with a soft Australian accent. He had a tanned weathered face and silver-colored hair. He had a trim build and wore a casual cream-colored front-button cotton shirt, unbuttoned at the top, with sandy-colored shorts and leather-strapped sandals.

"I understand that you want to talk about the Rawlings case. It was fifteen years ago but I recall the case quite well," Arthur said as he eyed his guests.

"We've uncovered new evidence on the Rawlings shooting, and we found the murder weapon while investigating the Tyler Whitford killing two days ago," Kelly revealed as she closely watched the retired man's reaction to the news. Fleming took a drink from his beer but his face didn't change expression.

"Hmm … Whitford, I recall that name. He was one of the men suspected in the embezzlement of funds from that software company. The man was Charles, though, if I recall correctly."

"Yes, you're right, Tyler was Charles' son. Tyler was killed with the same weapon that killed Mark Rawlings, according to ballistics. That fact placed enough doubt on the Terence Weiss conviction to overturn it and he's being released today."

Fleming stiffened, just a little. "All the evidence pointed to Weiss. We didn't have the weapon but all the rest of the facts pointed to him!"

"So what connection did you find between Weiss and Rawlings?" Simon asked as he noticed the waiter approach the table with the drink order. The waiter took the lunch orders and returned his attention to other tables.

"Weiss admitted that Rawlings owed him money. He also admitted that he had visited Rawlings at a house on Galiano Island and demanded payment. He said that he didn't kill him, but he had no alibi for the murder time frame. He said that he'd stayed at the Galiano Lodge that night, but no one could confirm that he was there at the time the ME estimated Rawlings' time of death," Arthur replied and then took a drink from his beer.

"Your report stated that no one was able to confirm the location of the crime scene where Rawlings was murdered, either."

"That's right. No blood was found at the waterfront home or dock, and none of the neighbors heard any shots either. The prosecution proved that Weiss had opportunity and motive, and they had the statement that Weiss had seen Rawlings that day. Weiss left fingerprints at the Rawlings house confirming that he had been there."

"Did you investigate anything concerning the involvement of Rawlings in the *DigiCast* embezzlement case?" Kelly asked, continuing to study the man.

"We looked around the Rawlings property to see if there was any evidence connecting him and or Weiss to the embezzlement, but found nothing. We were convinced that Weiss killed Rawlings and stuck to that conclusion."

"Is there anything else that you recall about your investigation that wasn't documented?"

"Hmm … the only strange thing was that Rawlings appeared to have sold the Galiano property to a Marriam Tremblay the year before he was killed. His bank records didn't show any transactions that you would've expected in a real-estate sale of that type. What's strange is that he had arranged for an automated payment of property taxes and utilities to be withdrawn from his bank account, which was sizable at the time. I don't know what the story is about that property now though."

"We went to see Weiss yesterday. Not a happy camper. What else do you know about him?"

"Not too much. He ran around with a bad crowd but I can't recall the name of the gang. It might be in my notes. I know he hates my guts, but that comes with the territory. You guys know that!"

The lunch meals arrived and were placed on the table.

"Do any of you need your drinks refreshed?" the waiter inquired.

"No, thank you. I have a few things to do this afternoon," Fleming replied and asked for the bill.

"One's our limit. Thanks." Simon looked up and smiled at the waiter.

"So, Arthur, do you live around here?" Kelly asked as she picked up her clubhouse sandwich.

"Yea, I've a place at Thieves Bay up the west side of the island. It's very quiet and private. I keep my boat there," he replied, grabbing a French fry from his plate.

"How are you finding retirement?" Simon asked as he took a drink from his beer.

"Oh, it's been about three years now and I find odd jobs to do. There are limited skills here on the island and there's always some handyman work around to do. I love my boat so I'm on it most of the summer months, rather than at the house," he replied as he poked at his salad.

"We appreciate you taking the time to see us. This case is full of surprises," Kelly remarked and took a drink from her beer.

"Funny how things work out! Humph ... I wouldn't have ever thought Charles Whitford was Rawlings' killer. He sure didn't leave any clues," Arthur said, shaking his head and taking another drink of his beer.

"The ferry back to the mainland doesn't leave until eight-forty tonight. Arthur, any suggestions as to where we can stop for a bite later tonight?" Kelly asked, changing the subject.

"Ah ... I'd say try the *Beach House Pub* at Browning Harbour. It's on North Pender and not that far from the ferry terminal. Food is good and it's a nice view in the evening. Can I do anything else for you two?" Arthur replied, looking anxious to leave.

"No, but you've been helpful. Thanks for your time, Arthur," Simon replied.

Fleming smiled and left the two detectives to enjoy their lunch and the warm day and went inside to find the waiter and pay for his lunch.

"Not a bad place to retire, huh?" Kelly asked Simon as Arthur disappeared inside the bistro.

"Well, with only two sailings a day, I see why most people have their own boat. I don't know if this place would be too quiet for me—I'm really a city guy!"

"You know, Simon, the name Tremblay rang a bell with me," Kelly said as she looked with a pensive expression at Simon across the table.

"How so?"

"I told you about the lighthouse earlier and the special oil painting Dad had given me. Well, the artist's signature was a 'J. Tremblay.' That's too much of a coincidence for me!"

"I think we need to take a look at that painting when we get back. What'da ya think?"

"Simon, something's up with that picture. We have to figure out what, and how it connects to our Whitford cases!"

The two finished their drinks, paid for their lunches, and headed back to the car.

"We got lots of time. We might as well explore the island while we're here!"

♓

Marcel Bessier was approaching Montague Harbour on the south side of Galiano Island in his yacht, the *Four Aces*. The marina had asked him to wait about half an hour until a berth for his forty-five-foot Bayliner could be vacated, as the harbour was busy. It was summer and the marina was one of the last large stops before crossing the Strait of Georgia to the mainland. Marcel had planned to stay overnight on his yacht but was going ashore for dinner, as he rarely cooked on the boat.

♓

The detectives joined the ferry lineup at Otter Bay about half an hour before the scheduled sailing. It was a Thursday night and it looked like the boat wouldn't be full. Everyone in the car was glad to be going home.

"Pender's a great place to visit, but it's too slow for me!" Kelly turned to Simon who was staring through the front windshield.

"I roger that. I loved the day and poking around the place. It's certainly an ideal spot to hide away and live a simpler life, but I wonder why Fleming chose this island to retire, as it's quite a slowdown for a detective. Humph!"

"Well if you're a boating guy maybe it's a good spot," Kelly replied. "And he was the assigned detective for the Gulf Islands as I recall."

The ferry began loading, but despite what Simon had figured the deck was almost full.

"There're still lots of pieces of this case that don't fit together. Why was Charles Whitford murdered and what triggered Tyler to go after Bessier with his dad's old Glock? It seems like Rawlings must've embezzled *DigiCast's* money, but no one's been able to find where he hid it. Was Weiss really involved with Rawlings and what's the story with Tremblay?" Kelly asked the rambling questions, working the disjointed facts in her head.

"Yea, then there's your lighthouse painting. Is that part of this mystery or something else?" Simon added to the list of questions. "And of course there's Fleming and his push to convict Weiss."

"Talking about Bessier, the missing Tyler Whitford keys are still bugging me," Kelly remarked as the pair sat in their vehicle waiting for the ferry to leave the terminal.

"Talking about bugging you, why did Weiss insist that he was intentionally framed by Fleming? Is it just a cop and suspect thing or was there another reason? I really couldn't get a read on the guy at lunch."

"Humph, me neither. I don't know if we made any progress today or not, but the trip was sure fun, eh Simon?" Kelly grinned.

♓

Elizabeth Richardson sat in her artist's studio fussing about the missing documents. She knew that there was nothing about her new identity in the old chest, but the documents certainly were a strong indicator that Joy Bessier hadn't drowned seven years before. Marcel could become dangerous if he suspected what had happened and was able to find her. She knew what she had to do, but didn't want to do it!

"I know that bastard had a gun in the safe in the study and I know the combination! I doubt he changed the house security codes either, thinking that I was dead," she thought to herself. "I still have the house keys, too. I have to get that gun to protect myself from him if he ever finds me! I'd better go and get it before he changes something."

She sat drinking a tea. The thought of returning to the West Vancouver house terrified her, but not as much as Marcel did.

"I'll get everything together and go tonight. I'd better book a room at Horseshoe Bay as I'm likely going to miss the last boat back to Bowen."

♓

Raj Jattan sat in a booth at the back of an Indian Restaurant on Marine Drive in West Vancouver, waiting for Lothar Zoric to arrive. Half a glass of red wine had been finished by the time Lothar showed and sat down.

"Sorry, Boss. I never get used to the traffic," the young man said as he removed his sunglasses.

Raj poured a glass of wine for Zoric. "Since Charles Whitford's dead and you couldn't find anything at his house, I did some research on that Bessier guy who shot Charles' son, Tyler," the East Indian said as he peered with his black eyes at the twenty-two-year-old, narrow-faced, thin man. Raj Jattan was a slender serious-looking twenty-eight-year-old man who had a black turban wound around the top of his head and wore a black pullover short-sleeved top.

"So how's that help, Boss?"

"Well, I'm told that Bessier is a big gambler and is into Jako Palma for a large lump of cash," Raj said flatly.

"Hey, Jako can be real bad news, Boss! He's some kind of heavy-weight in town."

"Well, I thought Jako could help us with our problem. I think Bessier must know something about our missing stuff. We've a meeting with Mr. Palma later tonight at the casino to see if we all can work together."

"I don't know, Boss; that guy's really trouble. Can't we go after Bessier ourselves?"

"It seems that Palma's looking for Bessier, too, and we don't want to get in the way of that. If Palma does Bessier I'll never find my money. I see no choice but to talk to Mr. Palma."

The meals arrived.

"I ordered for you, so eat up. The food's great here!" Raj said as the waiter refilled the empty wine glass and poured a second one for the new arrival.

♓

Arthur Fleming was on his forty-two-foot Nordic Tug trawler. The boat was tied up at his private dock that was separated from the local marina. The red-hulled boat had a teak galley, a small living area and a 28-inch flat-screen TV mounted from the top of the cabin. The boat had all the necessary electronics and Arthur could live on the boat comfortably when he chose. He had an appointment the next night at the old Rawlings place on Galiano Island and he wanted to ensure the boat was stocked and ready to go.

He had a modest house that sat secluded at the end of the dock. The private home was on a large lot and the neighbors were rarely seen as the tall cedar trees obscured the house from the road and the adjoining properties. Only the local residents used the marina and everyone kept to themselves.

"City cops. They're like ducks out of water out here! I sure don't expect to see those two out this way again," he muttered. "I never thought that the Rawlings case would ever surface again, though. It's good that I'm moving my merchandise tomorrow if they decide to snoop around some more." Fleming continued to talk to himself about his earlier meeting. "I'd better watch for Weiss. He could be a loose cannon now he's out of prison!"

♓

Sandra Vaughn was having a busy night at her poker table at the *West Coast Casino.* Many of her favorite players sat with large stacks of chips and were making large bets. Judge Anthony DeWit was doing very well and that was good news for Sandra. Thursday was his regular night and his luck was usually inconsistent, but he had a large grin on his face tonight.

He had already approached her and had made a room booking for eleven. He paid well when he was winning.

Raj Jattan and Lothar Zoric rode the elevator to the nineteenth floor of the *West Coast Casino and Suites* building. The meeting with Jako Palma had been arranged to be in Jako's private office that spanned the entire floor and included a private suite and entertainment room. The security guard on the ground floor had keyed the elevator access code to the nineteenth floor once the visitors had been appropriately frisked and access was granted by a call to Jako.

The elevator opened to the private foyer on the nineteenth floor and Peter Dobson escorted the visitors to the private office. The evening lights of the inner harbour were remarkable and the view from the office was second to none in the city. Jako Palma sat behind his glass-top executive desk and he was seen facing the view as the three entered the room. Peter moved to the back of the office and stood silently.

"You've requested this meeting, Mr. Jattan. What can I do for you two gentlemen?" Jako asked coldly as he turned in his chair. The forty-eight-year-old man wore an open collar black sport shirt, had jet black short hair and bushy black eyebrows. His eyes were cold and looked directly at Raj Jattan.

"Ah … Mr. Palma, I think we have a mutual interest in Marcel Bessier. He has something that belongs to me and I know you're interested in finding him, too. I thought that we could work together and get what we both want from him," Raj replied, trying not to appear nervous.

"Why come to me? You could find him yourself!"

"I know that you're looking for him and I don't want to interfere. I thought if we worked together it would be better for both of us!"

"What do you want him for?" Jako asked as he studied the East Indian.

"He's got some information I need."

"Yea, information about what?" Jako asked with a demanding tone in his voice.

"Some computer files that went missing and I think he knows where they are."

"What's in it for me? I could whack this guy and you'd get nothing!" Jako threatened.

"Look, someone stole fifty grand from me and I think Bessier knows where the information is or where I can find it. I'll give you half if I get the fifty K back!" Rattan knew very well that the actual amount was three-quarters of a mil, but didn't want to share the full amount with Palma, and figured that the fifty would be enough motivation to get Palma's attention.

"Hmm. Who's this clown with ya?" Jako glanced over at Lothar.

"Lothar Zoric, he works for me. He can work with you to help to find Bessier if you wish."

Jako frowned and turned to Peter Dobson. "Ya need any help, Peter?"

"I don't think so Boss but if ya want this guy to tag along, it's okay with me."

"Humph!" Jako reached over to his phone and buzzed the casino. "Hey send Sandra Vaughn up here on her break."

"I guess it's time to get Bessier in here then, eh Mr. Jattan? Peter, get these guys a scotch while we wait. We've ten minutes before our next guest arrives."

One of the casino security guards approached Sandra's poker table and whispered in her ear. "The boss wants to see ya upstairs at your break!"

"I've an appointment. Can it wait?" she replied softly.

"Ya want to tell Jako to wait?"

"Shit! Make arrangements to extend my break so I can keep my appointment when I'm done. I'm sure Mr. Palma would like to ensure his guests are kept happy."

"Ya, okay. I'll let your appointment know that you'll be a little late and that the room will be on us tonight."

Sandra held her breath as she took the elevator with the security guard to the nineteenth floor.

"Come in, Sandra. I think you can help us tonight." Jako Palma smiled and put his scotch glass down onto his desk as he saw Sandra enter the office.

"Yes, of course Mr. Palma. Anything you need," she replied, her heart pounding, as she had never met Mr. Palma in his office before.

"This is Mr. Jattan and Mr. Zoric. I know that Mr. Bessier's one of your favorite customers and he's one of mine, too, Ms. Vaughn. We need to see him right away and I believe that you know how to contact him. Is that right?"

Sandra looked at the room full of serious men. "Yes Sir, I think so."

She pulled her cell phone from her small purse and dialed the number. "Marcel, its Sandra Vaughn. Mr. Palma would like to see you ASAP," she said stiffly.

"Tell him I'm out of town," he answered.

"When can you get back here? I think it's important!" she asked, looking at Jako.

"Is he there?"

"Yes, Mr. Bessier, he's right here."

"Let me talk to him."

Sandra walked over to the large glass desk and passed the cell phone to Jako, who spoke into the phone, "Palma!"

"Ah … Mr. Palma. I'm working on getting your money and I should have it in a few days," Marcel explained.

"I need to see you now, Mr. Bessier!"

"Okay, but I'm on Galiano Island right now. It'll take me until late afternoon to get back to Vancouver. How about five tomorrow afternoon? That's the best I can do."

"You'd better be here, my patience is getting thin! The alternative won't be very pleasant." Palma growled and glanced over at Sandra.

"For sure, five." Marcel tried to sound upbeat but was annoyed that he had to divert attention and return to

Vancouver. He worried about his meeting with Palma and knew the command appearance was not a good thing.

Jako disconnected the call and handed Sandra her phone back across the desk. "Thank you Sandra, you may go and carry on with your business."

Sandra took the elevator down one floor and went directly to room E04 and knocked on the door.

"Sorry Judge, some panic upstairs. Okay now," she said as the door opened.

"Works for me Sandra, and they gave me this room at no charge for tonight. I've poured you a glass of wine."

♓

Elizabeth Richardson jumped into her car and headed for Snug Cove. She had a dark red wig on, wore wide dark sunglasses, black cotton pants and a black blouse. She looked like she was going to a funeral and took every precaution she knew in hiding her identity. She planned to take the eight o'clock evening ferry to the mainland and had thrown a cloth bag and flashlight into the back seat of her car. Her Kiew Road house keys were tucked safely into her purse.

It was just getting dark by the time Elizabeth reached the West Vancouver address. She knew the area well and knew of a good place to park her car out of sight from prying neighbors. She grabbed her green shopping bag, placed the flashlight inside and casually walked to the house and down the steep driveway.

Her heart was pounding and she looked for any sign of Marcel's car, as though she would recognize it anyway as it had been seven years since she had disappeared from his life. There was no car in the driveway and she assumed that he wasn't home. She walked very close to the shrubbery lining the driveway and sidewalk. It was hard for her to see her way on the blacked-out walkway, but she was very familiar with the route.

She stopped at the front door, listened but there was no sound. She pressed the doorbell, waited a minute but no one answered. She groped into her bag and found the house key and inserted it into the lock. She turned the lock, glanced behind her and listened. There still was no sound. She closed her eyes and took a large breath, running the security alarm code in her mind.

She entered the front door and went directly to the alarm keypad. "I sure hope Marcel didn't change the code!" she muttered as she held her breath and entered the six-digit code.

The small LED red light turned green and she quickly shut the door. She was in!

Elizabeth pulled the small flashlight from the green shopping bag and turned it on. The beam was narrow, but adequate for the job. She knew the safe was in the study and she wound through the rooms toward her destination. She noticed that most of her artwork was missing from the walls. "That bastard must've sold my work to feed his gambling habit!" she growled as she continued through the house toward Marcel's office.

She found the study and went directly to the large executive desk by the window. She pulled out the front drawer a short distance and reached under the desktop. She found a concealed button and pressed it. A wooden panel rose up and disappeared into the bookcase across the room. A safe was exposed that was pressed flush into the back wall. The face had a large dial and metal lever. Elizabeth walked to the safe and placed her small flashlight on the shelf so the face of the safe dial could be clearly seen. She rotated the dial in the combination of stops as she had done many years before. Completing the safe combination, she pulled the safe lever downward and pulled the heavy door open.

The safe had separator trays inside. The bottom floor of the safe had the loaded Ruger 38 pistol she was looking for. Additional shells were in a cardboard box at the back of the safe. She withdrew the light handgun and box of ammunition and placed them beside the flashlight.

Elizabeth saw a small package of $100 bills. "I'll take that for payment on my artwork, thank you very much!" She placed the stack of bills next to the revolver, then pulled the remainder of documents and a notebook from the cavity and looked them over.

"None of this stuff is of my concern!" she muttered quietly and returned the paperwork back into the safe. The loaded pistol, spare shells, and cash were placed into her green shopping bag. She closed the safe, rotated the dial a few notches and returned to the desk and activated the switch to close the sliding wooden panel.

She stopped for a moment and listened and could hear her heart beating quickly in her chest. The house was still quiet and she crept into her old art studio in the next room. Everything had been placed into one corner and her easels sat vacant of any work. A couple of small pieces of her finished work were stacked on the floor leaning against the far wall. "Hmm!" she muttered as she flipped through the canvases, selected one that pleased her and left the room for the front door.

Elizabeth reentered the security code to rearm the system, vacated the house and locked the front door. She was breathing heavily and walked quickly toward her car. No one saw her. The silence was unnerving. She placed her bounty onto the back seat floor, glad to leave, and headed toward Horseshoe Bay and her rented room.

Chapter Nine

Kelly went to visit her father. She had called the office the night before and told Captain Hollingsworth that she and Simon would be in the office late as they had gotten home just before eleven thirty the night before.

Westview Centre was one of the best facilities in the lower mainland to support and care for people with advanced Alzheimer's. His condition made her sad: she could no longer share with him the many good memories that they had once shared. She had been always his first consideration, even when she had been a rebellious teen. He had understood her pain and sadness in those years following his divorce and he had always encouraged her to follow her passion.

It was now her turn. She had been excited to tell him all about her discoveries, even though she knew he wouldn't understand. She took the photographs that she had found in his box of memorabilia, hoping that one of them would jog some past recollection, even for a short moment, but they didn't. She knew that the disease didn't allow such gifts, but she enjoyed her time nevertheless and promised him that she would return soon.

Kelly had promised Simon that she would pick him up before late morning. She found Simon standing at the transit station as agreed and he joined her in her car.

"Man, I was beat from yesterday. Good thing we didn't go into the office early," Simon remarked as he buckled up the seatbelt.

"I wanted to see my dad this morning and tell him the news about our strange case. He would've been so excited if he had understood what I was telling him, but I enjoyed telling him anyway."

"Well, I can't wait to get to your place and study those things of his more closely. There may be a clue there about Whitford, kiddo!"

They both entered Kelly's apartment and Hunter greeted the pair, nuzzling Simon.

"Hunter sure likes you, Simon," Kelly said while patting the dog on the head.

"Only because I kept slipping him cookies yesterday!" Simon grinned as Kelly shook her head in disapproval, but she knew the fact all too well.

The dining room table had all Kelly's dad's paraphernalia spread out. Kelly returned to the collection the photographs she had taken to show her father. Simon picked up the few photographs that Kelly had placed on a pile. He selected the photo with the group of five and the lighthouse, and turned the black and white photo over.

"Hmm … we know who all these people are now except the Joy woman. Any idea who Joy is?" Simon asked peering at the young face.

"Nope, not yet. My bet is she was the private secretary of one of the men in the photo but I'm not sure."

"The inscription sure is strange." Simon read it out aloud.

Georgina's place of note to view,
Marriam's place the point you Cain see,
To plot by the legend of Fisher's 3462
The captain's compass will be the key.

"Humph!" Simon thought for a moment. "What do you think that's all about?"

"You've got me! Put it aside and we can work on it later," she said as Hunter got comfortable under the table.

Simon selected another photograph. "You're sure cute in this one. I guess about five, eh?" he remarked, putting the photo down and picking up the snapshot with the two golfers. "One of these guys is in the other photo, so he's likely Rawlings. We know what Whitford looks like from a photo we saw at his house on Bowen, so it's not him. No names on the back, just a date," he said as he turned the photo over. "Any guess?"

"Nope—not a clue on that face either. It says that it's about one of Dad's company golf tournaments, but nothing else. Funny picture to have in this lot, neither Dad nor I are in it like the rest of them!"

Simon turned his attention to the oil painting lying on the table. "I like this painting. You say that there's something special about this work! Hmm …." He studied the artwork closely. "Did you notice this marking at the bottom of the lighthouse?"

"What marking?"

"See here, at the bottom of the lighthouse, there's a '55' and a 'W' painted in blue. I think that it was intended to stand out from the white lighthouse base," Simon said as he held the painting close to his face.

"Let me see that!" Kelly said sharply, took the painting from Simon and looked at the base of the lighthouse. "Yea, you're right! I wonder what that means," she said pensively as she placed the artwork back onto the table.

"Hey, I'll take a cell photo and we'll have it to study later," Simon said as he took the painting and placed it so that he could take the photograph and then turned the painting over, without thinking.

"Have ya ever looked at the back of this thing? It's labeled as *Georgina's Lighthouse* in black felt pen and there're strange penned numbers on the back, too!"

"No, what do you mean strange numbers?"

"See the numbers on the borders of the wide wooden frame? They look like they're placed in specific places and they've got to mean something! Maybe the numbers are connected with the riddle from the photo!"

"Hmm … it confirms the painting is of *Georgina's Lighthouse*, but we figured that out already. I don't get the numbers, though. Take a photo of those and we can work on their meaning later, too."

Simon took the shot and turned the canvas back over and placed it on the table.

"We need to go and see the lighthouse. I'm sure it must have answers to this puzzle."

"Okay, let's stand back, take a breath and look at what we've got," Simon said as he took a seat. "I say that we should work on the riddle from the back of the black and white photograph, first."

"Ah … okay," Kelly muttered and took a seat at the table. "There are four words with capitals in the riddle. We have Georgina's, Marriam's, Cain, and Fishers. These must either be names or places."

"We know that Georgina's is the lighthouse, so we have three left to work out."

"Marriam's is a girl's name and is too broad a search, so that won't help at this point; that leaves Cain and Fishers."

Kelly opened the lid of her running computer laptop. "Okay, I'll Google® 'Cain' first and see what we get!"

A list of mixed results appeared and she selected a number of page links, but nothing that fit the riddle seemed worth further exploring.

"Not that one. I'll try Fishers," she said and another mixed set of results appeared.

"Hey, let's try this link from the list. 'Fisheries and Oceans Canada.' That works with lighthouses and a marine theme." Kelly selected the link and the next page provided another inquiry search box.

"Hmm … I wonder what the '3462' in the poem means. It seems to me that it's associated with the Fishers clue." She keyed the digits into the inquiry field.

"Look, there's a chart number 3462." Kelly selected that link and a marine chart image appeared on the laptop screen. "This is a chart of the area around *Georgina's Lighthouse*! It's too small and unreadable on this computer screen. This website says that we can get this chart for $20, though." Kelly Googled® marine charts. "We can buy a chart at 'Black Fish Marine' on *Granville Island.* That's not too far from here."

Kelly dialed the listed contact phone number on her cell. "Yes, good morning. I'm looking for chart 3462. Do you have one in stock?" The conversation paused for a minute or so and Kelly sat and waited, staring at the computer screen.

"You do, great! I'm Kelly and will pick it up later this morning, okay?" she said excitedly as Simon sat and watched her. "I appreciate that. See you later." She ginned and hung up the phone.

"Simon, how about going to Mayne Island with me tomorrow and we can go and see the lighthouse and see where the clues lead us?" Kelly asked quickly, hardly able to contain her excitement.

"Okay, but we should go into the office later today and bring Captain Hollingsworth up to speed. This trip's still relating to the Charles Whitford murder, but we need his approval for an overnight trip if we end up staying there."

"Yea, yea … I know, I'll book the ferry for the first boat and you take notes on all this stuff!"

"I've the photos of the oil painting, so all I need is the riddle," Simon replied as he watched his partner load the BC Ferries website. "We can pick up the marine chart on the way back to the office. *Granville Island* is only about ten minutes from here and isn't too far out of our way."

♓

Sandra wanted to start early with her rowing routine. She had been fussing about her command visit with Mr. Palma and her role in setting up the meeting with him and Marcel Bessier. She hadn't been used in that way before, and she didn't like it either.

"The Judge was a good sport about the evening and he left me a good tip over my usual fee. I think he knew that I was stressed when I showed up at his room," she thought, then pulled hard on the oars of her narrow boat, and the lightweight shell moved quickly through the calm water.

Her mind wandered onto other thoughts. "I've got to get my head sorted out about Forsythe! I really like him but I've got to find a way to tell him about who I am and what I do. I'd quit if I thought that he would stay with me, and leaving the casino would be a good thing for me, too!"

Sandra's mind drifted back to the meeting with all the men. "I hope Marcel will be okay. Those guys last night sure didn't look very happy and Mr. Palma was cold and direct. Hmm ... I wonder if I'll see Marcel tonight at the tables." She continued her strained workout.

♓

Terence Weiss had enjoyed his first night of freedom. He stayed with Pits, an old friend who lived in the East Side of Vancouver. Everyone knew him as Pits as he had large pock marks on his face, remnants from some childhood illness, and he had always said that it was 'the pits' to have a messed up face. Pits was a member of the 'Los Chinche' gang. He was a large big-boned person and no one messed with him.

Terence needed a gun, and Pits had supplied a KAHR 9mm pistol without questions. Terence was on a mission and he was going to kill Fleming for what he had done! It was just going to happen earlier than he had initially planned. Terence had told Pits about his plans as they shared many beers the night before, and Terence talked about how pissed he was at Fleming and the bitterness seeped through each word.

Pits knew a lot of things about Fleming and told his friend Weiss that Fleming had got into the gun trafficking business in a big way and that Fleming mainly supplied the *Black Widow* drug gang with their weapons. The *Black Widow* and the *Los Chinche* were at war. Eliminating Fleming would certainly help the cause so far as Pits was concerned, so he told his friend that he would advise his *Los Chinche* buddies to watch for the *Black Widow*'s next trip to meet Fleming.

♓

Forsythe Harrison sat in his office at *Syms, Powell & Wells*, a small law firm located in the Vancouver downtown core. He had called Sandra's home number but she hadn't been home and he assumed that she had likely left for the Vancouver Rowing Club earlier than usual. He left a voice message, "Sandra, I think it might be fun if we spent Saturday together. I know it's your day off. Please call. Forsythe."

He had a framed photograph of himself and Sandra standing by her Sabot at the *Kitsilano Yacht Club*. The frame sat on his desk by his phone. He loved looking at her and she had such a large smile in the photograph. She was great fun and he wanted to see more of her.

Forsythe had returned to Canada to practice law. His parents lived in Vancouver and he wanted to be close to them. England was a nine-hour flight and it was simpler for him to move back to his hometown than to practice in Britain.

♓

Jako Palma sat in his executive office talking to Peter Dobson. "So what's ya take from last night's meeting with Raj Jattan?" Jako asked flatly.

"It seems to me like he's small time, Boss. I think that Zoric guy's a card short of a deck, too!"

"Yea, guys like that can screw things up at the worst time. I think you need to cut Zoric out of the picture. We'll deal with Jattan after we see where things go with Bessier and we get a better idea about the money he's looking for."

Peter Dobson was a tall six-foot-three muscular blond-haired man who had worked for Jako Palma for the past five years. He'd been involved in helping Jako with business problems before like Lothar Zoric, and knew exactly what needed to be done.

"I got Zoric's cell number. Leave the details to me, Boss. I'll be back by five to attend your love-in with Bessier," Peter replied coldly.

"I'm sure Bessier has a story for us. Ya take off and have ya butt back here by five," Jako instructed and then turned in his chair to look out the window.

Dobson left the office to prepare for what he had to do to handle Zoric. He punched in some numbers on his Blackberry®. "Hey Lothar, its Peter Dobson. I've been talking with Mr. Palma and we'd like you to schedule a flight to Galiano Island for tomorrow morning. Let me know what time you've reserved after you've made the booking. Come to the casino lobby at four this afternoon and we can work out the details of your assignment. Okay?"

"Sure thing, Mr. Dobson."

♓

Arthur Fleming wanted to be at Montague Harbour by dinner time. He had a favorite restaurant at the marina and he thought that it would be wise to have a good meal before his appointment at the Rawlings place at ten that night.

He hired Jordan Fisk to help when there were heavy shipments to handle. Jordan usually helped Fleming when there were handyman jobs that needed an extra set of hands. The young twenty-year-old man was happy to get any work and Arthur paid him well. Jordan never asked questions about the jobs, and stuck to doing exactly what he was told. The last two years had been very lucrative and Jordan looked forward to having another opportunity to make some good cash.

Jordan was a trim, thin, well-conditioned young man, dressed casually in an open unbuttoned red short-sleeved top. He had the hair on the side of his head cut short and the hair on top was long and mismanaged.

It was time for them to leave Thieves Bay and head to the marina.

"Cast off, Jordan, we're ready to go!" Arthur instructed and the young man jumped onto the dock and untied the red-hulled trawler.

♓

Marcel Bessier had made good time in crossing the Strait back to the Vancouver mainland. The late afternoon Friday exodus of boats was heading westward for the Gulf Islands, and his was one of the few that headed toward the mainland. He decided to fuel up at the *Fisherman's Cove Marina* before heading to his private dock just south of Eagle Harbour.

While the marina refueled his Bayliner, Marcel recalled that he should thank the young sales person who had stayed late the night of the incident with Tyler. Marcel entered the small sales office.

"Hey Mr. Bessier, sorry about the other night. I didn't know that guy was going to rob you!" the young man said, shaking his head.

"It's okay. Thanks for sticking around. Here's an extra C-note for your trouble." Marcel smiled and handed the man a one-hundred-dollar bill.

"It wasn't any problem. I hope you're okay and you're happy with the quick cleaning job and makeshift window repair!"

"Yea, you handled that just fine. I'm thankful that the boat took all the abuse and not me; anyway, I'll have it all fixed soon and the boat can be placed back on the sale board." Bessier smiled and returned down the gangplank.

It took less than fifteen minutes for Marcel to pull alongside his private dock in West Vancouver. He tied up the large boat and grabbed his bag containing the Tyler Whitford stash.

"I'll get this stuff into the safe before I go and see Jako. I don't want him getting his hands on this information. I might need the bargaining power later."

Marcel placed the bag on his office desktop, pulled the front drawer and activated the hidden switch. The safe appeared as the covering panel slipped away. He walked over to the bookcase, dialed the safe combination and opened the door. He noticed that his Rugger pistol and box of shells were missing. He stood staring in disbelief and thought back to the last time he had placed the gun in the bottom shelf.

"I know the damn thing was there!" He stood and thought what else he may have done with it.

"I'm the only one who knows it's here!" he yelled out and looked further around in the safe cavity. "My emergency cash is gone, too!" he growled, looking confused and then became very annoyed. He stood by the open safe and thought about what could've happened. It made no sense.

"The house alarm was set when I came in, and any B&E would've alerted the security firm. They haven't called, either."

he mused. Marcel went to the office desk and pulled the contents from the bag that he'd taken from Tyler Whitford's condo, and dumped it on the desk preparing to put it into the safe. He saw the plastic zip lock package with his wife's documents slide out of the bag onto the desk and peered at it for a moment.

"That bitch is alive! Of course, she must've come here and taken the gun and the cash! Charles Whitford's death has something to do with all this, and Tyler said that she likely didn't drown." He stood stiffly at the thought. "Damn, damn. When I'm done with Jako, I'll figure the rest of this damn thing out! I'll find her, that's for sure," Marcel yelled but no one heard him.

He put all the contents of the bag into the safe. "Well at least I've got five grand here she didn't get and I'd better change the house security code. I don't want her back in here again, that bitch!"

Marcel went into the kitchen to find the instructions on how to change the security code, as he had never done it before and had no clue how to do it.

♓

Lothar Zoric was at the casino lobby at the stroke of four as he had been instructed. He sat in one of the lounge chairs and waited for Peter Dobson to appear.

"Hey Lothar, stay seated and I'll join you." Peter sat in the soft bucket chair next to Lothar and placed a metal briefcase on the floor by the chair.

"Mr. Dobson, I got the flight booked as you asked. I'll be leaving Richmond on the seven thirty morning flight. I should be at Galiano by eight."

"Okay, good, and I'll be travelling with Mr. Bessier on his yacht and we'll see you at Galiano. Wait for me at the restaurant at Montague Harbour. We'll all go from there," Peter said, eyeing the young man who had his sunglasses wrapped around his neck.

"No problem, Mr. Dobson!"

"I need you to take this briefcase of files and documents to Galiano for me. I don't want Bessier to know about them right now. The case is locked and there shouldn't be any problem at the air terminal as it's a local flight." Peter handed the aluminum briefcase to Lothar. "Don't lose this and keep it with you at all times."

"What about a change of clothing and stuff?" Lothar asked, thinking that he would be away for more than a day.

"Don't worry about that! You might be back the same day and if not we'll sort out what you need in Montague Harbour if it's not on the boat," Peter smiled.

"Yea, that'll be fine," Lothar shrugged.

"Okay now, take off and I'll see you at the marina, probably late afternoon. I got your cell number and if there're any changes in plans I'll call ya."

Lothar smiled, got out of his chair and left the casino lobby with the briefcase. Peter Dobson watched the man go on his way. He smiled and took the elevator to the nineteenth floor.

♓

Marcel gave the keys of his red roadster to the parking attendant at the casino.

"Hey Mr. Bessier, we don't usually see you on Fridays. Something special up today?" the attendant asked as opened the door of the car.

"No, it's good to change routines sometime."

Bessier went inside and walked to the receptionist in the lobby. "Please advise Mr. Palma that Marcel Bessier's here for our appointment."

The girl smiled and buzzed the executive office.

A security guard appeared at the counter. "Mr. Palma will see you now, but I need to do a security check over here, please," he said and pointed to a place out of view of the patrons milling around in the lobby.

After completing the check for weapons, the guard went to the elevator and keyed his security code into the elevator pad, selecting the nineteenth floor. The door opened and

Marcel got into the car feeling very uneasy and he wasn't looking forward to the anticipated discussion with Jako Palma.

Peter Dobson met Marcel when the door silently slid open. "Mr. Palma's waiting for you, Mr. Bessier." Dobson pointed the way and followed Marcel into the office.

"Hey, Marcel. Want a scotch?" Jako asked as he sat back in a small sofa in his office.

"Yes, I think I will Jako, thanks."

"Peter, please get our friend Marcel a scotch, and one for me, too." Jako glanced over his shoulder at Peter Dobson standing by the front door of the office and then turned his attention back on Marcel."Take a seat, Marcel."

The two scotches appeared and one glass was handed to Marcel, the other placed on the glass side table beside Jako. Peter returned to his place by the office door.

"I hear that you haven't come up with your payment yet, Marcel. Dobson's concerned that you won't make your deadline. I thought that we should have a little chat about that."

"Yea, I'm working on it. I know that I'll have it for you before the deadline, Jako."

"We hear ya killed some kid and that he had some information as to where there's a large sum of cash. That right?" Jako asked coldly, as his black eyes peered at Marcel sitting in a chair across from the sofa.

"Ah … that's right, Jako. I was working on finding that money when you called. I think it's somewhere in a house on Galiano Island. Some embezzled cash from ages ago."

"Well you'd better be right or you'll run out of time, my friend. Maybe you should spend your short time finding another more plausible source of cash."

"I'm sure I'm right. The kid was serious."

"Hmm … you think it's somewhere in a house but that's all ya know, eh? I think that Dobson here should work with you and ensure that you find it." Jako smiled and looked Marcel directly in the eye. "We don't want to screw up now, do we Marcel, so Dobson here is going to be like your brother. He's going to stay with ya all the way."

"I plan to go back to Galiano in the morning. Mr. Dobson can meet me at my boat first thing," Marcel said nervously and then took a stiff drink from his glass of scotch.

"No, I think he should be your guest tonight. That'll make things easier in the morning," Jako replied as he continued to stare into Marcel's face.

"Ah … yea, sure Jako. No problem!"

"Okay, you guys get to know each other better. Peter, you keep me informed on how things go on Galiano."

"Right, Boss! Let's go, Marcel," Peter replied from the back of the room.

The meeting was over and Jako finished his scotch in peace as the other two left the office.

♓

Arthur Fleming and Jordan Fisk were preparing the trawler to leave Montague Harbour.

"Jordan, cast off!" Arthur yelled out from the pilot's bridge.

The young man pulled the ropes from the docking rings and then jumped aboard the boat.

"We've got to head through Active Pass. The tide waters are going to run fast tonight so be prepared," Arthur said as the young man joined him in the small cabin.

"Where're we going, Mr. Fleming?"

"Back to our house out by Whaler Bay. We've some customers that'll meet us there at ten!"

The Galiano house was in darkness when the forty-two-foot Nordic Tug reached the private dock off Cain Point. The two men tied up the boat at the far end of the dock.

"Wait here until I get some lights on!" Fleming instructed, then went ahead of Jordan to turn on a few lights in the house. The dim glow could be seen from the dock, which remained dimly illuminated. Jordan knew that he was expected in the house and he cautiously followed the dock to the garden path that led toward the back of the ranch-style home. Jordan joined his boss in the large family room.

"Ya want a beer, Jordan? There are some cold ones in the fridge," Arthur asked as he made himself a rum and coke in the kitchen.

Jordan went to the bar fridge, grabbed a Canadian® and pulled the tab. "Great, Boss!"

"We've got a little wait so enjoy your drink. We've a lot of heavy work to do soon."

It was very dark in the summer night. A couple of houses across the water on the small Gossip Island had lights, but it was very difficult for the occupants to see anything that Fleming was doing.

Arthur was on his second drink when the sound of another boat could be heard approaching the dock.

"It's time." Fleming gulped the remainder of his drink and as he went to meet the guests at the dock, he instructed, "Jordan, stay here!"

Arthur Fleming had been gone for quite a while. Jordan could hear the muffled conversation at the dock as he finished his beer, and eventually three men appeared at the back door.

"Okay, all's arranged. Jordan you help these men and get the boxes from the basement onto their boat. I'll be with you in a minute to help," Arthur instructed and then disappeared down the hallway and into a bathroom.

The men followed Jordan down a hallway and the basement door squeaked open. Arthur waited until he heard the men go down the stairs and then left the bathroom, walked into the kitchen, and placed his cash payment in his special hiding place. He smiled and then joined the men in the basement.

The two men from the visiting boat lifted a large wooden pine crate and Jordan noticed how their arms, covered with black widow spider tattoos, bulged as the guys lifted the heavy cargo. In less than an hour the loading had been completed and the visitor's boat engine noise faded into the night.

"Good work, Jordan. We'll overnight here as it's more comfortable than the boat and we'll head back to Thieves Bay in the morning. You've got to be careful going through Active Pass and I prefer not to navigate it at night if I have a choice."

Both men refreshed their drinks.

Chapter Ten

It was Saturday morning and the weather forecast was for a hot day for the lower mainland. Sandra was excited to be going on her first date with Forsythe that wasn't at the sailing club. He had suggested that they spend the entire day together and thought cycling around the city would be fun. She hadn't done that activity for quite some time and had pulled her bike from the locker in the garage of her condo complex.

She wanted to learn more about this gorgeous man. The biking invitation offered her a great opportunity to see if their relationship could move beyond sailing. He had promised that they'd still go to the late afternoon Sabot competition at the club, as neither of them wanted to miss that!

Sandra had gathered her biking gear and was ready to go by the time Forsythe buzzed her apartment. "Hey Sandra, it's Forsythe. I'll wait for you down here." The small speaker in the door pushed out the words with a muffled sound.

She quickly went into the concrete-encased garage and exited with her cycle in tow. "I'm ready. It's your date so you select a route." Sandra flashed a big smile.

"Well, I've already done fifteen minutes on this bike to get here so I guess we'd better do something easy to warm you up!" He jokingly poked her in the arm.

"Hey baby, I'm always ready! Where to?" she asked as she mounted her bike.

"I thought we'd start around Stanley Park and then try some of the dedicated bike lanes through the city. Let's go!" Forsythe directed his cycle toward the crossway leading to Devonian Park and the causeway.

♓

Lothar Zoric was running late. His flight was scheduled to leave Richmond for Galiano at seven thirty. He lived in a small basement flat in North Marpole and by the time he was finally ready to leave, it was already seven fifteen.

His seaplane flight departed from the southern shore of Sea Island in Richmond and there was no way he was going to make his flight on time.

"Oh damn, Dobson sure will be pissed I missed this flight," Lothar grumbled, checking that his cab was still waiting out in the street. "I know that airline doesn't have another flight until eleven twenty! Hmm … I'll call *Island Airways*. I know they've morning flights from the Bayshore downtown. Maybe they have earlier flights."

He called and booked a seat for the eight forty-five departure. It was Saturday and the *Island Airways* flight wasn't busy and there were seats available despite the late booking time.

Lothar grabbed Dobson's briefcase and ran to the taxi at the cub.

"Hey buddy, you're not going to make your flight!" the cabbie said as Lothar opened the back door.

"Yea, I know. I've booked another plane leaving from the Bayshore. It leaves at eight forty-five," he said in a rushed tone as he climbed inside the cab.

"You're lucky that it's not a rush-hour day, man!" the cabbie remarked as he picked his way down Granville Street heading for the downtown core.

♓

Peter Dobson was out of his bed early and fixing coffee at Marcel Bessier's large waterfront home in West Vancouver. "Hey Bessier, you look like shit!" he said as Marcel appeared in the kitchen doorway.

"Didn't sleep well. I don't usually have guests in the house," Marcel grumbled as he stood there in a bathrobe.

"Here, grab a coffee, you'll feel better. Get a move on, I don't want to get to Galiano too late."

"Hey, Dobson, why don't you stock the kitchen on the boat while I get cleaned up? We'll be on it for a day or so I expect, and I know I'm almost out of beer and scotch. You'll find a twelve pack of beer and a new bottle of scotch under the bar in the front sitting room. Oh … I usually eat out, so if ya want somethin' to eat you'd better check what's in the galley on the boat," Marcel said, taking his coffee and heading to his bedroom.

Peter grabbed his coffee and started to wander around the house, poking his head into the office down the hall. "Hey, Bessier this place must've set you back some! You could sign it over to Mr. Palma and have money to spare!"

"Ha ha, very funny, Dobson." A muffled laugh came from a bathroom down the hall. "I'm trying to sell that boat out there on the dock. It's worth enough to pay off your boss and then some, but it takes time to move those things. Besides, Jako only takes cash!"

Forty-five minutes later Marcel reappeared in the kitchen. "Okay, I'm ready; I assume that you've finished loading the boat so let's get on our way. We've some exploring to do!"

♓

Lothar Zoric had no problem making the eight forty-five morning flight at the Bayshore Hotel dock in Coal Harbour. The single engine DeHavilland Beaver was already at the dock. No other passengers were waiting and the pilot was not anywhere to be seen. Lothar was not a fan of flying and preferred to drive. He didn't want to start off on the wrong foot with Dobson so he agreed to fly ahead, even though it was outside his comfort zone. He was told by the ticket agent that the Beaver was the safest plane in the air, and that the design had been around for over fifty years. It was the most popular small commuter plane in Canada. The fact still didn't ease his anxiety about flying.

The pilot appeared on the walkway, unlocked the access ramp to the dock floats. "It looks like just you and me this morning, Sir. Walk carefully and we'll be off to Galiano in a moment or two."

The pilot looked too young in the eyes of Lothar, and he hoped the kid knew what he was doing. Lothar selected a seat in the front row, even though there was seating for eight in the small cabin.

The pilot climbed in. "The flight's only thirty minutes. Buckle up. It's a nice morning but safety first!" The pilot worked his way up the aisle and slipped into his pilot's seat. He started the engine and the floatplane taxied out into the inlet.

The aircraft pointed due west, the engine roared and the floatplane lifted smoothly off the water surface; Lothar watched the *Bayshore Hotel* become smaller as the plane climbed to its cruising altitude. Lothar's hands clutched the metal arms of his seat. His eyes bulged out and his heart felt like it was going to beat overtime. He wasn't having any fun.

Lothar noticed that Galiano Island was in sight and the floatplane began making its directional corrections to align for the landing at Montague Harbour.

The Beaver aircraft exploded in midair.

The explosion tore the fuselage in half and blew out the side and wing structure behind the cockpit. The burning plane dropped like a rock into the ocean in a ball of flame and smoke. The crash site was a half mile south of Helen Point on the western edge of Mayne Island, just minutes from the landing strip at Montague Harbour.

♓

Kelly and Hunter, sitting in the gray Taurus, waited for Simon outside his Chinatown apartment. He came out with an overnight bag, some Tim Horton's® donuts, and jumped into the front seat.

"Good morning, crew. I picked up something for the trip. Remember last time we almost missed the boat!" He smiled and opened the brown paper bag. "These are little guys and it makes them easier to eat when you're driving. I also packed a small bag in case we miss the boat or find something that demands an overnighter." Simon passed the paper bag over to Kelly so she could take a donut before she pulled from the curb.

"You're sure thinking ahead. I never even thought about that possibility of staying over! I did remember to book the ferry back from Mayne for seven forty-five tonight, though."

She changed the subject. "Simon, when we were on our trip to see Fleming you said that you seldom leave Chinatown. What's that all about?" Kelly looked over her shoulder to check for traffic and then pulled onto the roadway.

"As you know, I grew up in Chinatown. Dad worked in a small shop that imported things from China and Mom worked in a restaurant. The Chinese community is tight and everyone knows what's going on. You know, nothing goes unnoticed!"

"Not really, I don't—after my mother left my dad I seemed invisible to everyone around me, except for my dad that is. Your life was so different compared to anything that I remember!" Kelly finished her donut. "Got another one of those things in that bag?"

Simon held the bag open so she could take another and carried on with his story. "I love the life and the community culture. I became a cop to protect it from the violence that seemed to be creeping into its society."

"So, no love of your life, Simon? There's always a girl in the story," Kelly pointed out as she chewed the donut and watched the traffic.

"There was a girl in my early twenties. I guess a young love, you might say." He paused. "Her father had come to Canada with the *Bank of Hong Kong*. His wife had difficulties fitting into Canadian life and struggled with the language. They stayed only a short time and then they went back and took their daughter with them."

"And?" Kelly glanced over at Simon, her eyebrows raised.

"I eventually married when I was thirty-one, but my wife couldn't handle being a cop's wife and it ended after five years. I've adapted to being single now and I focus on the RCMP."

"You plan on staying single?"

"Ah … don't know. Life changes and these things seem to look after themselves. I just don't worry about it," he replied and looked inside the bag for another sugar donut.

The line for the Gulf Islands ferry was just as long as before, and being a weekend, the boat was again full with a waiting line already formed partly down the large lot for the next ferry.

There was plenty of time before the scheduled sailing and Kelly gave the woman at the ticket booth her pre-paid reservation number. Kelly drove her car to her place in line, and she and Simon took Hunter for a short walk. Everyone needed to stretch anyway.

The ferry left on time at ten ten, and the cars were jammed onto the small deck.

"Let's yank out that chart we bought and see if we can figure out how to read it," Simon suggested.

"Hey, okay, good idea! We can spread it out on the hood of the car." Kelly smiled, pulled the chart from its plastic cover, and stepped from the car.

The chart was about two-and-a-half feet by five feet in size. It had the chart number 3462 in large black, block letters on the top margin and "Fisheries and Oceans" printed in small print on the top border. The landmasses were colored yellow and the elevation of the land and the depth of the water were marked in ten-meter intervals. A large compass was printed in red and placed in the center of Saltspring Island, and was repeated over the Saanich Peninsula land mass of Vancouver Island. The international boundary between Canada and the United states was marked with blue dots.

"This is really cool! I see why a boater needs one of these to navigate around safely." Kelly folded the map into quarters and explained, "That makes it easier to read."

The top right quarter had all the island destinations of their Gulf Islands ferry route.

"Here it is, Georgian's Point!" Kelly's finger pointed to the entrance to Active Pass and the northern tip of Mayne Island. "We're going here first."

Simon pointed to the pair of landmasses to the south. "Here's Pender Island, where we were last trip." The Galiano ferry stop loomed into sight. Simon rolled the map and placed an elastic band around the circumference. "We'll be at Mayne Island soon. We'd better get back into the car."

The ferry began its docking maneuvers for Sturdies Bay. "Next stop's ours," Kelly said, watching the pier getting closer.

♓

Arthur Fleming was navigating his boat into Thieves Bay. It was late morning and he had other work to do at his house.

Arthur brought the boat alongside his dock and Jordan jumped onto the dock and tied up the boat on the metal cleats. "Great work last night, Jordan!" Arthur handed the young man an envelope. "Your payment's inside and I've given you a bonus. I'll need you again Monday. Can you be here by noon?"

"Sure thing. Thanks, Mr. Fleming."

Arthur worked his way along the dock toward his house and waved to Jordan as he left to go home.

♓

Harrison Forsythe's bum was getting sore from the entire morning's bike riding. "I don't know about you, but my butt needs a rest. Ah … how about lunch?"

Sandra felt the same, but didn't want to admit it. "Your call, your date! I'm really hungry, though," she replied grinning.

The cyclists had returned to Coal Harbour. "There's a great place to eat here where we can sit outside and watch the activity," Forsythe said as they locked their bikes on the railing and then found a comfortable seat at the outside bar.

"I'm glad this seat is wider than those tiny ones on the cycles. Surely someone can design something more comfy than those things we've been sitting on!" Sandra smiled, relieved to have a large padded seat as she got comfortable at the bar that looked over the inner harbour.

The waitress appeared and they ordered cold drinks and nachos.

"Having fun?" Forsythe started the conversation as he looked at Sandra and not the view.

The two drinks arrived and Sandra gulped a mouthful. "I sure needed that and it's getting hot today. Ah … you trying to wear me out, buddy?" Sandra asked, poking at her date.

"Just trying to work up an appetite!" Forsythe replied as he finished a mouthful of his cold drink.

"So lawyer boy, tell me more about you. All I know is you love sailing, can wear me out cycling and you've just joined a local law firm in town!"

"I grew up in Vancouver and my parents are still here. I wanted to be the best lawyer I could and with lots of hard work I was accepted at Cambridge. It's the second oldest university in England, after Oxford, and I wanted a place with a strong tradition."

"Why on earth come back?" she asked, studying him closely.

"I found that England's law community was too old school for me and with my parents still in Vancouver, I decided to come back here and practice."

"I didn't think Sabot sailing was big out there!"

"It's not! It's mainly sculling on the rivers over there. I learned that I liked Sabots when I was growing up here so I just picked it back up when I returned."

"You should join the rowing club at Stanley Park where I do my sculling," she suggested with an alluring grin.

The nachos arrived and they ordered another set of cold drinks.

"Your turn. You originally a Vancouverite?" Forsythe asked, looking at her smooth tanned skin and the shape of her sensual pink-painted lips.

"I don't usually talk about my family, as I left home when I was thirteen. My mother was a Native Canadian. She was Xwemelch'stn of the Capilano Nation. She overdosed four years ago and died. My father's white and grew up in North Vancouver," she replied and turned away from his gaze and looked over the calm water.

"I'm sorry to hear about your mother, Sandra. Where's your father now?"

"He's a mechanic and works in a small automotive repair shop in North Vancouver," she replied and pulled a cheese-covered chip from the pile of nachos and scooped some salsa onto it.

"Thirteen's very young. What did you do when you left home?" Forsythe asked and pulled a chip from the pile on the plate.

"Oh …." She hesitated for a moment and then looked back into his face. "I lived in the streets, mostly around Powell Street. I learned a lot from the runaways that camped around there and the homeless. I wanted to do better than that and took some programs that helped me pull myself together." Her heart started to beat quickly as she began to stress about telling her story.

"I can surely see that you did. You must be proud of yourself!" he said and took her hand and smiled.

"I am!" Sandra said proudly. "It's easier not looking native and having my dad's features I'd say, though I do miss my mother's Native culture a little. It was a big part of my life while growing up." Sandra looked saddened and Forsythe changed the subject.

"Well, I like you and also hope to spend more time with you!" he said and let go of her hand to take another mouthful of his cold drink.

"Me, too! Let's do another bike run around the park and that'll be all my butt can take today. The Sabot will be a welcome relief, having the wind to do the work."

Forsythe smiled and laughed.

♓

The gray Taurus SHO approached Georgina Point on the northern tip of Mayne Island. The lighthouse was easily seen from the road as Kelly turned the vehicle into the large parking lot. The lighthouse was a large tourist attraction in the summer, bringing tourist dollars to the small community.

Kelly took Hunter for a short walk before the pair of detectives started their tour of the grounds and heritage buildings.

"Okay, Hunter, you be a good boy!" Kelly signaled the dog to lie down in the back seat of the car, and she ensured that both back windows were partially down so that the hot day wouldn't overheat the interior of the car.

"Two tickets, please," Simon requested and paid the entry fee.

"When does the tour of the lighthouse begin?" Kelly asked the ticket attendant.

"Sorry, Madam. The lighthouse is closed to tourists. It's still operational and there's not a lot of room up there!"

"Hmm … is the lighthouse keeper here?"

"Yes, Madam, he's in the house over there." The woman pointed to the large white home to her left.

"Thanks." Kelly smiled and headed for the main building and Simon tagged along.

The magnificent property was on the rocky ocean shore. The square home was clad in white-painted wood siding and the entire grounds were beautiful and well kept. Numerous tourists were milling about the house and the large grass-covered property. Kelly eyed a room that had been converted into a gift shop and headed toward the cashier counter.

"I'm Detective O'Brian. My partner and I need to see the manager of this facility, please." Kelly smiled and pulled her detective's badge from her belt.

"Certainly, Detective, please wait here." The woman locked the till and disappeared down a hallway toward the back of the house.

A weather-beaten rugged man stepped into the gift shop accompanied by the cashier. "I'm Pat O'Flanigan, the lighthouse manager. Can I help you?"

Simon had joined Kelly at the gift shop counter, carrying the rolled-up chart under his arm.

"Yes, we're Detectives O'Brian and Chung. We're working on a number of homicides and we need to be able to have access to the lighthouse tower."

"What for, Detective? That's a strange place to deal with a homicide!" the short man quipped.

"Our investigation has led us to believe that there may be information in the lighthouse that'll help with our case," Simon interjected. "There's some missing money connected to the homicides and we've found some clues that we hope will lead us to the money and the perpetrator of the homicide."

"Clues?" The old man raised his eyebrows.

"Can you take us up there and we'll show you what we have? You might be able to help us unravel the clue," Kelly asked, teasing the man.

"Okay, follow me, Detectives. Did you hear about the plane crash this morning?" the lighthouse keeper asked as he led the way to the tower.

"No—what plane crash?" Simon asked, surprised. "Around here?"

"There was a commuter flight heading for Galiano Island and people say it exploded in midair and it crashed off Helen Point. They haven't found any survivors yet."

"Exploded!"

"It's been on the news, but no one knows what happened yet. Those Beaver planes are very reliable. The investigators are already at the site."

"Those guys figure things out quickly, so we'll know soon what happened," Simon remarked.

An old stone path pressed into the green lawn directed the short walk to the lighthouse tower. There was a constant breeze that swept off the point that cooled the heat of the day and the threesome walked along the open coastline. The salty air was filled with the scent of ocean life.

The path stopped at a steel door at the base of the painted white concrete lighthouse. Pat O'Flanigan pulled a bundle of keys from his pocket and unlocked the old door. The hinges of the door squeaked as the rugged old lighthouse keeper pulled the door open. He turned on the lights, motioned for the visitors to enter, and closed the door behind them. A narrow steel staircase wound around the inside circumference of the tower. Pat led the way upward.

"Small groups of tourists were allowed up here in earlier days, but with liability insurance and costs for tour guides, that practice has been discontinued." His voice echoed as the man spoke.

The tower was about four stories high and the assent was hard on the leg muscles.

The group reached the top and entered into a glass-enclosed round room. The large light was in the centre and there was a small walkway that wound around the inside edge. A door opened onto a small-railed walkway that ran around the exterior.

"What a unique view. I'd bet you never get tired of looking at this, eh Mr. O'Flanigan!"

"I'm an old salt and I never get tired of looking at the sea. So what are we looking for?" The weathered wrinkles on the man's face tightened as he smiled.

Simon pulled out his cell phone and found his photographs of the lighthouse painting. "This oil painting was done many years ago and it's of this site as you can see," he showed the lighthouse keeper. "What's interesting is that the artist placed a small inscription at the base of this lighthouse. See, painted in blue?" Simon pointed to the small markings.

"Yes I see, Detective. It looks like 55W," the man said holding the cell phone close to his face.

"Any idea what that message could mean?" Kelly asked, excited to be inside the lighthouse.

"It sounds like a direction to me. If this lighthouse's the reference point, then what we're looking for is fifty-five degrees west of here," the old man said and pointed to the bottom of the exterior glass. "Look, you see these markings on the edge of the glass going around the room?" He took the pair a few steps to the right. "Here! See this large 'N'? It signifies magnetic north. It's on all marine charts. The marks going around are minutes and degrees. If you go to your left, you are going west."

"I see. Since a circle has three hundred and sixty degrees, at ninety degrees we should find a 'W,'" Kelly remarked, interested in the explanation.

"Right, Detective. Your painting notation says to go only fifty-five degrees west."

Kelly started at the north marker and counted out the larger markings that symbolized a degree as she walked around the circumference of the lighthouse. "Okay, I'm at the fifty-five degree marker!" She turned her body to face directly out from where she was standing. "The painting must be referring to something out in that direction." She pointed in a direction across the water.

"Ah … can you help us find that spot on this chart?" Simon pulled the elastic off the rolled-up chart and looked at the lighthouse keeper.

O'Flanigan took the chart and placed the folded sheet on the lighthouse window. "There's not enough space to lay this flat in here!" he exclaimed, holding the map onto the glass with his hands.

He pointed to the large red circle placed on the Saltspring Island land mass. "See this marker, it's the same marking we just used in here. The star is over the zero, marking north. If you count fifty-five marks anticlockwise you will be moving in a westerly direction, just as your partner did in here." The man looked up from the chart. "One of you detectives hold this chart up."

Simon placed his hands on the top of the chart.

"Watch!" The lighthouse keeper counted the fifty-five markers around the red circle. "Here is fifty-five west. If you drew a line between this marker and the center of this red circle, the line would be the direction that you are looking for. Take that line and start it here." He pointed to the location of the lighthouse on the chart. "You're looking for something along that line; it looks like something on the northern part of Galiano Island, to me."

Simon took the chart off the glass window. "So something out there." He pointed out toward Galiano Island as Kelly had done.

"Looks like it, Detective." The old man grinned.

"I guess we've figured out the clue. Thank you, Mr. O'Flanigan. We're just learning how to read these charts," Kelly said with a smile, excited to decide what to do next.

"Glad to have helped. I don't get to work on many mysteries out here!" the old man laughed.

The three worked their way back down the winding staircase to the base of the lighthouse. The detectives shook the hand of the old man as they reached the steel door.

"We'll finish our tour now, thanks again. I loved the lighthouse. You've been very kind!" Kelly said, being the last to shake his hand.

"Let's go to the car and take a closer look at this chart, Simon! We can make that line he talked about and see what the detail might show."

Simon held the chart tightly clenched in his hand as they quickly cut across the lawn to the parking lot. He laid the folded sheet on the hood of the car and pulled his pen from his pocket.

"Here!" Simon pointed to the fifty-five degree marker as they had done in the lighthouse tower, and drew the line in black ink.

"Start here." Kelly pointed to Georgina Point where a small red symbol marked the location of the lighthouse.

Simon held his index finger straight and aligned it with the black line that he had drawn. Keeping his finger straight and aligned in the angle of the line he had drawn, he moved it up to the lighthouse point.

"Okay, the direction points to Cain Point and Whaler Bay." Kelly's eyes widened as the clue clicked. "Simon, get your notebook out and find the riddle!"

Simon withdrew the notebook and flipped to the page. He read the riddle. "Marriam's place the point you Cain see." He grinned. "Bingo, you're right. Cain in the riddle is Cain Point on Galiano Island. It fits! We should get off the ferry at Galiano Island instead of going home to Vancouver tonight."

"Yea, now all we've to do is find this Marriam's place. It must be at Cain Point somewhere!" Kelly exclaimed excitedly. "We don't have a last name for Marriam. Hmm …." Kelly pondered. "Simon, why don't you call Captain Hollingsworth and see if he can get a listing of all the property owners around

Cain Point, and maybe a Marriam will show up! He can get a road map and narrow the street names."

"It's Saturday!" Simon reminded.

"You know that the Captain is all cop first!" she smiled.

♓

Marcel Bessier and Peter Dobson started their route through Active Pass. A large ferry had announced its approach with a loud blast of its whistle and Marcel kept his yacht close to the shoreline to give the large vessel lots of room to pass.

"Between the active currents in here and the wake of the ferry, you have to be very alert in this narrow strip between these islands!" Marcel remarked as he carefully navigated his route close to the rocky shoreline of the island.

Peter Dobson sat back in his leather captain's chair and dialed a number on his BlackBerry®. "I should be able to get a cell signal now!"

"Hey JP, it's just Peter calling in. We'll be at the harbour in about half an hour or so." He listened to the voice on the other end.

"No, we've been out of contact and haven't heard about the plane explosion. Yep that was me. I had Zoric take a briefcase that had an altimeter and a timer. Fifteen minutes after reaching three thousand feet the timer was activated … boom!" he exclaimed. "Yea, well, the pilot was collateral damage. No one can trace that tragedy back to us and there's no evidence that they'll find. Brilliant, huh?" Peter listened to a comment and replied, "Okay, I'll call later."

Marcel clutched the large steering wheel of the yacht as he listened to the phone conversation. "You blew up that plane?"

"Just a message for you! Don't mess with me." Peter glared over at Marcel.

"Montague Harbour isn't much further," Marcel said as he took a deep breath and panicked inside his head.

♓

Terence Weiss sat at the kitchen table at Pit's place. He was looking for information about Arthur Fleming, using a laptop computer that was in the house. "Hey Pits, help me with this damn thing. I had no access to a computer while I was in the cage. I need to find where Fleming lives!"

"Use this Google® thing." Pits leaned over his friend and brought up the screen. "Put in the words you want information on in this box here. This site gets you web pages that have that word. The more specific you are in your choice of words, the better chance of getting something you're looking for."

"I'm looking for Detective Arthur Fleming. I want to find his address," Terence said specifically.

"Oh … try putting 'phone book BC' in the search." Pits keyed in the words.

"Great, I get all this shit. Which one should I pick?"

Pits looked at the computer results. "Ah … pick the 'myTelus phonebook.'" He waited for the next option. "Now pick 'Person' from the tab."

Terence keyed "Fleming." A long list of Fleming names were listed in the order of first initial.

"There's not too many names with the first initial beginning with an 'A.' You've your base list now my friend. He must be one of those!" Pits grinned and stood back away from the computer.

"Hmm … I'll have to call each one to either hear his voice or talk to them to see if they were an RCMP person. I'll need some excuse for the inquiry … hmm, thanks Pits!"

Terence began making his calls. "One of these must be my guy, unless his number is unlisted. I'll start with these and see if I can find the son of a bitch."

♓

Kelly's cell phone rang as the pair was exploring Mayne Island. "It's the captain," she said as she glanced at Simon. "Yes, Sir. Can you send the list to my phone, please?" she asked and smiled. "Simon, the property list is coming through." She waited to ensure that she had the list. "Thanks, Captain. Sorry about bugging you on your day off!" She hung up.

Both detectives looked at the list as Kelly scrolled down the file full of names. "These names are on Cain Road. Let's see what's here." She worked down the list and stopped. "Here we are. A 'Marriam Tremblay.' That's our name! The address is 3691 Cain Point Road!"

"Hey Kelly—Tremblay—isn't that the name of the artist that painted your picture?"

"That's right! Let's look at that signature again."

Simon found the photo of the painting on his cell and peered at the bottom of the artwork. "Here we are. It's a 'J. Tremblay.'"

"Right, and our house owner's an 'M' Tremblay. I wonder what the relationship is between the artist and the house owner." Kelly rubbed her forehead.

"Maybe some clue's in the house. Things seem to be coming together and the house looks like it could be the key." Simon sat and thought for a moment. "The ferry boat doesn't leave until seven forty-five. Let's find a place to eat. Fun, eh KO?"

♓

Sandra Vaughn couldn't wait to see Forsythe again. It had been only a few hours since they parted from their cycling date, but Sandra felt good about being with him. She still worried in the pit of her stomach that she wasn't going to be good enough for him. They were so different!

Her backside reminded her of how uncomfortable a bicycle seat can be but it still was the best date ever! Sandra arrived at the sailing club a little earlier than normally and had the Sabot ready and on the beach before most of the others. Her heart was pounding in anticipation of spending more time with Forsythe.

"Stupid, relax! We're just going to have fun sailing," Sandra told herself to calm down. Her body wasn't listening. He wasn't even there yet and she felt aroused just thinking about him!

"Hey, Sandra!" A voice came from behind her.

Sandra spun around, startled. "I didn't even see you come in! You're early, aren't you?"

Forsythe had a large grin, and his eyes looked directly at her. "I just couldn't wait!" He drew himself near to her and gave her a passionate kiss. She kissed him back.

"You're going to blow my concentration!" She smiled back at him.

"You've blown my concentration for some time now. I'm lost in you!"

He caressed her and gave her another kiss.

"Hey buddy, that boat will never get into the water if we do this all night. Let's get ready for racing!" Sandra tried to control herself and took a deep breath as Forsythe left for the locker room. She exhaled slowly. She was still wired and wanted him.

♓

Marcel tied up his boat at the public dock in Montague Harbour as he had just finished refueling. "Hey Dobson, there's a great restaurant in the marina. Let's get something to eat and we can discuss our plan for tomorrow."

They climbed off the yacht and walked up the hill to the pub side of the restaurant and sat at an outside table that overlooked the marina.

"I'll have a dark beer and the special." Peter Dobson craved a dark beer since Marcel had only light lagers on the boat.

"Bring me a scotch on the rocks and I'll have the special, too, please."

The pair said nothing in their seats and watched the late afternoon *GulfAir* single-engine commuter floatplane taxi out from its dedicated airline dock and leave for its early evening scheduled flight to Vancouver.

The drinks arrived at the table. "This place has been a zoo since the crash of the *Island Airlines* flight this morning off Mayne Island!" the waiter exclaimed, as he noticed the men watching the aircraft leave the harbour. "I hear that a salvage barge has been at the scene since late this afternoon. *Transport Canada*'s going to try and recover the wreckage and hopefully they'll find the cause."

Peter turned to the young waiter. "Have ya heard on how many there were on the plane?"

"I think I heard someone say that there were only two, thank God, the pilot and another, but there's been no official count yet," the waiter replied and left the table to serve another group who had just taken a table further down the outside deck.

"You know," Dobson leaned over to Marcel and whispered, "Zoric was supposed to have taken *GulfAir* but he missed it and took *Island Airways* instead. Ironic, you never know when your time's up!"

"Well helping it along isn't a good thing!" Marcel snapped back and glared again at the man that sat at his table.

"I meant the pilot!" Peter stared back at Marcel. "Let's hope it's not your time, eh. So what's the plan for tomorrow?"

"I've rented a car. My secretary has done the research and I know which address we're heading for." Marcel pulled a note from his wallet. "It's 3691 Cain Point Road. There's a road map on the boat and we can figure out later a route on how to get there."

"Good. What are we looking for?"

Marcel hesitated before he answered. "Uh … I'm not sure. I know that house has something to do with a large amount of money that was embezzled from a company fifteen years ago, as I told Jako. I know that a Mark Rawlings was involved and was murdered. Other than that it's not clear."

"You told JP that you were going to have his money in a few days. You're sure risking a lot on the unknown. That might prove to be very foolish, Mr. Bessier." Peter peered across the table.

"Relax, I'm sure that it's there somewhere. We'll find it. No sweat." Marcel took a drink from his scotch, realizing what trouble he was in.

The two meals showed. Nothing else was talked about and the two just watched the activity in the busy marina.

♓

The gray Taurus drove off the ferry at Sturdies Bay on Galiano Island.

"Simon, punch in 134 Madrona Drive in that GPS, please. We've an overnight reservation at the *Galiano Lodge*. They said that it was less than ten minutes from here."

"I think we should meet for breakfast at about seven. I've booked the seven thirty ferry for tomorrow night and that should give us all day to figure this out." Kelly was pleased with herself that she had everything under control.

"Well, at least I thought about a change of clothes. You'd better hope the hotel has a small shop to buy things. If we're lucky they have stuff for dogs, too. The ferry boat sure didn't have anything for an unplanned overnight stay!" Simon smiled and was happy that he had brought an overnight bag and was able to give Kelly a poke.

♓

Sandra and Forsythe were finishing their meals at the sailing club.

"We sure were off our game today!"

"Well, if you concentrated on sailing and not me, we would've stayed out of the water. I don't remember the last time I ended up in the bay!" Sandra replied in a teasing tone.

"I didn't think you had all your attention on the race either! I didn't think I was that good looking," Forsythe teased right back.

"You know," Sandra decided to change the subject before she blushed with the attention, "I'm considering quitting the casino. I was pressured by the boss to influence a customer, a Marcel Bessier, to attend a meeting. I don't think I should've been involved."

"Hmm, what was the meeting going to be about?" Forsythe asked, being curious about Sandra's concern and unusual comment about work.

"I'm not sure. There were a lot of unhappy-looking men in the room. I figure it isn't going to be a friendly meeting."

"What does that have to do with your job dealing cards?" Forsythe asked as he looked at her a little confused.

"Oh … ah, Mr. Bessier's a regular player at my table." She paused as her heart rate began to increase. "Some men give me their private numbers and my boss asked if I had Mr. Bessier's. I admitted that he had given it to me some months ago, so I was asked to call him at that number," Sandra said, guarded about her answer.

"Hmm … why would regular players give you their private phone numbers?"

"You know, wealthy guys think that they can pick up girls because they have money. We're told to be polite and take the numbers."

"I get that! Why did you keep it?" Forsythe continued to prod.

"Well ah … I figured you never know when you may need an influential lawyer and Mr. Bessier is a very influential man in this town. It was long before you and I met."

Forsythe scrunched his face. "Do you feel threatened? Is that why you're thinking about quitting?"

"I just don't feel comfortable being used that way. I'm still not sure. Let's drop this now, okay?"

"I'm really concerned about you, that's all, Sandra," Forsythe said in a consoling tone.

"You know I'm not from a happy family situation, and that I'm something other than what people think. The club would shit if they knew my heritage!" Sandra blurted out.

"That doesn't matter to me. You're the person I care about, not your family or background."

"Forsythe, won't your family freak when they find out you're dating someone like me? Parents have expectations, and I'm sure they have great ones for you."

"We've our own things to work out together first, don't you think?" Forsythe pointed out. "Let's go for a walk on the beach. We can't miss an evening like this sitting here!"

The pair got up from their table and left the club crowd behind. Forsythe took her hand and Sandra turned as she felt his fingers mingle with hers. He pulled her to his body. "I want you. I feel a lot for you." He kissed her. "I want to be with you!"

"I want you, too!" Sandra held his hand tightly as they continued their stroll on the sandy beach.

"I live just over there on Beach Avenue. Will you come over there with me tonight?" Forsythe asked in a whisper.

Sandra paused before answering. She looked directly at him. "I want to, I really do but I need to work some things out in my head first. Can you give me a bit more time, Forsythe?"

He smiled, but was disappointed. "Sure, take all the time you need."

Chapter Eleven

Kelly O'Brian was up before seven and had already left the hotel room to take Hunter for his morning walk. Kelly had purchased a local t-shirt and she and Hunter left the full parking lot of the quaint hotel, Hunter keeping pace with Kelly's light jogging along the main road. There wasn't any sidewalk but there was little traffic in the morning and they ran on the pavement. The ferry used by the morning tourists who needed to reach the mainland wasn't scheduled to leave until eight twenty-five, so the exodus hadn't really started. The day began warm and sunny, promising to again be very hot by noon.

Simon waited for the pair to return. He was hungry and knew the day would be full and he always made a point to have breakfast if he could. "Hi guys, ready to eat?" Simon asked as he spotted the two returning from their short trip around the area.

"Just give me ten. I need to freshen up after our run. Won't be long!" Kelly said somewhat out of breath.

Simon stared at Hunter and smiled as he followed his partner back to her room. "Yea sure, we know better don't we, Hunter?"

"Hey Simon, why don't you let the local detachment on the island know that we're in town? It's proper protocol and all," Kelly yelled from the bathroom while stepping out of the shower.

"Good idea." Simon found the local yellow pages and found the number. "Good morning, Officer. Is the Captain in yet?"

"Sorry, Sir, this is a small office and there are only two officers here. Can I help you?"

"Yes, of course. I'm Detective Chung and my partner Detective O'Brian and I are here investigating a homicide in West Vancouver."

"West Vancouver—you're a little out of your area, Detective. What's up?"

"We just wanted to advise you that we're on the island and that our investigation is taking us to a Marriam Tremblay's home on Cain Point Road. We likely will be there most of the day."

"Thank you for advising us, Detective Chung. We know that property. Sometimes we're called about disturbances and unusual activity at that location, but we haven't found anything out of the ordinary."

"Great, if we find anything of interest we'll advise you." Simon gave the officer his cell number.

♓

Sandra had been awake most of the night. She had tossed and turned thinking about Forsythe and their intensifying relationship. She had never thought about what would happen if she fell in love with a guy, and how to deal with her extracurricular business activities at the casino. This man was like no one else she had ever met, and he certainly didn't travel in her typical crowd. She didn't want to screw things up!

"It's time!" she told herself. "I should go and visit my dad."

Sandra hadn't seen her father since her mother had passed. It wasn't his fault, but it was a messy time. Sandra had lived alone without either of them for many years after she left. The pain of her youth rushed back into her consciousness and tears began to form in her eyes. "Damn, I have to move on! Seeing Dad is one of those things I must do before I can move ahead with Forsythe."

She skipped doing her morning rowing workout and focused on getting ready to see her father.

Sunday morning traffic in Vancouver was unusually light over the *Lions Gate Bridge* as she drove to North Vancouver. It was summer and many people were on vacation away from the city.

Her red Fiat was parked outside of her father's rented suite before she realized that she had arrived. The small North

Vancouver house was built in pre-war times and her dad had rented the bottom single-bedroom basement suite. Sandra sat in her small car parked outside the house for some time, debating with herself if it was the right time or not to go inside. She took a deep breath and headed for the side basement-suite door and knocked.

The side door opened. "Hi Dad, can I come in?"

Her father stood surprised for a moment at the young redhead standing in his doorway, then regained his composure. "Sandra, yes of course, come in!"

Sandra entered the small apartment. "It's been a long time." Sandra paused and took another deep breath. "Too long, Daddy."

The man in his mid-fifties was at a loss for words. He just looked at his daughter. The room was silent.

Sandra found a seat in the small sitting room and sat down. "I'm figuring it out and I need you in my life now. I'm sorry for not being with you after Mom died. I just couldn't then!"

The man smiled and sighed, "I know. Things have been tough for you. You couldn't embrace your heritage and with your mother's problems I understand that. I'm happy that you're safe and well. I've been worried about that, you know." He paused and looked at the young woman that she had become. "You're so beautiful. Are you still alone or is there someone in your life?"

She smiled. "I think that there's someone, but I'm scared that he'll leave when I tell him about some things." She looked down at the floor sadly. "Not good things. He's such a wonderful man."

"What kind of things, Sandra? Young love can overcome many things. It did with your mother and me many years ago."

"Ah … just things. I'm planning to change my life though, for the better. It's been tough but I know I can make it work."

"This visit's your start, right?" Her father looked at her. "Look at me, Sandra! I know that you haven't wanted me involved in your life but I miss you and wish that things had been different."

She raised her head and looked at his face, wrinkled and worn. "I wish that now, too."

"Life's about change. Things about us change, we react to change, and we learn how to deal with change. Love will change you and your man, too. Don't be afraid of it, embrace it and learn to go with the flow of it. I do love you and I'm always here for you, Sandra. Make the changes you need and make a better life." He paused with tears in his eyes. "I wish that I had been there for you when you needed me but you made that choice, not me."

Sandra got off the sofa and hugged her father. "Thank you, Daddy, I know I did. I love you, too. I'll be back soon and we can spend some time together and get to know each other again, if you'd like."

"I'll like that." He gave her a kiss on the cheek.

Sandra turned and left her father standing there watching her leave, glad that she'd come.

♓

Terence Weiss joined the lineup at the Tsawwassen ferry terminal, planning to take the next Gulf Islands boat at ten that morning to Pender Island. The ticket agent told him that the sailing was already full and that he would be able to take the next one that wasn't until six o'clock that night. He parked the old Chevy he had borrowed from Pits in the lane for the late sailing scheduled for Pender Island and didn't know what he was going to do all day. He called his hotel and advised them that he was going to be late and then checked out the availability of something to eat at the concession stand.

♓

Forsythe had gotten up early and gone for a run. Sandra had filled his thoughts all night and he kept thinking about things that she had said. He was concerned about her having phone numbers from wealthy gamblers and thought that wasn't wise for a young beautiful woman to do.

"I want to be with her. I have to find out what's going on, though! I think I'll go to the casino and see for myself what's going on over there," he told himself as he pushed his body into a sprint.

Forsythe returned home and planned how he was going to watch her without being caught.

♓

Simon checked out of the Galiano Lodge, paid the bill and took the receipt. "I'll expense this when we get back," he said, shoving the papers into his wallet.

"We don't have a warrant or anything, so we'll have to be careful today." Kelly turned to Hunter. "You, too!" and headed for the parking lot. The group loaded their few things into the car and Kelly put Hunter into the back. Kelly started the Taurus and pulled out of the parking lot, as Simon entered the destination on Cain Point Road into the GPS.

"Turn left 200 yards on Sturdies Bay Road," the woman's synthetic GPS voice advised of the pending direction change.

"I love the voices they choose for these electronics! You note they are all female though, eh Simon? It must have something to do with women's sense of direction," Kelly poked fun as she reached the intersection and turned left, heading northwest as instructed.

Simon shook his head and knew better than to make some comeback remark.

"Turn right 300 yards on Cain Point Road." Kelly smiled at the instruction and complied. "Yes madam!" she quipped.

The morning ride was on a typical Gulf Islands road flanked by trees and low brush, now in full summer foliage. Many signs warning of deer crossings dotted the shoulder, and the pavement followed the contour of the rolling hills.

"Turn right in 100 yards," the GPS voice announced another correction in the route. The road wiggled northward and glimpses of the ocean could be seen through the thinning tree line.

"You've reached your destination." The road curved away, ending 100 yards further ahead.

"Yep, here it is, 3691," Kelly said excitedly. "We found it!"

She turned the gray sedan into the driveway, which worked its way along the side of the house and down to the water's embankment. Kelly parked.

The modest rancher had brown-stained cedar siding that was weathered and sun bleached. The grounds weren't well kept and all the bushes were overgrown.

"Hunter, you stay here. We'll see if anyone's home," Kelly commanded, exiting from the car.

The pair of detectives found a stone walkway that ran from the rear door to the private dock. It didn't connect to the driveway and the visitors had to walk across an overgrown lawn now full of crabgrass to reach the back door. Simon knocked on the rear door. There wasn't any answer.

"I'll go around to the front, Simon."

Kelly walked back to the driveway and found the stone walkway leading to the front door. She found the doorbell and pushed the button. *Ding-dong.* Kelly heard the announcement inside clearly from the front porch. She waited. There wasn't any answer. She tried again. *Ding-dong.* No one answered.

Kelly returned to the car and let Hunter out. "Don't go too far, Hunter," she instructed and rejoined Simon. "No one's home! Let's look around."

Simon cupped his hands and peered into one of the large glass windows that overlooked the dock and narrow waterway. The morning easterly rising sun lighted the large sitting room inside and it was quiet. He proceeded to the next set of smaller windows and looked through the glass as before. "Kelly, an office is here at this end."

Kelly joined Simon, went to the adjacent window and looked into the bright office. "Hey Simon, look—this smaller window isn't locked, see the handle's still up."

She took the edge of her car key and placed it under the lip of the metal frame and pulled the window forward. It moved slightly open. "Simon come and help me here; this window's stiff. It'll take both of us to yank it open!"

"What are you doing?" Simon asked as he glanced around to see if anyone was watching.

"Trying to get in, dummy! We have to see what inside so …." she replied and looked up with a childlike grin.

"Humph!" Simon grunted, joined her and they pulled the window open large enough for a small person to crawl through.

"You're the smallest one here, partner!" she laughed.

"You're suggesting a B&E, detective?" Simon sarcastically asked, shook his head and took off his belt, holster and service weapon and then handed them to Kelly. The thin Chinese man headed through the open window head first and placing his hands on the office floor, wiggled his body through the opening.

"You okay?" Kelly asked with a chuckle as Simon got to his feet and saw her ginning at the spectacle.

"Next time it's your turn!" He smiled back and headed for the rear door.

"You're lucky that there's not a house alarm!" Simon poked as he unlocked and opened the back door and took back his gear that Kelly handed to him.

"Hunter!" Kelly called and the dog promptly came to her side. "Lie down and wait here." She motioned with her hand; the dog obeyed and lay beside the walkway. The detectives entered the home and left the rear door open.

♓

Marcel Bessier and Peter Dobson had a quick breakfast of coffee and toast on the Bayliner and then walked the steep hill to the marina to find the car rental office.

"I asked for a midsized car. We're looking for *Galiano Car Rentals.* The agent said we could find the office behind the marina's restaurant." Marcel puffed out the words in short sentences, breathing heavily as the pair reached the marina at the crest of the hill, where they spotted the rental office.

"I'm Marcel Bessier," he said still out of breath. "I've a car reservation," he told the young woman at the desk in the small office, who looked barely twenty years old.

"Ah …." she muttered as she checked the daily log. "Yes, Sir. Sign here."

Marcel signed the document, slid it back over the counter to the woman, and the two men were given keys to a Camry. "You'll find it to your left. It's white," she said with a smile.

"Oh … do you have a map of the island?" Marcel asked as he grabbed the keys from the counter. "I left mine down on my boat at the marina and I don't want to go back and get it!"

"Yes, of course," the woman replied, and grabbed a map from under the counter to hand to Marcel.

"Thanks. We're visiting a friend here. He lives on Cain Point Road. Could you mark that on this map for me, please?"

"Sure. That's a nice part of the island and you'll love the views up there." The young woman marked the road with a pen. "It should only take you about fifteen minutes or so to get there from here."

"Thanks. We'll have the car back long before you close," Marcel said noticing the closing time posted on the door.

Marcel noted that the car was outfitted with a GPS as he settled into the driver's seat. "We won't need that now!" he grunted, "I don't like them anyway. Those voices are irritating!" He handed Peter the map. "You navigate."

Peter Dobson didn't like being told what to do by Marcel. Peter knew that Marcel wasn't in control but didn't like it anyway. He settled for the current arrangement, at least for the moment.

The trip was just as the rental agent had said and in short order the white Camry came to their destination. Marcel abruptly stopped the car for a moment outside the house and then carried on to the end of the street.

"What are you doing? You passed it!"

"I know—look, there's a car in the driveway. We can't just barge in when someone's home."

Marcel turned the Camry around in a neighbor's driveway and drove a number of houses down the street and parked.

"Look, there's a private dock out back. Why don't we get the boat, come back and watch from some vantage point from the water side. We know where the house is now and we might be able to get in later. Let's go," Peter commanded, as he didn't want to be seen too interested in the house.

Marcel put the Camry in gear and headed back to the rental office.

♓

Sandra volunteered at the *Greater Vancouver Food Bank* and tried to go each Sunday. She often arrived before lunch and helped out for a number of hours before she had to get ready for her shift at the casino. She knew the location very well, as she had often had to stand in line for food herself many years before. Helping out was one way that she felt she could pay back the generosity she'd received when she had been in need.

The demand for food exceeded the availability of products on the shelf and Sandra often donated cash when she was there to help make up the food packs.

"Hey Sandra, good to see ya today! There's a big line already and we can't put the packages together fast enough. You know where to go. Thanks for showing up," a voice drifted from the packaging room.

Sandra remembered the many days when food and shelter was all that she thought about. The visit always reminded her about how far she had come and how lucky she really was to have come through her ordeal as a happy and self-reliant woman. The line seemed to get longer each time that she showed up to help. The scene was depressing, but she felt better to be able to contribute in some small way.

♓

Jako Palma sat at his office desk watching the activity in the inlet. He watched the flurry of activity at the *Island Airways* boarding platform in Coal Harbour. A Beaver aircraft sat tied up at the dock, which was unusual. He knew why. The airline had been grounded, resulting from the explosion of their commuter the day before.

His office phone rang and he turned away from the window and picked up the receiver. "JP, here."

"Jako, its Raj Jattan. Lothar hasn't reported in yet. What's up?"

"I don't know either. Dobson hasn't called me yet either. I'm sure they're all busy with Bessier. I'll find out and get back to you, okay?"

"I'm running out of time finding that information I need," Raj pressed, sounding stressed.

"I know, Raj. It's under control. We'll talk later, I've a meeting." Jako hung up and smiled. He returned to watch the activities at Coal Harbour.

♓

The Tremblay rancher was beautiful inside. It was tastefully decorated and it was evident that a woman didn't live there.

"This looks like a guy's place," Kelly commented standing in the large sitting room. "All I see are sports things, golf trophies, and golf photos over there. Of course, there's fishing stuff over there. What's with the stuffed fish? Only guys like those mounted on their walls!"

"It's not the cleanest place, either. Women hate that!" Simon remarked and wandered into the kitchen. "Nice appliances," he muttered and opened the refrigerator. "Someone's living here and there's lots of beer," he opened the freezer, "and frozen food, too. This dishwasher hasn't been turned on for some time, though." Simon noted the hardened food on a few dishes.

Kelly peeked into the large bedroom. "The bed's made!" she called out just as she spotted a painting over the bed. "Hmm." She got close to the oil painting and looked for the signature. "Simon, this painting's done by J. Tremblay, too."

The picture was of three boats tied together in a quiet cove somewhere and the picture had a brass name plate on the wooden rustic frame. "Good Friends" was etched on the metal. "Well, we're certainly at the right place."

Simon pulled his notebook from his pocket. "Let's look at the riddle."

"Can we go for lunch first and come back? We'll have lots of time anyway this afternoon," Kelly suggested as she joined Simon in the kitchen.

"Okay with me, KO, and I suspect that Hunter is looking for something to eat, too. I'll leave this back door open so we can get back in later, if the owner doesn't show." Simon put his notebook back into his pocket. "It's a dead bolt anyway!"

"I asked the desk clerk at the hotel where the best place to eat around here would be, and she said the *Whaler Bay Pub*. She told me how to find it. We go back down this road to the first intersection and take Whaler Bay Road."

"Humph. We won't need that female GPS then!" Simon remarked as the group got into their places in the unmarked police car.

The trip took less than ten minutes. The pub overlooked a marina nestled in the small narrow bay.

They returned to the Tremblay house an hour and a half later.

"Pub food is always great. I sure was hungry," Kelly remarked as they approached the Cain Road house.

"Me, too. The beer wasn't hard to take, either."

"No car's here yet! We should be able to spend time in the house without interruption," Kelly said, turning the Taurus into the driveway.

"I'll check," Simon said, exited the passenger seat and disappeared as he went to the front door. He returned to the car a minute later and said, "There's no answer, the owner's still not home. Let's go around back."

The back door was unlocked as they had left it and the pair entered the sitting room and sat down. Simon pulled his notebook out and read the riddle out loud.

Georgina's place of note to view,
Marriam's place the point you Cain see,
To plot by the legend of Fisher's 3462,
The captain's compass will be the key.

"The only part of this riddle we haven't figured out is the last line. The captain's compass will be the key," Kelly repeated the final line of the puzzle.

"Even though marine charts have keys and there are compass-like markings on them, I don't think the clue is about something on a chart. We've done that chart thing already," Kelly mused as she looked around the room.

"Well, let's take the line literally. There must be a captain's compass around here somewhere. It's likely one of those small things like an old pocket watch, you know—hikers use them." Simon placed the notebook back into his pocket. "Where would be the most likely places to find a pocket compass in this type of place?"

"I'd say in this sitting room or in the office where you crawled through the window." Kelly started to walk around the room. "Hmm … it's not in here that I can see."

"In here!" Simon shouted from the office. "It's a big mariner's ship compass on the side table."

Kelly joined Simon in the office and saw the large compass that was encased in a brass ring and was set with gimbals so that the compass could remain level, counteracting the roll of a ship.

"Cool. This thing must be quite old. I can't believe that we didn't notice it before." Simon stared at the device. "So what's the key all about?"

Kelly sat in the old office chair. "Don't know. Let's think for a minute."

♓

Marcel Bessier was piloting his Bayliner through the small narrow channel between Galiano Island and Gossip Island. "The gray car's still in the driveway," Marcel called out to Peter Dobson, who was sitting in the back lounge of the yacht having a quick beer. "I think we should carry on and tie up at Whaler Bay around the point," Marcel suggested, looking at his marine chart and noticing the marina marked in the small bay.

"It's close to here. Why don't we just overnight and see if that car's gone in the morning?"

"You're cutting it tight leaving it another day!" Peter warned, shaking his head as he joined Marcel in the pilot's cabin. "It's your ass and I don't care one way or the other."

"Yea, I get that!" Marcel glanced over at Peter. "We should look around in the daylight so going tonight isn't such a good idea as the house lights might attract someone's attention. Let's see what's at the marina, and then we can decide."

"What if that gray car belongs to the owner? Then what are ya goin' to do, Marcel?" Peter asked as he crushed the empty beer can in his fist.

"Ah … let's talk about options later. I need to concentrate. This passage is very narrow and shallow in places and it's low tide right now," Marcel said, carefully watching the depth sounder.

♓

Simon and Kelly sat in the office staring at the large dusty brass compass. They didn't notice the Bayliner pass by the window as it travelled up the narrow passage past the house.

"Will be the key, will be the key!" Kelly repeated the last line of the riddle. She went over to the compass and picked it up. "My God, this thing's heavy!" The compass started to spin around as she turned around to look at Simon holding the compass's outer case. "Simon, this thing's not reacting to my movement. It looks like the gimbals are stuck." She simulated the roll of a boat but the compass didn't react.

"Hmm!" Simon took the heavy object from her and carefully rotated it over as he placed it on the floor. He laughed. "Guess what's under here?"

Kelly looked at the underside of the compass. "A key—it's taped under here to the gimbals' frame!" she exclaimed as Simon pulled the key away from the tape, got off the floor and placed the compass back onto the side table.

He placed the key in an evidence plastic bag. "It looks like a key to a safe!" He sat back down and peered at the silver-colored key. "This whole thing's certainly not been very easy to figure out."

"You know Simon, I've been thinking. This place is definitely a guy's place, right?"

"Sure seems so to me, KO. What's bugging you?"

"The owner's name's Marriam and that's a woman's name. Why is a man living in a woman's place and there's no sign that a woman lives here?"

"Hmm. That key must've been here a long time, too. The tape was very hard and brittle. It was difficult to pull the key away from the brass frame. The photo with the riddle was taken when you were five or so, right?" Simon thought about the timing of the photo and the key. "We'll have to think about those facts later and see if we can figure out how they connect. So far as the man living here and not a woman, maybe the guy's a relative or something!"

"Hum ... yea maybe. Let's go. It's very hot in here and I think we've got all we'll get from here for now. We found the key anyway!" Kelly said as though she was talking to herself as Simon closed the office window that he'd crawled through earlier.

"I'll have to leave this back door unlocked as it's a dead bolt and must be locked with a key from outside. I don't want to go through the window again and the front door's the same! I doubt there are B&E issues around here anyway. I'll leave my card on the table in the kitchen in case the owner comes back and finds the place open." Simon said as he pulled a card from his wallet and placed the key in his pocket. "I'd better not lose this!"

"Let's head back to Sturdies Bay and get something to nibble on for the ferry trip back. There's not much to buy on those small boats."

Kelly saw the long line waiting for the next ferry as she arrived at the ferry terminal. "Uh, oh! It looks really busy, and it's Sunday night. Everyone's going home and we don't have a reservation!" Kelly sighed as she reached the ticket booth.

"Sorry Madam, the boat's full for tonight. I can provide you a ticket for the morning boat leaving at eight twenty-five. Do you want to buy the ticket now?"

"I never figured on this amount of traffic. Yes, please, I'll take the morning ticket," she replied, pulling her credit card from her wallet. "Hey guys, we'll have to wait until the morning."

Kelly grabbed her ticket and her credit card from the attendant, turned the car around and headed back to Galiano Lodge.

♓

Sandra was having her shower before dressing for work. She felt that the smell of the food bank always got into her clothes and skin and she always felt better after her shower. Her mind wandered back to thinking about Forsythe again.

"I want to be with him, and he wants to have sex with me soon, too; the way that he looks at me!" She tried to work through the issues in her mind that she had about being with him. "I don't want him to be just another guy and I do want things to be special and romantic." No easy solution to her dilemma came to mind. She got dressed and headed out to the casino a little frustrated at herself.

♓

Terence Weiss drove off the small Gulf Islands ferry at Otter Bay on Pender Island and was hungry by the time he had reached Browning Harbour. He checked into his Beach House B&B room and walked down to the pub.

It was almost eight thirty in the evening by the time he sat down at a table on the outside deck.

"The kitchen closes in half an hour. If you want something to eat I suggest you order right now, Sir," the waiter suggested, standing with a menu in his hand.

"Yea, just got off the ferry. Is there any of that roast beef special left?"

"Sure is!" the waiter replied.

"I'll have that and a pint of cold beer, anything dark on tap will do."

A few minutes later the beer was delivered to his table. "Pender Island's beautiful this time of night." The waiter smiled and left the table as he saw Terence staring out at the few boats anchored off shore. The sun would be gone soon and many of the boats had already turned on their running lights as they sat on the calm water. It was restful and Terence was glad his long day's trip was finished.

♓

Forsythe was having dinner with his parents and they were always happy for him to come and visit. It was Sunday, so they put on a feast, as they always did on Sundays. He was an only child and they usually spoiled him. They lived in a beautiful large estate in Point Grey.

"So, Son, are you enjoying your practice here?" his father asked while pouring white wine into a crystal wine glass.

"I'm still getting settled, Dad. I love the work, though, and the bustle of the city."

"Your mom tells me you're seeing a girl! Has it been long?"

"Yes Dad, she's the girl that I sail with on Wednesdays and Saturdays at the club in Kits." Forsythe replied and then took a sip of his wine.

"Becoming more than sailing partners are we?"

"Ah … I think so. She's wonderful, Dad. You'll need to meet her and I like her a lot!"

"Dear, you haven't known her for very long!" His mother caught the conversation from the kitchen.

"You know, Mom! You just know right away," Forsythe smiled. "We're just dating!"

"Just be careful. Lots of women would love to land a handsome lawyer with money!" she retorted.

"Ah … Mom!" Forsythe rolled his eyes.

"Tell us a little about her, Son." His father smiled and peered at his son.

"Oh! She's beautiful, of course, and tall like me. She loves the water and racing Sabots and she does sculling in Coal

Harbour almost every morning!" Forsythe answered excitedly and took another sip of his wine.

"What does she do for a living?"

Forsythe hesitated for a moment. "She works at the new casino on the waterfront. She says it's only for a while and she's planning on changing jobs soon." He took a breath. "We've just started dating beyond sailing at the club. Just let's see where it goes, okay?"

"No more questions then!" His father looked up at his wife and they all sat for dinner.

Forsythe didn't want to tell his parents too much about Sandra yet. He was just working things out himself and was planning to spy on Sandra at her workplace. He didn't feel very good about that, but he had to know what she was doing with men's phone numbers and what was really going on at the casino. Their discussion about the pressured phone call concerning Mr. Bessier didn't sit well with him, either.

Forsythe finally said good night to his parents about ten. He didn't change and headed directly for the *West Coast Casino.*

"Good evening, Sir." The parking attendant took the keys of the old silver Jag from Forsythe. "Good luck, Sir." Forsythe was handed the parking slip and the car disappeared into the underground parking lot.

Forsythe had never been to this casino before. He took the escalator to the second floor. He looked about to see if Sandra was within sight but he couldn't see her. His heart started to beat faster, worrying that she would see him snooping around.

The casino was busy and noisy. He walked slowly around the large room, frequently checking that his girlfriend didn't catch him skulking about. He spotted Sandra in the back of the casino by the large glass windows that overlooked the inner harbour. She was dealing cards to the six poker players sitting in front of her. He watched from a place behind the dollar slot machines. He pulled his body out of sight and ordered a beer from a waitress who walked by.

He frequently poked his head around the corner as he sipped on his beer and slowly played the slot machine. He looked up again and she had gone, replaced by another dealer. He didn't see her, and a number of the players at her table had left their seats.

"Humph!" he muttered and asked the next waitress who passed by. "Do the card dealers over there take any breaks? I've noticed that some have been replaced." He pointed to where Sandra had been dealing cards.

"Yes, Sir. Those dealers get to have an hour break at eleven each night." She smiled. "Can I refresh your beer?"

"Ah, sure. Okay," he replied and the waitress took his empty glass.

Forsythe waited for his beer and then started to look around for Sandra. He couldn't find her anywhere and became concerned. "Hmm, she should be somewhere about!" He decided to go to the cash cage. "I'm curious, where do the poker dealers go when they're on their break?"

The casher looked at him closely. "You're not a regular here, eh?"

"No, just checking the place out before I spend my money," Forsythe replied with a smile.

"Oh! Well the dealers have a special lounge that they go to when they're not on the floor. Are you looking for anyone in particular?"

"Ah … no it's okay. Thanks," Forsythe replied and walked away from the small wicket. "Hmm … a special lounge! I wonder where that is and why they're provided with that. Strange thing!"

Forsythe returned to his dollar machine and waited for Sandra to reappear. "Hmm … yes, strange thing indeed!"

Sandra replaced the temporary dealer at twelve. The table of the original players reassembled and the game continued. Forsythe decided to go home.

Chapter Twelve

A man with light-colored graying sandy hair and appearing to be in his early sixties sat at his desk reading legal documents. He owned the law practice and now only handled the affairs of long-term clients. He was reviewing Charles Whitford's official Last Will and Testament that he had been instructed to execute upon specific criteria. The will was dated the week after Joy Tremblay had been declared as missing and presumed drowned, seven years ago. Charles' instructions were very clear and explicit. He had left two sealed envelopes with the lawyer, one addressed to his son, Tyler Whitford, and the other addressed to Patrick O'Brian, and the lawyer had been instructed to wait one week after Charles' death before executing the will and sending out one of the letters. The week delay had been debated at the time and Charles had been adamant that he had wanted the lawyer to have adequate time to get all the death documentation together and details of all Charles' assets compiled before deciding which letter was to be mailed out.

The lawyer had been instructed that upon the passing of the seven days, he was to decide which one of the two letters to send, and to destroy the other without opening it. Today was the day that the lawyer had to begin executing Charles Whitford's Will and to decide which letter to send.

Tyler Whitford was to be sent the letter if he was alive and competent to handle his own affairs, in which case the O'Brian letter was to be destroyed. Charles had told his lawyer that he knew Tyler had been involved in risky activities, and therefore had prepared the alternative letter for Patrick, while hoping that Patrick's wouldn't need to be sent.

The news of Charles' death and the Tyler Whitford killing was common knowledge, and the lawyer knew that it was time to execute Charles' instructions. He ensured that he had received adequate documentation of both Charles' and Tyler's deaths and he destroyed Tyler's letter as instructed and then prepared a covering memorandum addressed to Patrick O'Brian.

The lawyer placed the memorandum, and the sealed letter that had "Patrick O'Brian" hand-written in pen on the face of the envelope, into a large brown envelope and told his secretary to post the package to an address suite in Marpole.

♓

Kelly O'Brian and Simon Chung sat in their car in the Sturdies Bay ferry lineup early. They didn't want to miss the morning sailing, as there were only two scheduled for that day.

"It's bazaar that Whitford's gun that was used in the Mark Rawlings murder would lead us on this mysterious tour. We seem to have more blanks to fill in than answers at this point!" Simon said as he sat in deep thought looking at the small ferry begin its docking routine.

"Yea, and now we've a key and nothing to help us find where it belongs!" Kelly said, her eyes glazed, thinking about the facts that she knew already.

The car radio played softly in the background and was keeping the car occupants entertained while they waited in line. Neither was really listening, their thoughts focused on the Whitford case, when they heard a news bulletin interrupt the music station.

Transport Canada has released their preliminary findings of the Island Airways crash over Mayne Island yesterday morning. They've been able to recover pieces of the plane's fuselage and rear cabin section. Their spokesperson has told us that the tidal waters and heavy ocean currents in that area have made salvage difficult and many pieces of the aircraft may never be recovered. Transport Canada has confirmed that the midair explosion was not due to any malfunction of the Beaver single-engine plane. The type and location of the blown-out fuselage indicates that a bomb had been detonated in the front portion of the passenger cabin. Island Airways will be able to resume service later this afternoon as the disaster doesn't appear to be a fault of the pilot or the aircraft. Transport Canada also indicated that a review of its domestic security policies will be undertaken later this year. The suspect passenger has been identified as a

Lothar Zoric. The search for the flight recorder and the explosion device continues.

"Hmm … sounds strange to me! It doesn't sound like a suicide nut-case to me, but more like a calculated hit!" Simon's thoughts jumped to the news report.

"Pretty ugly I'd say, taking the innocent life of the pilot! Whoever it was only cared about the kill or the contract. Our RCMP task team will have their hands full with that one!"

The ferry arrived and the detectives knew that they had a full day ahead with reports and working out the unanswered questions of the Whitford case and the *DigiCast* mystery.

♓

Marcel Bessier and Peter Dobson were up early to get a start looking for the money at the house on Cain Point Road. They chose to eat breakfast at the Whaler Bay pub and were back on the Bayliner before eight.

Marcel started the yacht's engines and Peter untied the boat from the dock at the marina.

"The plane crash was the buzz in the restaurant this morning. It didn't take those guys long to identify Zoric and figure out that the crash was caused by a bomb that he brought aboard," Marcel commented to Peter with a disturbed voice as the boat pulled away from the mooring.

"It's just risk management, Marcel. That's what I do, eliminate problems!"

It was a short hop to the Cain Road house dock. There wasn't a car in the driveway and the house looked void of activity.

"Okay, let's tie this thing up and find the money! It won't take long to see if you're right or not," Peter said in a threatening tone as the boat drifted toward the dock.

The yacht was quickly secured and the two men walked quickly to the back door of the rancher.

"Hey, this back door's unlocked! That makes it easier for us," Marcel told Peter Dobson as he pushed the door open and entered the back room. The pair quickly looked about the sitting room.

"Let's start in the kitchen over here," Peter muttered, entered the bright room and then exclaimed loudly. "Shit!"

"What's up, Dobson?"

"The cops have been here!" he growled and handed to Marcel Simon Chung's card that had been left on the kitchen counter. "They must've been the people at the house yesterday! How'd they know about this place?"

"Beats me!" Marcel assured him.

"I certainly hope for your sake that they haven't found the money or whatever you're looking for Marcel, or you're screwed."

"We'd better go through everything! I hope we find something obvious like a safe or a hidden locked drawer or something!" Marcel paused, "I also hope the owners don't show up."

"Yea, for their sake!" Peter started pulling everything out of the cupboards and drawers and let it all dump onto the floor.

♓

Elizabeth Richardson had been worrying all weekend about Marcel Bessier. Having his gun in her bedside table didn't help her feel safer and she jumped at every sound outside her usually quiet house.

She felt better being at work. It helped her to think about other things and her busy schedule afforded no time to stress about the unknown. She had committed to an art exhibition and she still had a number of pieces to complete.

No one had recognized her coming or going from her old home in West Vancouver, and that was a good thing. She decided to carry on with her new life on Bowen Island and put the past back where it had been, in the past! It was easy to say, but her mind was no longer at ease.

♓

Jako Palma appeared at his office later than usual. He noticed that his secretary had left him a phone message on his desk from an earlier call that morning. "Please call Mr. Jattan. It's urgent," the note read.

"This guy's going to be a big pain in the ass," Jako mumbled under his breath as he sat down in his office chair. "I'd better call or he'll do something unpredictable." He looked up the number and dialed.

"Hey, crap your bed or somethin'? Ya sure called early! What's the panic, RJ?"

"You lied to me! You said you didn't know what Dobson was doing with Zoric! You had Lothar murdered, you bastard!"

"Hey, get a grip! It was Dobson's call. He thought Zoric was a loose cannon and would put us all at risk. He was just protecting you from a potential problem and you should thank me! Remember, Zoric screwed up the Whitford thing, so it's better that he's out of the picture anyway. Saved ya a bullet, RJ!"

"You should've talked to me first! Lothar usually delivered in the end," Raj spitted out, annoyed.

"Okay, okay. Relax. It's done now," Jako said calmly with a smile.

"If Dobson's such a hotshot, what has he found out so far?" Raj asked angrily.

"Relax man, he's still with Bessier! We'll know tonight and I'll let you know as soon as I do. Bye." Jako hung up, not providing another opportunity for further discussion.

♓

Terence Weiss had purchased a detailed road map of Pender Island while waiting for his ferry the prior day. He knew exactly how to find Flemings' house at Thieves Bay. He wasn't in a hurry and took time to have a full breakfast in the pub at Browning Harbour. "Another day or so won't matter! I've waited a long time already!"

It was going to be another hot summer day, and Terence was glad that the abundance of trees would keep him cool while staking out Fleming's place. He jumped into his old Chevy and headed across to the south island. It was Monday and the weekend traffic had disappeared. It was quiet and there was little local activity was on the road. The calmness of the island seemed to stream through the open car window and the old car followed the wiggly pavement around the rolling hills.

Glimpses of the ocean began to appear and Terence knew that he was getting close to his destination. He pulled onto the side of the road and grabbed another look at Fleming's address, then pulled back onto the pavement. He drove slowly, trying to find the house numbers; they were difficult to find or read, making his search for Fleming's place slower than he expected.

"Ah, there it is!" he told himself out loud. He drove a few driveways down the narrow road and turned the old rusted white Chevy about. He drove toward the marked marina a short distance away and left the car outside of the "members only" parking area, then headed back to Fleming's address on foot.

Terence pulled an old baseball cap further over his face, wanting to remain unseen by anyone, and frequently scanned the area for approaching vehicles or pedestrians as he slinked his way along the quiet road. It was desolate and no one else seemed to be about. He reached Fleming's driveway and cautiously walked toward the house, which was secluded, from the roadway.

He found a car in the driveway and Terence assumed that his target was at home. He crept to a side window, peeked in but saw no movement. He approached the corner of the house and eyed the private dock and the moored red trawler tied up at the dock and saw movement of two men on the deck of the boat. One was a young man and the other was Arthur Fleming! He was sure of it, as he had Fleming's face burned into his memory. Terence crouched in the bushes and watched.

♓

Jordan Fisk and Arthur Fleming were preparing the trawler for another outing. Arthur planned to pick up another arms shipment that night and everything had to be ready and in proper order. These pickups were tricky and dangerous. He was pleased that Jordan had done this task before. It wasn't the type of work for a novice.

Jordan cast off the lines and Fleming pulled the trawler away from the dock.

♓

Simon Chung and Kelly O'Brian arrived at the West Vancouver RCMP precinct late in the morning.

"Good morning, you two. Come into my office and update me, please." Captain Hollingsworth was anxious to hear what the pair had been doing for the last few days.

"As you know Cap, the Whitford cases are connected to the old Rawlings murder case from fifteen years ago. We now strongly believe that Charles Whitford was the person who murdered Mark Rawlings. We also think that the murder of Charles Whitford must be connected to money embezzled from *DigiCast* in the early 1990s," Kelly summarized.

"We've also discovered that *DigiCast* was Kelly's father's company!" Simon added.

The captain said nothing for a moment. His eyes narrowed as he looked at Kelly O'Brian. "I'm sorry to hear that, Detective. Can your father help us with this, Kelly? I know that he's ill."

"No, Sir. He has advanced Alzheimer's and he can't. We've been using some old records of his and some family mementos that are providing some clues, though," she replied sadly. "I ah … keep my father's condition very private, Sir."

"Yes of course, I'm sorry. How much money are we talking about?" the captain asked stone-faced and shifted his attention to Simon.

"We don't know that, either, Captain, but we've another clue." Simon placed the key on the captain's desk. "This key, we think, has been hidden since Rawlings' murder. It looks like it's for a safe, but that's all we know at this point."

"Hmm … where'd that key come from?" Hollingsworth asked, eyeing the key in the plastic bag.

"It came from Marriam Tremblay's house, one of those addresses that was on the list you sent us over the weekend." Kelly eyed her captain but he didn't comment further.

"Tyler Whitford must've found out about the embezzled money from something that he found in his dad's house. I don't get how Bessier fits in yet. We're still missing something," Simon said, rubbing the back of his neck.

"The clue to Charles Whitford's murder must've been at his house on Bowen Island. We must've missed something when we were there and I'll bet Tyler knew about some hiding place of his dad's and waited until we left!" Kelly sighed.

"Everything seems to lead back to Charles Whitford! Look into who he worked for. Maybe something will pop up," Captain Hollingsworth suggested, glancing back at Kelly.

"Another thing, Cap. The house on Galiano that's owned by a Marriam Tremblay; it's being occupied by a man. I'd like to check the hydro and property tax records and see who's paying those bills. I think that house is connected to all this somehow," Kelly replied seriously.

"Okay Kelly, I'll get those records for you. Carry on looking into Charles Whitford."

The pair of detectives returned to their desks on the other end of the room and they both sat down.

"I'll be glad to get onto the Bowen ferry; it'll sure be cooler there than in here," Kelly muttered as she checked her voice messages.

"Detective O'Brian, I've been directed to you by your switchboard and I've some information about Lothar Zoric, the man who was killed in the *Island Airways* crash," the woman's message played.

Kelly looked at Simon, dialed the number captured by the recording, and put the call on speaker.

"Hello," a woman's voice answered.

"Are you the woman who left the phone message at my RCMP office this morning?" Kelly asked, a little puzzled.

"Yes, Detective. My name's Sandra Vaughn. The newspapers reported that you were one of the detectives looking into the Tyler Whitford killing that happened on Mr.

Bessier's boat. I thought you might be the best person to talk to about Mr. Zoric."

"I don't think I'm the right detective to talk to, miss. That case is being handled by our downtown office but I can give you the number."

"Well, I think it involves Mr. Bessier. You're looking into that shooting case, aren't you?" the soft voice came through the speaker.

"Okay yes, I'm investigating that case. What information do you have?" Kelly asked as she glanced over at Simon.

"I just heard about Mr. Zoric and the plane crash investigation on the radio this morning."

"And?" Kelly frowned.

"Well, I was called into my boss's office Thursday night. I work at the *West Coast Casino and Suites* and there were four men in the room when I arrived. There was a meeting in progress and I was introduced to Mr. Zoric and Mr. Jattan. I was pressured to call Mr. Bessier to attend a meeting with those men and my boss, Mr. Palma. None of the men looked very happy."

"Pressured you how, Ms. Vaughn?"

"Well, when there's a room full of unhappy men and they want you to make a phone call, you make it!"

"Sorry Ms. Vaughn, I don't follow." Kelly shook her head and scrunched her face.

"Oh, I had Mr. Bessier's cell phone number and my boss wanted me to make the call."

"What makes you believe that any of those men had anything to do with the plane crash?"

"I don't know for sure. I'm a little nervous around Mr. Palma, though. I thought the information might help, especially since it involves Mr. Bessier, and Mr. Zoric was in the room at the time."

"Thank you, Ms. Vaughn. By the way, you said there were four men in the room. You identified three, so who was the fourth man?"

"I'm not sure but I know that he was one of Mr. Palma's men. I've seen him before but don't recall his name. Sorry."

"Are you going to be all right? You sound very upset, Ms. Vaughn."

"Sure. I think so. The crash was an awful thing and I thought that I must tell you about the meeting."

"Good. Don't tell Mr. Palma that you called us. We'll look into this information and thanks again for coming forward." Kelly disconnected the call, got up from her desk and headed toward the back office. "Simon, come. I need to update the Captain." Simon tagged behind.

She knocked on the door and the captain waved the pair in.

"Captain, there could be a possible link with Marcel Bessier and the *Island Airways* plane crash! A woman just called saying she met Zoric, a Mr. Jattan and her boss Mr. Palma on Thursday night. They seemed to be very anxious to have Mr. Bessier attend a meeting at the *West Coast Casino and Suites*. It's a thin connection but I doubt a coincidence."

"Okay, Detective, it's definitely interesting timing! You guys continue with Whitford. I'll call downtown and advise them of the possible link with those other men."

♓

Sandra Vaughn still didn't feel very settled after her call to Detective O'Brian. The whole Zoric and Bessier thing really bothered her. She never had felt in danger before, even when she had lived on the streets. She knew that this was different.

She needed a friend to talk to. "Hey, Forsythe. Sorry to call you at your office."

"Any time, Sandra, you know that." His calm voice sounded reassuring.

"You know that I said I was planning on leaving my job, right?"

"Yea, I remember. Is there a problem?"

"I don't know, but I'm feeling unsettled. Remember I told you about Mr. Bessier and I called him at the request of my boss, Mr. Palma?"

"Yea, I know! I didn't like you having those guys' phone numbers!"

"Well, I think one of those guys in that meeting had something to do with the bombing of that *Island Airways* plane that crashed. The passenger on that plane was Mr. Zoric and he was in the Thursday night meeting and he was one of the men looking for Mr. Bessier."

"Do you know for sure?"

"No, but I just told the cops."

"Okay. Be careful. Let the cops do their job, Sandra!"

"They said not to tell Mr. Palma, so he won't know that I leaked the information of the meeting about Bessier and Zoric."

"Good. Just do your job. No changes to your normal routine and we'll work out what to do."

"Thanks, Forsythe. I trust you," she said, still feeling stressed about it all.

"Me, too." They both hung up.

Forsythe sat in his office chair thinking about the call. "I don't like the sound of this one bit! I think I'll go and watch Sandra again later tonight. I'll see what's going on and check that she's all right. Maybe I can help her with all this."

♓

Terence Weiss had remained motionless and hidden in the shelter of the heavy bushes at Arthur Fleming's house for some time, and finally decided that it was unlikely the trawler would be back soon. He called Pits on his cell.

"Hey Pits, it's Terence and I'm here watching Fleming's place. I think he's planning another one of those gun runs we talked about. You want to let your *Los Chinche* guys know? I'll bet the sale and transfer will be in a couple of days. See if they can get a line on it. Talk later man."

♓

Peter Dobson was becoming tired of looking for something that wasn't likely there. The majority of the house had been trashed and nothing had been found that could lead to any cash.

Marcel Bessier was still thrashing about in the basement and Peter decided to contact Jako. He decided to send a text so as not to alert Bessier about his call. He pulled out his Blackberry®, still hearing Marcel making a racket in the basement.

"Jako. Bessier's drawing a blank. Looks like a bust here. Instructions?" He pecked out the message, pressed send, and set the BlackBerry® to vibrate.

Buzz, buzz. Peter looked at the return message.

"Got another rush job for you Monday. Bessier's time's up. He's just a liability. Do your thing."

"Okay, book me a flight from Galiano tonight. Advise airline and flight." Peter keyed his reply, pleased to be done with Marcel Bessier and the fruitless search.

Peter Dobson pocketed the phone and walked down the staircase to the basement.

"Find anything down here, eh Bessier?"

"I don't get it! There must be something here," Marcel bellowed in frustration.

"You've run out of time, man," Peter said coldly; he shot Marcel twice and the bleeding body fell to the basement floor. "What a fuckin' waste of time!" Peter spit out the words and placed his revolver in his back belt underneath his light jacket. He shook his head and walked out of the house toward the Bayliner.

"I didn't think I was going to have to run this fuckin' thing. Damn!" Peter grumbled and thought about how to get to Montague Harbour to catch the plane back to the mainland. "I can't navigate those waters through Active Pass on my own to get to the flight on time! Hmm … I'll have to go back to Whaler Bay and find a car I can heist over there!"

He untied the boat, jumped aboard, started the engine, and slowly headed the yacht toward Whaler Bay.

The telephone rang at the local RCMP station on Galiano Island. "Hello. RCMP. Can I help you?"

"Yes, I've just heard gun shots a couple of houses down the road on Cain Point Road. Come quickly!"

"Are you sure it was gun shots?"

"Pretty sure, please come now," the panicked caller insisted.

"We'll be there in ten minutes, Madam."

The officer yelled at his partner. "Shots heard on Cain Point Road! Let's go!"

An elderly woman stood in her driveway when she spotted the flashing lights of the RCMP white vehicle. She frantically waved at the car as it approached.

"Officer, I think the man took the large boat that was at the dock a few doors down!" she yelled and pointed to the house.

"What direction was the boat headed?"

"Up the narrows toward Whaler Bay," the woman said, almost out of breath.

"Okay, go back inside your house. We'll look after it!"

The woman ran back down her driveway and the officers went to the suspect house.

"We've been called to this place before," an officer said to his partner as the squad car drove into the driveway.

"Yea, and a couple of detectives from the mainland were here yesterday, too. They called in to advise us that they were on our turf. Let's see what's happened here!"

The two uniformed officers drew their weapons and with caution approached the house.

"If our perpetrator took a boat, then he must've left through the back door. Let's enter through there," one officer suggested. He walked to the back of the house, and as he peeked through the open door, saw nothing and entered. "Clear in here!" he yelled out. His partner joined him and the pair surveyed the house that had obviously been searched, because everything was strewn all over.

"Someone was looking for something, eh?" an officer muttered as they worked their way through the house, trying not to step on anything on the floor.

"Nothing up here and no sign of a shooting either! Let's check downstairs."

The pair worked their way to the basement. "RCMP, anyone down here?" an officer yelled. There was only silence.

The first officer down the staircase saw Marcel Bessier lying on the floor in a pool of blood. The officer carefully approached the motionless man and checked the body's pulse. Blood had run down the dead man's face and his shirt was blood-soaked from two shots in the chest.

"Call the ME. We've a gunshot victim here!" the officer exclaimed as he noticed that the basement was a mess and had been tossed like upstairs. "Someone was pissed that they didn't find what they were looking for, eh?"

"Looks like it! Tell the ME that I'll have to drive to Whaler Bay. That was the direction the woman pointed and our perp may still be there with the boat! You stay here and I'll be back shortly."

"Okay, partner. Be careful. The guy's armed and he's had a good head start!"

The officer ran upstairs, jumped into his RCMP cruiser and pulled from the driveway squealing his tires. The officer headed for Whaler Bay with siren blaring, about five minutes at full throttle.

Peter Dobson knew that he had little time to get to Whaler Bay, tie up the boat, and disappear before the cops showed. The gunshot echo was loud in the basement and he knew that someone must've heard it!

He had watched Marcel maneuver the large yacht the day before, and the space that they had been moored at was still empty at the marine dock. "Shit!" Peter growled as he almost overshot the dock and was thankful that the space was at the end of the dock rather than between other boats. He aligned with the dock, cut the power and ran off the bridge of the boat down to the main deck. He grabbed a bow line from the front starboard side and as soon as the dock surface appeared he jumped and quickly tied the one line to the dock cleat. The boat was still moving and almost broke the line as the dock strained to stop the yacht, pulling the dock against the restraining pole anchors. Peter had no time to fuss with finishing tying up the boat and left the stern of the yacht to drift into the open marina.

Peter sprinted along the wooden dock and up the loading ramp.

"Hey! You haven't secured your boat! Hey you!" Peter could hear the yelling of boaters as he darted out into the parking lot. He heard the siren of the approaching RCMP vehicle and slipped into the bush at the end of the parking lot by the side of the pub.

The RCMP officer slammed on his breaks at the edge of the parking lot. He saw no one running, but noticed boaters straining to pull the yacht into the dock by its bow line.

The officer vacated his car and ran down to the gangplank toward the group of boaters fighting with the yacht.

Peter saw his chance and started to work his way from behind the pub and then stopped. He smiled as he peeked out behind one of the parked cars and noticed that everyone was watching the activity on the dock. The RCMP officer had joined the group and the RCMP vehicle was still at the end of the parking lot, door open.

He walked slowly, acting as any other marina customer who was watching the activity on the dock, and headed directly toward the RCMP vehicle and glanced inside. They keys were in the ignition and the lights were still flashing.

Peter jumped into the driver's seat and drove the cruiser out of the parking lot. He saw the officer running back yelling, but he couldn't stop Peter Dobson.

Peter figured out how to turn the flashers off and he drove normally down the road toward Sturdies Bay. He knew he had to quickly ditch the police vehicle and knew that there would be many vehicles from which to choose in the small town. He heard a second RCMP vehicle scream toward him so he parked the RCMP cruiser in one of the backstreets of the shops and took off on foot to steal a suitable replacement.

In less than fifteen minutes, Peter was driving toward Montague Harbour in an old blue Chrysler. His BlackBerry® vibrated, and he pulled over to check the text. "Island Airways at 1600 hours."

Peter grinned. He had just enough time to make the flight and get off the island.

♓

Kelly and Simon reached the Charles Whitford house on Bowen Bay by midafternoon.

"Hey Simon, we're getting to know our way around here!" Kelly noted as she came to the rear door of the Bowen Bay waterfront home. "Simon, someone's been here! The stuff from the boat shed is all over the lawn and the back French doors are open!" Kelly exclaimed as she entered through the open back door and gasped. "Holy shit, Simon—look—this place has been tossed!"

"Certainly someone's been here since we left and I doubt it was young Tyler who left this place like this. He must've known where his dad's things were," Simon remarked as he shook his head looking at the mess.

"You never know. Maybe not, but I doubt he'd trash the place looking. I wonder what the intruder was looking for!"

"Let's hope we can find some paperwork on who Charles was working for. The office is the best bet to start."

The officers made their way around the debris looking for the office.

"We need his company files. Look for storage boxes of folders or file jackets," Simon said while trying not to step on too many things that were scattered on the floor.

Kelly's phone rang. "Hey Cap. What's up?"

"I got those files you wanted on the Tremblay house. You'll never guess who's paying the bills!"

"Surprise me."

Hollingsworth laughed. "Get this! The trail was tough to track but it turns out that retired old Arthur Fleming's paying the bills from some obscure back account, online."

"That's crazy! Why?"

"Don't know, but the Rawlings automated payments stopped when his account was frozen after he was killed. Fleming continued after that." The captain paused, "Bazaar, huh?"

"We'll have to put Fleming on our radar. Thanks, Captain."

"Why would Fleming care if the power and taxes were paid? This case sure is weird," Kelly suggested again to Simon.

"Let's see. Rawlings was killed for something, likely involving the embezzled money. Fleming's either involved in that, or knew the house was going to be empty and is using it himself. Power and taxes must be paid in order to have the services provided," Simon replied.

"Okay, but Fleming has his own place on Pender," Kelly reminded Simon.

"That's what he said, but maybe not."

"Simon, it does seem that Fleming's mixed up in this as well," Kelly said as she looked around the office. "The way this case is going, I'm not surprised. One twist after another."

"Keep looking for the paperwork. This Whitford guy must be the key to the whole thing," Simon remarked as Kelly's phone rang again.

"Man, you're popular, KO!" Simon smiled.

"Kelly O'Brian."

"Officer Hastings from Galiano Island. You called me yesterday informing me of your visit at the Tremblay house."

"Yes of course, Officer Hastings. Why are you calling?"

"We found a murder victim in that house earlier today. He was shot twice in the chest. He's a 'Marcel Bessier' according to his ID."

"Bessier!" Kelly yelled out.

"That's right, Detective. The suspect killer took a yacht from the Tremblay house to Whaler Bay, but we lost him."

"That was likely Bessier's boat. Where is it now?"

"It's been secured at Whaler Bay; and Detective, the house has been trashed, too. Bessier or his killer must've been looking for something. It's a major mess!"

"Okay, secure the house, too. I need to check a few things out here. I'll get back to you later."

"Thanks, Detective O'Brian." Hastings hung up.

"My God, Simon! Bessier's been murdered at the Tremblay place! The bodies are sure mounting up!"

"Look, there's nothing here in this house. Let's get back and work the case after we have dinner, okay?" Simon needed to have some time to work the pieces. There were still lots of pieces that didn't fit.

Chapter Thirteen

Terence Weiss had learned how to wait and be patient. He had planned his revenge on Arthur Fleming and he knew that his chance to get even would eventually come. Finding Fleming was the hard part—execution of the man who had framed him would be the easy part. It was simple. Fleming had stripped Terence of his life, now Terence was going to strip Fleming of his. It only seemed fair and just!

Terence hadn't heard from his friend Pits yet. He knew the *Los Chinche* gang would find out if there was an arms buy in the works. If there was, they would certainly interfere with the deal if it did involve the *Black Widow* gang. The *Los Chinche* needed the weapons to continue their war with the *Black Widow* gang. Terence knew that involving the *Los Chinche* could only increase the chance that Fleming would be eliminated; it was a risk he would have to take, because Terence certainly preferred to have the pleasure himself.

The old Chevy worked its way down the winding island road. It was getting to be late afternoon and the narrow roadway was coming into shadow as the sun touched the treetops. There were few cars on the road and Terence had to head back to Port Browning to find any place to catch a meal.

♓

Raj Jattan had just received a report from his computer expert. Raj had given Charles Whitford's laptop to the expert to see if the password encrypted files could be accessed. Raj was very upset. Multiple attempts to disable the password activated some Trojan program that had wiped the data drive clean. There now was no way to recover the information that once was on the machine. There was no way to find the hidden Charles Whitford bank accounts and the missing funds either. He needed the backup CD-ROM that he knew Whitford had created. Raj knew that he would be held accountable once the *East Indian Community Fund* charity that he administered discovered the accounting omissions and false transactions.

Raj Jattan had become skeptical that Peter Dobson would be able to find the missing data disk. It was now clear that it had been a mistake to get Jako Palma involved. Zoric had been right about that.

"One more day! I'll give Dobson one more day! If I don't get that information I'll have to think of another plan. I'd better get things together just in case." Raj knew that his time was running out and relying on Peter Dobson wasn't comforting.

♓

The sun was disappearing behind the mountains that towered over the Vancouver north shore by the time Kelly and Simon got off the Bowen Island ferry. The ferry had been full of tourists and the deck had been completely full of vehicles. The pair decided to drive as far as West Vancouver before stopping for dinner.

"There's a fabulous fish place just down here in Dundarave. You like fish Simon?"

"You bet!" Simon replied, realizing at the same time that he was somewhat famished.

The establishment was a fish market and a restaurant. Locals could buy fresh fish and homemade fish products or elect to stay and have a meal prepared. The small place was buzzing with people when the two detectives arrived.

"Is there a table upstairs? I love your upstairs—it's so quaint," Kelly inquired at the hostess desk.

"Yes, we've a place available. Just take those stairs and a waitress will be with you shortly," the young woman replied with a smile.

The narrow staircase opened to a cozy room in an attic-like setting. There was only one unoccupied table and the pair took their seats.

"Wine?" the waitress inquired as she handed them menus.

Simon looked at Kelly and she smiled. "Okay, a cold house white, please."

"How are you holding up, KO? This must be difficult since this case seems to involve your father's old company,"

Simon asked, concerned and knowing that Kelly was becoming personally involved.

"I'm good. I've been working on and off trying to figure out things about my early life with my parents. I've never really understood what happened to Dad's business and I hope that this case leads to some answers and some closure for me. The whole case seems to be going in circles, but we're making progress, I think."

"We'll find the answers! They're out there." Simon sounded reassuring as the wine appeared and two glasses were poured.

"You want to place your orders now?" the waitress asked, and then waited for the two as they quickly flipped through the menu and made their choices.

"I received a call from downtown while we were on the ferry. The information you took from that Sandra Vaughn created a lot of interest. It turns out that Jako Palma, who runs the *West Coast Casino and Suites*, is an influential underworld boss. We haven't been able to stick him with anything solid over the years but have suspected him on contracting numerous hits and threatening many prominent citizens," Simon said and took a sip of his white wine.

"So it's likely that he contracted the hit on Lothar Zoric!"

"Likely, though no one's sure of the connection. Zoric hasn't been seen as one of Jako Palma's boys."

"Hmm … maybe a new recruit?"

"Why terminate him then?"

"Got me! Maybe he screwed up," Kelly shrugged her shoulders and took a sip of wine.

"The lab boys have been given some materials that were recovered from the plane crash that may provide leads to the bomber. They're working on that now," Simon continued.

"The key we found at the Cain place is bugging me! There must be a clue we've missed that's connected to the key. There's been a clue for everything else, eh Simon?"

"Okay then. What clues and information have we gathered that we haven't used yet?" Simon pulled out his notebook.

"Well, the photo I have of people in a house celebrating must've been taken at the Cain place. We know all the faces there, and the photo of the baby we surmise is me."

"The picture of the golfers is still an unused clue. That one seems out of place," Simon noted.

"Simon, pull the photos of the oil painting. Check we've covered all that information."

He pulled the cell phone photo from the file. "The artist, J. Tremblay. We know that this person is connected to the house, because an 'M. Tremblay' owns the place."

"Yes, and the picture of the lighthouse on Mayne Island. We know about that clue, too."

"Ah, the back of the painting had the name of the lighthouse and three numbers. We haven't accounted for the numbers written on the frame." He handed Kelly the phone so that she could see the photo.

"Strange way to put numbers! We have twenty-six and sixty-nine on the right frame and thirteen on the left frame." Kelly took another drink of the wine and stared off into space, thinking.

Their meals arrived at the table and the mystery was placed aside.

"You know KO, I believe you've become a great detective. Your cases have been complex and you've handled them professionally and with an uncommon sense of ingenuity," Simon remarked as he took a sip of his wine.

"Why thank you, Simon. That's a great compliment coming from you! I really do love my work and you're the best partner any cop could ask for, I believe that!" She grinned at Simon.

"So, have you started dating again? Your time's now you know," he asked, changing the subject.

"Ah, my time will be when I feel I've got myself together. Ricardo last year was too soon and I realize that I need to know myself before I can be ready to know someone else."

Simon laughed, "If I were only younger!"

"Simon, you need to find a nice girl in your own community. Be happy. Life's too short, you know. This detective thing, being a passion, is just one aspect of who we really are. You need to share things with someone. I've still got lots of time," Kelly replied.

"And I don't?" Simon jabbed and laughed.

The wine was good and the atmosphere seemed to bring the two partners closer. Kelly looked away and changed the subject. "The Bessier thing's very sad. He was a funny bugger but didn't deserve being shot to death. You know, the missing Whitford keys are still strange. I'd bet Bessier took them before we arrived on scene that night. I wonder why."

"There! That's what I mean. You're always thinking! We should get a warrant and check his place out." Simon picked up his cell and left a message with the captain. "Hey Cap, Simon. I think we should check into Bessier some more. Can you get us a warrant for his house? KO and I would like to snoop around a little. Ah, say we suspect he has the missing keys for the Tyler Whitford killing and we need to close that loose end." Simon ended the call and placed the cell back into his pocket.

"Talking about thinking!" Kelly looked directly at Simon. "The numbers on that painting have been running around in my head, too. Can they be numbers for a safe combo? We've a key and maybe they're the combo!"

"That's brilliant, KO! The first number must be a turn to the right, the second a turn to the left and the last a turn back to the right! Just like a combination sequence!"

"Yea, all we've to do is find the safe!" Kelly said, excited again and laughing.

"Let's go. It's time to go home. We've had a full day," Simon said, looking for the waitress.

♓

Arthur Fleming had anchored his trawler in Campbell Bay on the northern side of Mayne Island.

"I think we should review the plan for tonight. It's dangerous and we need to be on the same page," Arthur said, pulling his marine chart out that covered the area and laying it on the table in the stateroom of the boat. "Jordan, tonight's plan is similar to the last one we did except that it will be with a smaller freighter. That means that this vessel will be less stable in the water during the shipment transfer, making this more difficult than the other time."

Fleming pointed on the chart. "The freighter will be coming up this channel here as before. Rosario Strait, and will track along the American side of the international boarder." Fleming dragged his finger along the dotted line on the chart.

"Okay, I see." Jordan said with close attention.

"The freighter's headed for the Vancouver harbour and our shipment must be removed before it reaches the Canada-US line, up here."

"So what's the issue?" Jordan asked with a beer in his hand.

"Even though it's summer and the waters are relatively calm, the wake produced by the freighter will make it difficult for me to keep this boat steady. The freighter's travelling speed will act like there's a wind blowing the shipment while it's being loaded down onto our boat by their hoist."

"I understand. We must match the freighter's speed and maintain control of our roll and pitch while handling the freighter's wake as well."

"Very good, Jordan! The beam on this boat is thirteen feet and narrows a little at the rear deck. We've got to land the shipment on the upper eleven by fourteen-foot top deck. The load will be packaged on an eight-by-eight pallet and should have three layers of two-by-four wooden crates."

"So we've got to get this eight-by-eight-sized pallet onto our boat without wrecking everything up top or hurting ourselves." Jordan nodded his head.

"We've been given a specific radio channel to communicate with the skipper of the freighter. We must get the timing just right and have the freighter drop the load just as we are fully upright between rolls. Jordan, you'll have a voice connection to the freighter and it's your job to advise the crew handling the crane on aligning the drop and when to release the load. I'll be able to hear your conversation as I pilot this boat."

"Yea, and all in the dark, right," Jordan replied, a little concerned with the task, and took a drink from his cold beer.

"We must be on the starboard side of the freighter, where there's no chance of being seen from Saturna Island. The freighter's scheduled to be past the San Juan Islands and along its straight course by two thirty in the morning. That's about seven hours from now; get a rest and no more beer. It's a tough job and there's an extra bonus in this for you. Any questions?"

"Sounds like fun!" Jordan forced a smile and gulped back the remainder of his beer.

Arthur felt like having a beer, but he had to be focused and knew that he couldn't have one. It was essential that he was very alert. He set his alarm for twelve and tried to get some rest himself.

♓

It was fifteen minutes before the *Island Airways* Beaver was scheduled to leave Montague Bay. Peter Dobson thought that it was ironic that it was the same airline that had taken Zoric's life. That didn't bother him.

He spotted the large barge, carrying the damaged airplane fuselage, sitting at the far end of the harbour. The wreckage looked mangled and the large hole that had twisted metal jutting outward was a clear indicator of where Zoric had been sitting with the aluminum briefcase. Coast Guard and *Transport Canada* vessels were staggered throughout the marina's docking floats. He'd overheard the mixed conversations in the bar while he had a quick beer before his flight. He noted comments that pieces of the explosive devices had been found and the cops were following up on suppliers.

Peter was sure that his tracks had been covered and didn't think anymore about the random discussions at the marina bar. He had another assignment and he was glad to be leaving the quiet island.

He thought about the Simon Chung detective calling card at the Cain Road house. The reason the West Vancouver cop was there was a complete mystery. It no longer mattered. He was on to another job.

Palma wanted to see him the next morning. The flight was on time and he liked that; punctuality and reliability.

♓

Sandra Vaughn missed having Marcel Bessier at her table of regular poker players. His seat was empty. She knew that he must've had his meeting with Jako and she was worried for him. She liked the man. She liked lots of her clients. It was still a busy night, and as Marcel was her regular eleven o'clock customer she didn't have an appointment at her eleven o'clock break.

"Just as well," she told herself. She wasn't in the mood to have sex with any of the men at her table anyway. The whole Jako Palma thing was messing with her head and she just wanted to be with Forsythe.

She didn't see Forsythe peering at her from the slot machine room. She gazed over the room filled with gamblers, wondering how many more of them had issues with Mr. Palma.

It was break time and her relief dealer had taken over the table. None of the players at her table left and all continued with their games. No one was ahead tonight yet everyone thought that the evening was their lucky night!

Sandra sauntered over to the bar. "Quiet night for you tonight, eh Sandra?" the bartender turned his attention to her.

"May I have a white wine, please? Every night can't be a winner!"

Sandra sat, happy for the break and also happy not to pretend that she was having a good time.

"Sandra Vaughn?" a man wearing a dark suit and dress shirt inquired as he found a seat beside her at the bar.

"Ah … yes. Can I help you?"

"Maybe we can help each other," he answered without looking directly at her.

"Sorry, I can't see anyone tonight."

"Well, I've a lucrative proposition for you," he said and smiled as he turned to face her.

"Yea, like lots of guys in here, I bet you do!" She turned away from the man.

"Look, there's ten grand in it," he replied in a low cold tone.

"Ten grand!" she turned back toward the man, curious at what he wanted and whispered, "Do you want me to rob a bank or something?" Sandra hesitated and looked up at the man. "What do you want?"

"Look, this isn't the place to have this conversation." He paused, "All I know is that you're friends with Judge DeWit and you would likely want to keep that arrangement private. I've been watching you for a number of weeks now. I get the program."

"So?" Sandra stared at the man. She didn't trust his type of people. Her gut told her that.

"Relax." The man flashed a private investigator's badge under the counter, then continued.

"I'd like to talk to you. Not now and not here. It must be after seven, though. I have commitments during the day I must attend to. I know Wednesday's your day off. How about then?"

"I don't know, and I don't know you!" Sandra snapped her answer.

"Cautious. Good. Here's my card. Check me out and call to confirm a time." He slid his business card on the bar counter and then got up and left the bar.

"Edgar Logan, Private Investigator."

Sandra slipped the card into her purse and returned her attention to her wine.

Forsythe witnessed the discussion at the bar. He saw the business card go into Sandra's purse and the man leave her alone at the bar.

"Hmm … I wonder what that was all about. This whole place is unnerving and I don't feel that Sandra's safe here!" he muttered and continued to watch Sandra until she returned to her poker table.

Forsythe was worried. He also wasn't sure how he felt about what Sandra was doing. He suspected what she did when she wasn't at the tables but tonight had been a surprise and things didn't happen as he had expected. He hated the thought that he had been wrong about her. He cared about her and was struggling with the facts and what he was going to do about them.

He knew that he wouldn't be watching her if he wasn't concerned about her, or was it because he didn't trust her? "I've got to sort this out. It's driving me crazy!" he muttered and decided that he had seen enough and went home, confused as to what to do next.

♓

The bedside alarm rang and Arthur Fleming turned, rolled over in his berth, and turned it off. It was time to get ready. "Time to rock and roll!" He shook Jordan in the berth next to him. "It's time to set up the gear!"

All the radios were tested and life jackets had been put out before Arthur had taken his nap.

The crackle of the trawler's radio sounded. "This is Northern Star," the voice was clear through the speaker.

"Happy Hunter, come in Northern Star," Arthur rushed to answer the call on the marine radio.

"We're running late. ETA expected at three thirty, repeat three thirty, over."

"Read you, Northern Star. Plan in motion. Over and out," Arthur responded and hung up the mike.

Jordan looked curiously at Fleming. "Happy Hunter! What's that?"

"I just wanted a call sign that couldn't be traced, that's all."

"Ah. We've got more wait time, eh boss? I'd just like to get on with it!" Jordan exclaimed impatiently.

Fleming smiled. "Me too, Jordan, me too."

The wait seemed endless in the dark of the night as the trawler bobbed on the ocean, even though the trawler's cabin lights had been turned on. The time finally arrived.

"It's time to go!" Fleming started the Cummins engines of the trawler. "Pull the anchor and ensure that it's secured. We don't want that thing thrashing about. It could get rough in the channel later."

Fleming turned on the boat's running lights and headed the trawler out toward the shipping lane. There weren't signs of other vessels. That was good.

"We want to go to the southern end of Saturna Island. That's where the freighter will make its last course correction," Fleming said, looking for marker buoys in the darkness. There were very few lights that could be seen on the coastlines of Saturna Island as Arthur Fleming worked his way toward the agreed intersection point.

The crackle of the radio sounded again. "This is Northern Star, over."

"Yes, Northern Star. Happy Hunter, over."

"We're approaching our last course correction off Patos Island, over," the radio crackled again.

"Roger that Northern Star. We can see your running lights. We'll be at your stern in ten. Suggest time to reduce speed to less than five knots, over."

"Roger that Happy Hunter, over and out."

The trawler maneuvered behind the large freighter as it loomed in the darkness. Even at five knots the wake was substantial and the trawler increased forward speed to improve control. Fleming brought his trawler amidships, staying about twenty feet from the steel hull.

"Happy hunter in amidships position, over," Arthur reported.

Jordan turned on the upper deck lights. He saw the freighter upper lights turn on high above him and he could see the large loading crane begin to lift the loaded pallet over the side.

The trawler was rocking with the force of the freighter's wake. It was critical to remain in sync with the large vessel and Jordan clenched his teeth.

"Beginning cargo transfer, over," the voice from the freighter advised through the speaker.

"Okay, over," was all Jordan could spit out.

The crane lifted the cargo over the side of the large hull and began to lower the shipment downward and the movement of the freighter started to twist the load in the draft of the rushing air. The shipment continued its downward descent. The trawler hadn't changed its position and the load was dropping well behind the trawler.

"Hold the drop, Northern Star. Uh, Happy Hunter throttle back and allow us to drift back closer to the load, ah over," Jordan directed and focused on the load swinging on the side of the steel-hulled freighter. The freighter moved forward relative to the trawler as Fleming reduced the trawler's speed. The hanging shipment loomed closer toward Jordan and hung positioned above the boat's rear upper deck.

Fleming watched from the pilot station, but it was difficult to see everything from his vantage point and Arthur had to rely on Jordan. His Nordic Tug was becoming less controllable as it approached the stern of the larger ship. It started to rock back and forth more violently in the churning wake of the freighter.

"Okay Happy Hunter. Far enough! Maintain position, over." Jordan directed as he took a large breath. His heart pounded and his adrenaline rush tensed his arms. "Northern Star, you've about ten feet to lower. Slowly, we're rocking heavily out here, over!"

Fleming fought to maintain control of his trawler.

"Five feet, four three, hold." Jordan counted out as the pallet and cargo were just clearing the upper stainless steel railing of the rocking trawler.

"Northern Star, we've only one shot at this. When I say go, drop the load two feet then disconnect the line," Jordan instructed from the upper outer deck as he held onto the thin metal railing.

"Roger that Happy Hunter, over."

The radio went silent. The trawler rocked to starboard and on the boat's return to center, "Drop!" Jordan yelled.

A loud crash was heard by Fleming on the upper deck. The load was dropped and slid to the port side as the boat rolled over. It was stopped from going overboard only by the light stainless steel handrail that wrapped around the upper deck.

"Drop completed Northern Star. Good night, over!" Jordan announced as his heart pounded rapidly.

The freighter increased its speed as Fleming steered the trawler eastward away from the freighter's hull; the boat stabilized as it moved away from the wake of the larger ship.

Jordan turned off the bright upper deck lights and the trawler was reduced to darkness, marked only by the small red and green running lights in the darkness of the night. He pulled a large gray tarp over the shipment and secured the load.

The trawler was already north of Galiano Island by the time the transfer had been completed.

"Holy shit that was some ride, eh Arthur? Wow!" Jordan exclaimed, still pumped with adrenaline as he joined the captain of the trawler in the pilot's cabin.

"Great work kid! Look, it's now too late to go to Galiano and unload. I'm going to return to Campbell Bay and we'll stay there overnight. We can celebrate and have a drink when we anchor there in about half an hour." Fleming paused with a huge grin on his face, "Fantastic work kid!"

Chapter Fourteen

Sandra Vaughn was out on her scull early. The summer heat had made her bedroom hot and she hadn't slept well. Her head was full of Edgar Logan and Forsythe Harrison. She had tossed and turned thinking about what she was going to do. The heat was just an excuse she used to explain to herself why she hadn't slept.

The fresh morning air and the serenity of the calm ocean inlet water helped her to ease back and put her thoughts aside. She worked her way toward the *Canada Place Convention Center* and passed the casino. Her thoughts immediately jumped to Jako Palma and how scared she had become about him. She wanted to quit, but she told herself that it had to be after the Zoric situation had cooled off!

Life had become complicated. She felt trapped and she hated not being totally honest with Forsythe. She worked her frustrations out on the small boat and pushed herself until she couldn't take another stroke. She sat motionless as the scull drifted and came to a stop in the southern part of Burrard Inlet. She closed her eyes and let the soft tidal waves drift her. She sat in the scull in the middle of Coal Harbour, took a deep breath, and then she slowly exhaled. "It'll work out. Be patient," she told herself.

♓

Detectives Kelly O'Brian and Simon Chung were at their office working on their backlog of reports. There were many of them to do. Simon had to refer to his notes to ensure the reports that Kelly was preparing were complete. They usually were, but he liked to check anyway.

"Hey, you two! I got your warrant for the Bessier house." Captain Hollingsworth waved the paperwork at the two detectives. "He lives on Kiew Cliff Road."

"Cap, what are we going to do if the place is alarmed?" Kelly inquired as she had never faced that situation before.

"Call out our SWAT team. They've an expert who can disable the alarm usually before it triggers. Here's their number," the Captain replied and Simon took the number to make arrangements for the specialist to meet them at the house.

Kelly grinned at Simon. "Let's go. I've always wanted to see one of those waterfront estates!"

The candy-red BMW roadster was in the drive as Kelly drove their vehicle into a spot behind the spots car.

"We'd better wait for our SWAT guy," Simon advised eyeing the estate.

Kelly sat in the car, fidgeting. "I guess we'll never find out what happened to the Tyler Whitford keys!" she muttered as the SWAT Hummer rolled in behind the pair of cars. The officer got out.

"Thanks for coming quickly." Simon handed the officer the warrant. "We need to enter, but suspect there's an alarm. High-priced neighborhood and all," he said as he grinned. Simon was handed back the warrant and he stuffed it into his pocket. "Okay then."

The SWAT officer worked quickly on the door lock and had opened the front door without incident. He quickly spotted the entry alarm noticing the red blinking light of the alarm and pulled the face cover off. In less than fifteen seconds the alarm had been disabled.

"Okay guys, the place is all yours," the officer announced.

"That was fast! Thanks," Kelly remarked.

"No problem." The officer handed Simon his card. "Call if you need anything else." The officer turned and headed toward his Hummer.

The pair of detectives entered the large foyer and closed the door.

"Wow, what a way to live! It must be something else to have the bucks for this place!" Simon looked through the large plate glass window that overlooked the private dock and spectacular waterfront view.

"We'll never know about it—that's for sure on a cop's income!" Kelly remarked wide-eyed.

"Where do you want to start, KO?"

"There must be a safe here somewhere. Let's search for it first. Ah … let's find the office."

The two split up to search different parts of the sprawling rancher.

"Hey KO, help me in here!" Simon yelled a minute later.

Kelly joined him in a large study overlooking the ocean. "Better view than our office, I'd say," she paused, and then asked, "what are you thinking?"

"I'll bet there's a safe hidden around this bookcase; let's take a very close look."

"Ah … okay Simon, you take one side of the bookcase, I'll take the other."

The detectives pulled each book and framed photograph from each shelf, one by one. They inspected each shelf looking for an indication of a hidden safe or panel or something.

"You know," Kelly said standing back and looking at the bookcase, "the bookcase design is a bit strange, don't you think Simon?"

"Strange how?" He joined her in the centre of the room.

"There're two bookcases separated by this solid face between them. Doesn't that seem odd?"

"Not really. Maybe there's a beam or post there and the two bookcases are placed on either side of it."

"Yea maybe, but high-end homes like this are carefully designed … no posts that are unnecessary there." Kelly walked to the solid wooden face. She peered closely at each panel. "Come here, Simon! See—this panel doesn't fit like the others, and it has small scratches on the edges!"

Simon joined her and looked closely at the panel. "This panel's also pushed further in than the one above." He looked and the panels were staggered in depth from one shelf level to the next.

"Hmm … I'll bet it's a false face. We've got to find the activation switch to raise this panel. Check the shelves on either side. Look for a small button or something!"

Each partner took a side of the shelving unit and started to take the books out again.

"Simon, I doubt that it's here though. We've already looked closely at these shelves!" Kelly paused and stood in thought.

"If it's not in the shelving unit the only other place for a switch must be the desk!" Simon moved toward the large wooden desk and pulled the chair out. He got on his knees and looked under the desk. "Nothing obvious under here!"

"Ah … I think the key word is 'obvious,' Simon. Pull the desk drawer out from the desk and take a look!"

Simon got off the floor and pulled the desk drawer out, lifting it off the rail stop and then placing the small drawer on the desktop. He got on his knees again and took another look. "Bingo! You got it, KO!" Simon exclaimed and pressed the small button. A small panel in the bookcase raised and exposed the safe. "Slick!"

Simon got onto his feet and both detectives walked to the safe in the bookcase.

"A dial safe—none of that electronic stuff. Must be a number of years old, eh Simon?"

"I know a few things about safes, especially about these dial types." Simon bent over and looked underneath the handle.

"Simon, what are you looking for?"

"This type of safe usually has a manufacturer code stamped underneath on the pull handle," he said as he placed his head as far into the small cavity as he could.

"Yep. Get a pen and write this down." He spoke with his face still looking up into the small space.

Kelly went to the desk drawer on the desktop. She found a pen and paper. "Shoot!"

"Uh, CD1993 … V … 376329 … SR," Simon said and pulled his head out.

Simon pulled the SWAT officer's card from his pocket and picked up his cell. "Hi, it's Detective Chung. You were just at the Kiew Cliff home in West Van." Simon listened and then continued. "Yea hi, I've a Sentry dial safe here. I've the manufacturer's code. Can you use your protocol and get the combo from the manufacturer?" Simon asked and then smiled. "Great! Ah, yea the code's CD1993 … V … 376329 … SR. We'll hang here and wait for your call, thanks." Simon hung up the call and looked at Kelly who looked perplexed. "Kelly, the SWAT guys have a protocol where they can get the combos from manufacturers if they provide proper documents or if there's some public safety risk," Simon explained.

"How'd you know that?" she asked looking impressed.

"Remember, I've been around a while! One of those experience things I'm to pass on to rookies, you know," Simon laughed.

♓

Peter Dobson found Jako Palma going through business reports at his desk.

"Hey Jako, last month's financials finally come in from finance?" Peter asked as he went to the sideboard to get a coffee.

"Yea, looking really good. All departments are up. How was your flight last night?"

"Better than Zoric's the other day, I'd say," Peter laughed as he poured his coffee. "So what's the panic, JP? Somethin' going down?"

"Yea, I think it's time to close a loose end. Raj Jattan's pressing and is likely to go off the deep end. You know, risk management."

"What about the girl?" Peter asked as he walked toward Jako's desk with his black coffee.

Jako paused for a moment. "She can wait. I don't want any questions right now. Let things cool and she can be dealt with later. We know where she is and I want Jattan dealt with first."

"Can we afford to wait?"

"We can't afford to rush! I'm not sure she's put the pieces together yet anyway. We'll watch her closely for the next few days."

"You're the boss. What plan have you got for Jattan?"

"Draw him out to the Charles Whitford place on Bowen. Remember, he's the one who told us all about Whitford. The heat's off that place and it's at the quiet end of the island—I looked on Google®. Besides, out of town is better."

"Works for me, Jako!"

"I'll tell him that you got some info from Bessier and the clues at Charles' place. His guy Zoric missed it and we're just trying to help! You'll meet him there."

"What time ya got in mind for the setup, boss?"

"Say nine tonight? Time for the ferry trip, travel to the house and it'll be getting dark. You can get to the house early and wait for him. Be quiet this time. The gun noise out there can be heard for miles."

"Okay boss, set it up!"

♓

Terence Weiss thought that he was going to play his waiting game smarter today. He sat in his old Chevy by the Thieves Point marina and waited for Fleming in the car. He knew that there would be lots of time to prepare once the trawler appeared at the mouth of the marina. Besides, it was more comfortable to wait in the car than to sprawl in the woods all day. He had brought a lunch and a cooler of beer as he knew that it might be a long wait.

He sat and recalled his time in the slammer. The damp, cold cell and open toilet. No dignity and everyone had to prove that they were tough to survive. He did his time, not because he deserved it, but just because this bastard Fleming wanted to get an easy collar.

Terence was ready to go back to that cell, if need be. Fixing Fleming would make the repeat sentence worth it. He had survived before. It would be a cake-walk a second time.

♓

Simon's cell phone rang. He and Kelly were sitting in Marcel Bessier's family room admiring the spectacular early morning view. "Chung here!" He smiled at Kelly as he listened. "Hey, great work. Let me grab by notebook. Hang tight." Simon pulled his notebook and pen from his coat.

"Right." He paused, waiting for the combo.

Simon scribbled the three numbers in the notebook and hung up. "Here we go, let's try these."

He got up from the sofa and returned to the study safe. Kelly followed him as he dialed the numbers written in his book and pulled the safe's lever down. "Our SWAT guys are great," Simon muttered as he swung the door open and he looked inside.

They both pulled on a pair of rubber gloves.

"Hey KO, there lots of stuff in here! Clear a space on that desk and I'll pass you what's inside."

Simon pulled the contents out of the safe, one article at a time and Kelly placed the items on the office desk. "Okay that's it; let's see what we have." Simon kept his notebook open. "I'll note the inventory and you go through the stuff."

"One. Here's a pack of cash. Looks like about five grand." She put that aside.

"Two. A CD disk in white sleeve." She put it aside.

"Three. Here's a pile of IOUs. These are gambling IOUs, with various lenders' names. A number of these are to Jako Palma!" She put the pile of notes aside.

"Four. A plastic Ziploc bag with the following contents inside." She opened it. "Ah … a driver's license, Care Card and five credit cards, all belonging to a Joy Bessier." Kelly replaced the items, re-zipped the bag and put it aside.

"Five. Another plastic Ziploc bag with the following contents inside." She opened it. "A couple of newspaper article clippings." Kelly unfolded one. "This article is about the Rawlings murder fifteen years ago. We'll go though these later." She replaced the clipping and put the bag aside.

"And last, six. Another plastic Ziploc bag with the following contents inside." She opened it. "A birth certificate for Marriam Tremblay!" Kelly looked at the document very closely. "The parents are listed as Mark Rawlings and Joy Tremblay and ah ... the child was born the 19th of March 1980." Kelly stood stunned, and just stared at the document. "Huh ... that's my birth date, Simon! What a coincidence, eh?"

Kelly pulled the office chair closer and sat down. She was stunned and had tears running down her face. The room went silent. Simon found an easy chair in the study and sat down.

"It can't be me! My father's Patrick O'Brian not Mark Rawlings. It must be some coincidence that the birth date is the same as mine! I'm confused." Tears streamed down her face. "What's all this stuff doing here anyway?"

Simon waited, and then commented. "Bessier must've got this from one of the Whitford men! Maybe that's what prompted him to look for the *DigiCast* money."

"That must mean that this stuff had originally been at Charles Whitford's place and Tyler must've found it after we left." Kelly said with a sniffle. Her eyes were red from the tears.

"If Joy Bessier drowned seven years ago, how could Charles Whitford have ended up with her driver's license and credit cards?" Kelly pushed her tears aside and looked up at Simon.

"Only one thing comes to my mind ...." Simon was cut off in mid-thought.

"Joy Bessier didn't drown!"

"It fits, KO."

"Except it doesn't explain why Joy Bessier or Charles Whitford had the birth certificate for Marriam Tremblay!" Kelly thought about what she had just said. "Unless Joy Tremblay, the artist who painted the lighthouse piece I have, is Joy Bessier, the famous West Vancouver artist! Tremblay must be Bessier's maiden name. Joy is the mother of Marriam and that's why she had the birth certificate of her daughter, Marriam, when she skipped out on Marcel."

"I don't know! Where does your father Patrick fit in all this then?"

"I'm confused. Marriam has my birth date! I can't concentrate on this situation now. What else do we have that's outstanding?" Kelly frowned.

Simon flipped through his notes. "Ah … we've Arthur Fleming's financials that are still outstanding, and also we don't have an understanding of what his connection is to the Cain Road house on Galiano," he replied and flipped more pages. "Also outstanding, includes the photo of the two golfers at the *DigiCast* event, the silver key, and the combination to an unknown safe."

"Yea, the golfers. Hmm, there were lots of photos of golfers and golf trophies at the Cain house! One of those may be the clue that links the photograph to the rest of the clues. We've go to back to Galiano now, Simon!" Kelly stood up, grabbed her phone. "Hey Captain, KO! Things are coming together. Can't go through it all now, but can you book Simon and me the next flight departing from the Bayshore dock to Galiano, then the next return flight?" She paused for his answer. "Thanks, text me with the flight times. We're leaving the Bessier place now. Oh … can you please get a locksmith out here with a uniform officer, too? We need to change the lock so we can get in later."

Kelly hung up the phone and faced Simon. "Let's hustle. We've a flight to catch!"

"Hold up there, detective. Let's put this stuff in a bag first! Can't leave five Gs around and you'll likely want some of this other stuff to look at later!" Simon called out as Kelly was halfway out of the room.

"Right, right! Find a bag in the kitchen. Go, go! I'll get the car started," Kelly yelled back.

Simon smiled, shook his head and pulled the wastebasket from under the desk. He placed the evidence inside and rushed out of the house, slamming the door behind him."There's a bag in the car," he muttered.

The gray Taurus sped down the expressway toward the *Lions Gate Bridge.*

Simon's cell rang. "Chung!" he answered and then paused. "Hey Cap. Yea, she's okay. A little wired I'd say, but okay." He smiled at Kelly, who was concentrating on the road as the car flew down the highway.

"We should be on the eleven twenty *Island Airways* flight. That'll be tight—Simon can you have them hold it if we're a few minutes late? Tell them RCMP business." She quickly glanced over at her partner with a determined look on her face.

Simon smiled and returned to his call. "Cap, you're the best. Thanks." He hung up. "Hey, don't kill us before we figure this out!" Simon cautioned.

"Ha, ha. Hang tight! I always wanted to see what this car could do!" She stomped on the accelerator and turned on the siren. "Policy, going over the speed limit calls for the siren! I've always wanted to do this in this beast!" Kelly said with a grin.

"Hey don't forget the flashing lights. They're fun too … and policy," Simon laughed as they screamed down the highway. "I'll make that call to *Island Airways*."

♓

Forsythe Harrison sat in his office mulling over things in his head. He looked at the time.

"Sandra will be done with her morning row by now! Time to call." He picked up the phone and dialed her number that he now knew by memory.

"Hello, Sandra," was the greeting he heard as she answered.

"Sandra, its Forsythe. I need to see you. Can we meet for lunch?"

"Sure. What's up?"

"Just meet me at one of those park benches across from your place. Say just before noon. Okay?"

"Park bench. Noon. Got it. See you later."

Forsythe darted out of his office. He had less than an hour.

♓

Jordan and Arthur were more exhausted from the night's arms transfer than they had realized. The silence of the bay allowed the men to sleep until midmorning. Arthur woke up, startled that it was already so late in the morning.

He went to the upper deck to check on his cargo. It was safe and well wrapped. "Good lad!" he commented to himself.

Jordan heard Arthur on the upper deck and jumped from his bed in the rear stateroom. He remembered that he and Arthur had celebrated their successful adventure and his headache attested to the late night.

Arthur came into the room. "We'd better fix something to eat. We won't be leaving here until seven tonight. We've a lot of work later unloading this stuff." Arthur's hangover reminded him that his heavy drinking days were over. He reached for a juice in the fridge. "I'll have a beer later," he said as he saw Jordan scrunching his face as Arthur poured juice into a glass.

"Don't just stand there. Your mom taught you how to make an omelet, didn't she?"

"Uh … it has eggs, right?" Jordon looked lost.

"Okay watch. I'll show you just once."

♓

Sandra wanted to check out Edgar Logan before she met with Forsythe. She pulled his card out of her purse and dialed the phone number.

"Logan Investigation. How may I help you?" a woman answered.

"I'm looking for some investigation help." Sandra thought about an excuse to call. "How long have you been in business?"

"Quite a while honey. Some boyfriend problem or somethin'?"

"Ah, no I need to find someone. Do you do that?"

"Sure thing. Do you want to talk to Mr. Logan, the boss?"

"No. Not now thanks. I'll call back." Sandra hung up satisfied with the information that she got.

♓

The gray police car roared and screeched to a stop at the Bayshore Hotel. Kelly turned off the car emergency lights and the siren. The parking attendant met the car wondering what was going on.

"Where can we leave our car for a few hours?"

"You can park it in the lower underground. Just take a parking slip and we'll deal with the fee when you return."

"Thanks." Kelly zipped into the garage and found an empty spot.

"We'll just make the flight!" she said excitedly as though she had run all the way and not driven.

"You go ahead; I'll get a bag for the evidence and I'll be with you in a minute!" Simon said as he jumped out of the car. "Go!"

Kelly ran up the parking ramp. The *Island Airways* float plane was waiting.

"Are you the detectives I've been waiting for?"

"Yea … my partner's coming!" She flashed her shield as she saw Simon run up behind her with the bag of evidence.

"Okay," Simon said out of breath. "I left the cash in the trunk!" he grinned.

"Let's go. We're running a little late. We land at Montague Harbour in thirty minutes," the pilot said and turned heading for the plane that was tied at the dock.

The rental car turned into the driveway of the Marriam Tremblay house on Cain Road and parked at the end by the waterfront. The two detectives jumped out of the car and walked quickly to the back door.

"Simon, the backdoor's still unlocked." Kelly opened the door and stood in disbelief.

"Oh my God, what a mess!!" She stepped into the sitting room. "Bessier has pulled everything out. Look at the kitchen!"

Simon shook his head. "You're looking for golfing stuff, right?"

"Uh, yea. I saw most of it over there." She pointed to the end wall of the sitting room. The old photographs and tournament awards were still on the wall. Kelly knelt down and started to pick up the golfing memorabilia from the floor. As she placed the items back on the shelf she studied each one closely.

"Simon, this one is the only one that has two names on the engraved plate." She stood up and handed the golf trophy to Simon. "All the others only have Mark Rawlings' name."

Simon took the trophy. "*DigiCast* Classic 1986 Mark Rawlings and Victor Catroppa," was engraved on the small brass plate.

"We need to figure out who Victor Catroppa is and where he fits into all this." Kelly sat down. "He must be the other man in the photo we've got!"

"Look, we've about five hours before our return flight. Why don't I put that award into the car and we can spend about an hour quickly straightening up this place."

"Okay. I'd feel better leaving this house cleaned up. We can grab something to eat after."

♓

Sandra's apartment overlooked Devonian Harbour Park. She was concentrating on getting dressed and she didn't question why Forsythe had selected that park to meet her before lunch. He was making an unusual effort to meet her during working hours. That was a first!

She left her apartment and walked across the busy street to the park. A man was sitting on the park bench, facing toward the harbour, and she knew that it was Forsythe. She came around the bench and sat next to him.

He handed her a large bouquet of purple lilac flowers. The fragrance was strong and filled the surrounding area with its sweet scent.

"They say that the color and type of a flower are old symbols that express people's feelings." Forsythe looked at her face. "These are the symbols of a person's first emotion of love." He paused. "It's not my first emotion of love for you, but it's the first time I've shown it in public!"

He took her hand and gently kissed her, and then he smiled.

She sat frozen in her place. She couldn't find the words and continued to look directly at him.

Forsythe sat silent for a moment, and then took a large breath. "I know about the other men Sandra. I know about your hourly night breaks at the casino."

She was going to say something. He held his finger to her lips. He continued, squeezing her hand. "I know that you must've been worried about telling me. I didn't like it when I figured it out, but it's okay for me now."

"I've been trying to think of a way to tell you." She began to cry. "It didn't matter to me before, you know. It was just a way to get what I wanted. To feel I wasn't dependant on anyone anymore and it was my choice each time." Tears began streaming from her eyes. "I never thought about what would happen if I met someone like you. You're more than I ever dreamed. This seems unreal, what's happening to me." She took a breath and continued and sniffled.

"I haven't wanted to have sex with you before you knew. I wanted you to know that you're the only man I want to be with. Oh … it must sound so hollow."

"None of it matters, Sandra. Only you matter to me. The rest is just us getting to this point. It's time to end it and quit," Forsythe said softly. "I'll be here for you."

She looked down at the flowers. "I can't yet. I'm concerned about my boss, Jako Palma. I went to the cops and told them things about his business. He won't like it if he finds out and if I quit … it'll not look very good. The timing is wrong."

"I'm very concerned about your safety, Sandra. Come stay with me," he urged, caressing her hand.

"Give me a little more time, Forsythe. I've got to work a few things out myself."

"Are you sure?" He used a finger to wipe the tears from her cheek.

"One more thing, Forsythe. I must miss our sailing tomorrow evening."

"Why? You never miss that event. Never!" He looked concerned.

"Sorry, just something I promised. That's all." Sandra kissed him and got up from the park bench. "Thanks for the flowers, they're beautiful. I'll call."

She turned and walked back toward her apartment. Forsythe watched her until she had disappeared into the building.

♓

Peter Dobson had parked his car in the driveway of the Bowen Bay house on the waterfront and then entered the house.

The late afternoon's sun was almost blinding as it came through the large windows of the study of Charles Whitford's place. Peter was looking for the best place to hide so Raj Jattan wouldn't see him upon entering the house.

Peter picked up some things that had been scattered on the floor. "I can't trip over any of this. It's best just to get it out of my way." He placed a few things back onto the shelves. "That's better. No surprises."

Peter found the bar and poured himself a scotch. He surveyed the back rooms, imprinting in his mind the layout and position of the furnishings as he worked his plan through his mind.

"Nope, that won't work!" He changed his mind on his plan and took another drink of the scotch.

Peter looked about the room and saw the large sea trunk. "That'll do!" He walked over to the chest and pulled it from the wall, and opened the lid. Peter knew about the data CD disk, as Raj Jattan had been very specific as to what he wanted. Peter purchased a box of blanks that were packaged with white protective envelopes. He had brought one with him and placed it on the desk. He then found some books in the bookcase and started to place a half dozen of them in the chest. He inserted the blank disk in the front cover of the last book, placed it with the others in the chest, and closed the chest lid.

"That'll work better!" Satisfied, he refreshed his drink. He sat and waited in the other room for Jattan.

Peter turned on a light in the far side of the sitting room. The sun had dropped below the horizon and the room had quickly become dark. He heard a car turn into the driveway and knew it was time.

The East Indian man was short and stocky. His red short-sleeved shirt and red turban emphasized the graying manicured beard. "What's all the mystery and why meet here, Dobson?" he asked as he entered the room and saw Peter sitting, drinking a scotch.

"I finally got Bessier to tell me where your precious data disk was and I thought that it was fitting that you took possession of it yourself. I'm not your delivery boy! What was all the fuss about anyway?" Peter asked as he put his glass of scotch on a side table and got out of his seat.

"Charles Whitford was our bookkeeper accountant. He was able to move funds from the charity I manage and put the money into some personal account. He worked the transactions to look as if I took the money! The only proof I have that Charles took the money is his private account and transaction details, which I believe are on the data disk. Without that proof, I've got a big problem!"

"So that wasn't the money Bessier was looking for!" Dobson exclaimed, surprised, and he slowly walked toward Raj Jattan.

"I don't care how you want to do this Dobson, so long as I get the information on the data disk. Where is it?" Raj demanded loudly.

"You want a drink first? The scotch is smooth!" Peter watched the anxious man.

"After I get the disk! Show me where he told you to look," Raj yelled.

"Okay, okay. Relax. Let's go." Peter led Raj into the study. "He told me that it's in here!" Peter lifted the lid of the old sea chest. "It's slipped into one of these books, I understand. Well, that's what he told me anyway."

Jattan smiled and bent over to look inside the open chest. He pulled the first book from the row and opened its cover. The white CD sleeve with the disk was inside and slipped from the book onto the floor of the chest. "Ah," Raj muttered and leaned further over to retrieve the CD.

Peter pulled a switchblade from his pocket and the long narrow blade shot from the hilt of the handle. He stabbed Jattan in his side and pushed the blade in deep to its end.

Raj turned his head in surprise and tried to stand up, but couldn't. "What are …." he started to say as Peter stabbed Raj a second time in the side of the neck and Jattan fell forward head first into the chest and slumped across the old wooden box. Peter pulled out the blade, wiped it on the Indian's shirt, retracted the weapon and returned the knife to his pocket.

Dobson knew that he had killed the man, but checked his pulse anyway. "That fixes that risk!" Peter washed the blood spatter from his hands and face in a small sink by the bar. He then returned to the sitting room, turned off the light, and sat to finish his scotch in the dark.

♓

It had become dark by the time Arthur Flemings' trawler reached the Galiano Cain Road dock. The illumination from the running lights didn't help much to light up the dock, making the approach tricky.

"Jordan, you tie off the boat as I get the house open and the lights on!"

Arthur found the back door unlocked. "Why's this open?" He turned the door handle and became concerned that someone had broken into the house. He turned on the sitting room and kitchen lights. Things didn't look out of place so he returned to join Jordan at the trawler.

"I think someone's been in the house. We'll have to look about after we get this stuff stowed in the basement."

"Sure thing, Mr. Fleming," young Jordan replied as he worked his way to the top deck and began to remove the tarps and the cargo's securing lines.

"Come down and get some lifting straps. We've to remove each crate individually. Use the trawler's hoist and electric downrigger," Fleming instructed.

Jordan grabbed a half dozen nylon straps and returned to the upper deck.

"Wow, these boxes are heavier than others we've brought here!" Jordan remarked while placing a strap under each end of the first crate.

"Yea, we've a different product this time. Be careful that you get the strap in the middle of the crate, otherwise the box won't lift properly."

The hoist hook was placed into the rings of the straps and Jordan carefully lifted the box and swung the crate to the dock. Fleming unhooked the straps and Jordan prepared for the next box.

It took over an hour to unload the shipment from the Nordic Tug.

Each man grabbed one end of the first crate and carried it to the sitting room.

"I'll take a breather here. Jordan you go downstairs and get the lights turned on."

The young man turned into the house hallway and flipped the hall lights on. He opened the basement door, turned on the staircase lights and upon reaching the basement, turned on the bright working lights. Jordan stopped in his tracks; his eyes wide open.

"Hey, Mr. Fleming. You need to come down here quick!" Jordan screamed and backed away toward the staircase.

"Okay Jordan, what's the fuss?" Arthur asked as he started down the stairs. Fleming didn't need any explanation. There was blood everywhere and the room was a mess!

"Well that explains why the back door was open!" Arthur walked to the dark red stain on the concrete floor. "Someone was looking for something! Look at the stuff all about the floor," he said staring at the blood stains. "Maybe the person was killed when it was found!"

"Jordan, we know there was nothing down here! Maybe it was just a murder made to look like something else. I'm sure many people know that I'm not here all the time. Hmm … just a place of convenience," Arthur tried to rationalize the situation.

"If that's so, where's the body, Boss?" Jordan asked, his eyes still wide with shock.

"Hmm … good question, a very good question." Fleming thought for a moment.

"Jordan, just clean up the mess so we can finish unloading. We only need our cargo to be here for two days anyway," Fleming said, now feeling nervous about the time frame.

"You want to leave the shipment unattended?" Jordan asked surprised as he looked around at the things strewed around the room.

Fleming stood for a moment then answered, "Nope, you're going to stay here. I'll do what I need to do back at my house at Thieves' Bay, then I'll come right back. Let's get our stuff moved."

The crates were heavy and it took the two men over an hour and a half to get the shipment stacked into the basement.

"Let's have a drink. I hope our visitors didn't take your beer from the fridge," Fleming said, out of breath, exhausted, and needing to rest. He turned out the basement lights and returned to the sitting room. Jordan found his beer in the fridge and Arthur found his scotch and poured a drink.

"I think I'll stay overnight with you tonight in the house and you'll only have tomorrow by yourself. Okay?"

"Works for me, Boss, but it's spooky that someone was killed here."

They both sat saying nothing more, just finishing the rest of their drinks, thinking about the next few days ahead.

Chapter Fifteen

Elizabeth Richardson was at work but was still distracted by concern about Marcel Bessier. She had become very nervous and jumped at every sound and noise. She hadn't been sleeping well and it showed on her face: she looked tired and exhausted. She wasn't her usual chipper self with the tourists either, and spent her breaks alone, lost in thought. She picked up an unfolded daily newspaper as she cleared one of the tables.

Upon glancing at the front page, she stood shocked as the headline jumped out at her.

"**Prominent Lawyer Murdered**." Beneath the headline in smaller print was, "*Marcel Bessier found shot to death on Galiano Island.*"

She thought that she was going to faint and found the closest unoccupied chair and sat down. She couldn't bring herself to read the article and hung her head and wept. Her quiet sobs filled the café but she couldn't contain the emotion. It was tragic; she never wished this on Marcel. He was a jerk and nasty at times but he didn't deserve being murdered. Tears streamed down her face.

Someone purchased a hot coffee, placed it beside her on the small table and left, not saying a word. Elizabeth looked up to thank the person for the coffee, but she was alone. She took a tissue from her dress pocket, wiped her face and sat silently, sipping the coffee.

As she sat, her mood changed. Her sadness passed as she realized that she was finally free from the man who she had so long feared. She no longer had to be afraid, or to hide. The thought caused her to take a deep breath. She could resume her real identity now and knew what she had to do.

♓

Kelly was just returning from her morning walk with Hunter. The city was alive with people taking advantage of the wonderful cool early morning. She stopped by her mailbox and grabbed the stack of mail and flyers. She placed the stack of mail on the kitchen counter and proceeded to get ready for work. She was excited to begin the day. There was a new clue to unravel and she could feel the Charles Whitford case finally coming together.

She poured herself a coffee while sitting at the table in her underwear and grabbed the stack of mail.

"Hmm … what's this one, Hunter?" The dog looked up at her. "It's a package for Dad! I can't believe that those people in Marpole still have our forwarding address!" She flipped through the rest of the envelopes. "Bills, bills, bills, and junk mail. Humph."

She set aside her dad's envelope. "I'll stop and see Dad tomorrow. I owe him a visit anyway."

Kelly picked up Simon in the gray Taurus at the transit station as usual.

"Ready for a new day? We sure have lots of stuff to sort through today. It's great to be a detective!" she said in a cheery tone as Simon quickly slipped into the front seat.

"Topped up and ready to go I see," Simon replied; he was glad to see Kelly back to her normal enthusiastic self.

The Captain saw the two enter the room. "How'd that flight to Galiano work out?"

"Great—thanks, Cap! We think we got the break we've been looking for. We'll follow-up on that later."

"You've the information on Fleming you wanted. The link's in your e-mail."

Kelly opened the e-mail. "Ah … yea it's here. Thanks, Cap." She selected the embedded link.

"Simon, this guy's sure doing very well as a retired detective. See these large cash deposits? One hundred and fifty grand here and look—almost two hundred and seventy-five grand here." She pointed to the entries on the screen. "Hmm

… he's sure up to something! With him paying the bills at the Cain house and all of these large deposits, it smells of some type of trafficking to me."

Kelly looked up from her computer monitor. "I think we should ask the local uniforms to set up surveillance out at Cain Road for a while. Maybe they can pull some officers from some of the other islands for a few days, eh?"

"Okay KO. You set that up. The officer over there seems to like you!" Simon smiled.

She smirked and made the call.

Simon spread the bagful of evidence taken from the Bessier house on his desk. He took the CD and placed it into the computer drive. A listing of files appeared on the screen.

"Very good!" Simon smiled and selected the first file.

"Password Please," flashed on the screen.

Each consecutive file selected requested a password.

"Great! It's a job for IT," Simon muttered frustrated.

Kelly finished her call. "It's all arranged. The guys over there will set it up for a few days and see what happens. They're itching to find out what's going on at that house anyway. What are you doing?"

"I tried to see what was on the CD disk from Bessier's safe but the files are password protected. I'll get the IT guys to look into it and maybe they can bypass the security hoops."

"You know, Simon, the birth certificate we found kept me awake all night."

"I figured as much." Simon looked up at her and smiled.

"If Marriam Tremblay was born on the same day I was, and Joy Tremblay is the woman in Dad's photo at the lighthouse, then …."

Simon interrupted, "Then we still have a mystery to solve. The birth-dates are coincidental, nothing more! Marriam's father was Mark Rawlings and your father's Patrick O'Brian. There's some link with *DigiCast*, and we don't know what it is, though it's strange I grant you!"

"Okay, you're right. Victor Catroppa is the only key left." Kelly paused and took a breath. "Well, I mean him and the safe of course."

"I feel like one of those small ping pong balls in an arcade machine, bouncing from one clue to another, ringing a few bells but not making the big score!"

"Well partner, all the bells have to go off soon and we'll find out the prize, eh?"

"Let's draft our reports, and then we can work on the Catroppa thing."

♓

Sandra was out of her apartment early. She sat on the park bench across from her condo and watched the large cruise ships return from their Alaska circuit. The ships were huge and she watched the thirteen-story liner ease into its *Canada Place* berth.

She wasn't in a mood for rowing today and she had hated telling Forsythe that their sailing date was cancelled. She didn't like it and she knew that he didn't either.

Sandra had a headache and a slight hangover, likely from the bottle of wine she drank by herself the night before. The morning fresh air didn't help. She wasn't sure if the throbbing was from the wine or the discussion with Forsythe. She had to get her act together if she was going to be alert when she met with Edgar Logan.

♓

Kelly was working on her reports when her cell rang. "Detective O'Brian."

"Good morning, Detective. It's the RCMP office in Galiano."

"Ah yes. What's up?"

"We've the results of the prints we took from the perp at the Cain house. You know he stole one of our cruisers. Well, we lifted prints and got a hit."

"Great. I wondered how soon it would be before you got something," Kelly said and looked at Simon who was still slowly pecking out his report.

"The prints belong to a Mr. Peter Dobson. He's not a nice guy according to his rap sheet. The ME's extracted the bullets from Mr. Bessier. I'll courier them to your office and you can have the CSI guys take a look. The ballistics may tell us more."

"Great work. Thanks. We'll put an APB on Dobson from this office." Kelly hung up and noticed that Simon had stopped his typing. "Simon, our guy who whacked Bessier is a 'Peter Dobson.' I'll get the notice out with his photo. Also, I was told we're getting the slugs from the crime scene. I'll have the front desk watch for them and send them to ballistics as soon as they arrive."

♓

Terence Weiss was sitting bored in the old Chevy waiting for Arthur Fleming to appear. He was becoming worried that he had been spending too much time in the area and people would become curious as to what he was doing there. The car wasn't exactly nondescript, either. He decided to lift the hood of the car and make it appear as though he was having engine problems. There had been a few people who had walked past his car up the small road that serviced the marina and some others who were milling about on their boats who could see the small parking area where he sat and waited.

He was playing some game on his BlackBerry® when the Nordic Tug appeared in the mouth of the small marina heading for the dock that Terence had seen the boat tied up to earlier. He promptly turned his BlackBerry® off, exited the Chevy, and quickly walked toward Fleming's house. As he made his way along the paved street to the back of Fleming's house, Terence watched the trawler work its way into the small bay, targeting the private dock. He had lots of time to find his entry to the detective's old house. Windows had been left partially open and he had entered the property the day before and had left himself an open door at the back.

Terence slipped down the driveway and entered through the open rear door, locking it behind him. He had already made himself familiar with the layout and had selected his place to hide inside and wait for his prey. He watched Fleming through the front window and noticed that the detective tied up the large boat by himself. Terence smiled, screwed the silencer onto the HAHR 9mm gun that he had got from Pits. He returned to the kitchen and waited, crouched behind the side kitchen wall. He heard the front door unlock and Arthur enter the front room.

Arthur Fleming tossed a black plastic bag of empty beer cans and bottles on the floor. He turned to close the door and stopped, stood still and listened.

"Who's there?" Arthur shouted, pulling his service pistol and pointing the barrel toward the ceiling. He listened, but there was nothing. His cop instincts took over and he quickly moved to the sitting room wall.

Terence crouched behind the wall of kitchen cabinets and knew that he wasn't in the best position. He rolled his eyes as he had unintentionally moved his foot when it cramped in the awkward stance, the sound warning Fleming of an intruder. His heart raced, and his mind feverishly tried to determine his next best move. He remained motionless and heard Fleming's footsteps slowly advance toward the kitchen.

Arthur lowered the barrel and now had it pointed directly into the kitchen. He stood still again and his eyes darted around the open space. He slowly advanced. The muzzle of the pistol poked past the edge of the wall.

Terence saw that he had no option and darted out from behind his hiding place and grabbed the muzzle of the pistol with his left hand. He held his firearm in his right. The motion pulled both men to the ground with a thud and both bodies scrambled for control as they rolled on the floor. Fleming forcibly swung his fist around and hit Terence's wrist, knocking the heavy gun from the intruder's right hand's grasp. The weapon spun away from either man's reach, slid across the floor, and rested on the far side of the kitchen floor.

"Fuckin' bastard!" Terence screamed as both men fought to get control of Fleming's gun, now encased in clenched fists. Terence was the younger and stronger of the two men and he was slowly overpowering his opponent. "Fuck with me, will ya!" Terence yelled.

Fleming strained as both men rolled on the floor, struggling for control, and he knew that he had little strength and time left. He realized that he couldn't overpower Weiss so he dropped his left hand and reached down, pulling his knee upward as Terence struck him in his face. He was losing the battle for the weapon and blood began to pour from his eye. With one last effort he stretched his arm; his left hand grabbed his small concealed ankle pistol. He pointed it directly at his assailant and fired twice.

Terence momentarily released his crushing grip on Arthur and Arthur pounded Weiss's wrist with the butt of the ankle pistol. Arthur rolled away from the bleeding intruder and shot Weiss a third time.

The loud sound of the gunshots had made his ears hurt. He lay on the floor exhausted, turned and saw Terence Weiss motionless and bleeding out onto the kitchen floor.

Arthur staggered to his feet and took a moment to regain his breath while holding his gun. He peered at the well-toned tall man, bent over and checked for a pulse. Terence was dead and Arthur knew that he was lucky to have survived!

The seasoned detective knew that the loud gunshots would've been heard by anyone at the marina. He had to call 911 and alert the local RCMP of the fatal shooting. He called the number.

"Yes Sir, Mr. Fleming. We've received a number of calls about gunshots at Thieves Bay. We've already dispatched a car. Has anyone been injured?"

"Yes, I shot the intruder. He's dead, but I'm okay," Arthur replied, still winded from the struggle.

"Give me your address and I'll divert the officers directly to your location."

Arthur provided the address, and knew that it would take a short while for the RCMP officers to get there. There was only a small contingent of police on Pender Island and he knew Thieves Bay was some distance from their centralized office. He knew how to handle the situation once the squad car arrived. He grabbed a beer from the fridge, returned to the sitting room and waited.

"Man, I'm sure glad Jordan wasn't with me! Who knows what would've happened?" Arthur muttered as he pulled the tab on his can of beer.

Arthur knew that he had to be back to Galiano by late afternoon the next day and that he had to wrap up this entire situation today.

He took a long drink from his can of beer and glanced at the body on the kitchen floor. Seeing Terence reminded him of the old Rawlings case and he remembered that he and Rawlings had got started working together trafficking goods. They started off their business relationship doing small jobs; Rawlings had turned out to be a good partner and they both knew that they had a good thing going. Rawlings' place had been perfect, too, with its private dock and secluded locale. He also recalled how he had become upset about Rawlings' murder and became driven to find the person responsible. Of course, Terence Weiss had been the likely candidate, and the evidence collected certainly pointed that way. Charles Whitford hadn't even been on the radar screen!

The white RCMP squad car with its flashing red and blue lights turned into Flemings' drive and two uniformed officers walked quickly to the back door.

Arthur heard them arrive and he met them with the door open. "He's in here! He attacked me—we fought and I shot him."

One of the uniforms eyed the gun with the silencer that was on the floor under the far kitchen counter. "That weapon's his?"

"Yes. My old service weapon is over on the other side of the kitchen floor and I shot him with this one!" Arthur handed over the small ankle pistol, then paused. "I had my service weapon drawn but he grabbed that and we struggled for control. I had to use the ankle pistol in self-defense."

"Do you have permits for these guns, Mr. Fleming?"

"Yes, I'm a retired RCMP detective. I put this guy away fifteen years ago and I understand that he was just released."

"Ah, payback time, eh Fleming?" the officer commented as he made notes of the conversation.

"It comes with the territory, Officers. You guys know all about that!"

"Yup, sure do. The ME will be here shortly. He was up island when you reported the shooting."

The officers gathered their crime scene kits and began recording the scene and taking the required photos. "We are the ones to do most of the work out here, ya know. It's not like the city guys who have separate teams for each step."

"I'm sure that's more interesting, though. You see most of the case right through, start to end. That's how it was when I was on the force workin' the islands." Arthur stood and watched the officers go about their business.

The medical examiner arrived, did his cursory investigation, and bagged the body. "The mess I'll leave for you, Mr. Fleming." he said coldly as the body was carted out on a gurney by the two officers.

"I think we've everything we need right now, Mr. Fleming. How's the best way to reach ya if we need to talk later?" one of the officers asked as he returned from the driveway.

"I'm in and out. Here's my cell." Arthur wrote his number on a sheet of paper and handed it to the inquiring officer.

The police contingent and medical examiner left the scene and Arthur walked into the kitchen, found his scotch and poured himself a glass. He took a deep breath, entered the sitting room and sat down. He hadn't realized how unnerving the brush with death had been. His hand shook as he picked up his drink. "I'm getting too old for this shit! Maybe it's time to finally retire."

♓

Kelly O'Brian typed "Victor Catroppa" into the internet inquiry. She was familiar with using the online telephone directory service to find people.

"Eh, Simon, there are only two Catroppas listed in Vancouver. One of these is a business, 'Catroppa's Antiques' and the other 'V Catroppa'. I guess we have our guy!"

"Ah … try the antique store first. Where is it?"

"It's on Dunbar Street off the 400 block," she replied as she wrote the address and phone number in her notebook. "It's time to pay the man a visit and see what he has to say!"

The small antique business wasn't busy when the detectives entered the store. The opening of the door set off a small brass bell hung at the top of the sill, announcing their entry. An elderly man came from a room behind the counter. "Can I help you two?"

"We're Detectives Chung and O'Brian." Kelly showed her gold shield that was clipped on the front of her belt. "We think that you may be able to help us with one of our cases."

"Certainly, Detectives, and how may I help you?"

"Did you know a Mark Rawlings?"

The old man stood for a moment. "I haven't heard that man's name for a long time, Detective. He used to be one of my golfing partners, ah … maybe fifteen years ago now. Someone murdered him, you know!" the old man said as he raised his eye brow.

"Yes, we know that he was shot. What can you tell us about him?"

"Hmm … we went to high school together and we both liked to play golf. We played together for years. He was a good golfer and was always able beat my game, but we made good golfing partners. We even won a trophy together once, I recall."

"Do you know anything about him having a child?"

"A child, oh my goodness no, he never said anything about that! I don't believe that he ever married and he kept to himself a lot. We talked about sports and golf mostly. He was doing quite well in his company but something happened and his company went out of business. He left some things here, and of course never picked them up."

"Things! What type of things?" Kelly asked, surprised, and glanced over at Simon who stood silently during the conversation.

"Oh, I'd have to look for them now. I've lots of stuff, as you see. It's been a long time, but I never throw out anything. I'm sure it's here somewhere," the man said as he scratched the side of his head.

"We'd love to see them. When can we return?"

"Oh … well, ah … let's see. Give me a few days," the man said looking pensive. "Will Friday be okay? I should be able to find Mark's things by then, I think."

"That's perfect. We'll be back on Friday. Thank you Mr. Catroppa."

The pair of detectives smiled at each other as they left the antique store. "Neat place. Can't wait for Friday!" Kelly exclaimed.

♓

Sandra Vaughn found the building address in East Vancouver that was on Edgar Logan's business card. It wasn't the best part of town but Sandra knew this area quite well from the time that she had lived on the streets. It was getting late, but the sun hadn't yet set behind the mountains and long shadows sprawled from the buildings across the street.

It wasn't difficult to find a parking space and she parked her red Fiat outside the building's red brick entrance. She entered the front and looked for Mr. Logan's office.

Forsythe Harrison waited until Sandra had entered the building, and then parked his silver Jag a block further down the street. He had been very concerned about her change in plans about skipping the sailing meet. It wasn't her nature to pass up on any sailing opportunity. He continued to think about her report to the police about Jako Palma and how scared she seemed. He had to ensure that she was safe and wanted to know the reason for her cancelled date.

Sandra found "Logan's Investigations" etched into the glass window of a small office on the second floor. She entered and noticed a stocky woman in her mid-forties with wiry red hair, sitting at an old steel desk scribbling some notes in a file folder.

"Oh … I'm looking for Edgar Logan," Sandra told her as the stocky woman looked up from her task. "I'm Sandra Vaughn and he's expecting me."

"Sure thing, honey. I'm Janice and he's in the office behind me. Just go in!" The woman smiled and eyed Sandra.

Edgar Logan was sitting behind his small wooden desk. He had dark eyes, wore heavy black-rimmed glasses and had brownish skin. His shirt collar was open. The office was hot, stuffy, and untidy.

"Take a seat please, Ms. Vaughn. I'm sorry about all the mystery but that's the nature of my business," Edgar said, looking up at the visitor.

"What's your interest in Judge DeWit and how does that concern me?" Sandra asked as she sat in an old uncomfortable chair.

"I've been investigating the Judge for some time. My client's name isn't important but we need some information that we believe is on Judge DeWit's iPhone®."

"Information on his cell phone! How do you expect that I'm going to get that for you, Mr. Logan?"

"I know about your regular arrangement with him on your Thursday night breaks. His wife has girls' night and he comes to play cards and be with you at the casino. I don't care about your business, Ms. Vaughn, but I need the information on that iPhone®," he said, peering over the top of his glasses.

"How do you plan for me to get this information without him knowing?"

"I've this little device." Edgar pulled out his desk drawer and placed on the desktop a small black box with a cord hanging out one end. "You plug this end into the iPhone® and when this small light turns green, you're done and can unplug the cord from the cell. Simple!"

"What does that thing do?"

"It has some electronics to copy and download all the data from the phone. It's very small and you should be able to hide it in your purse."

"What if I don't want to do this for you? It's an invasion of his privacy, and illegal!" she asked as she studied Logan's face.

"Well, there's ten grand to start, and I'm sure the cops would be interested in the extra type of business you girls are doing at the casino!" he paused and smiled. "Look, you find an opportunity tomorrow night. It takes less than one minute. You meet me here noon Friday with the data and I'll give you your cash and forget everything else. Simple." Edgar slid the device toward Sandra.

"I want fifteen grand. I don't like this stuff and messing with Mr. Palma's not a good idea, Mr. Logan. You want this so bad, then pay me for my risk."

"Look, it's a double deal. You get his cash for the hour and you get mine." Logan looked at her for a moment. "Okay, twelve grand."

"He'll know it was me!" Sandra exclaimed nervously as she glanced down at the small device on the desk.

"No, not a chance," Edgar replied.

Sandra snatched the black device and placed it into her purse. "One time! Cash, right?"

"Look. I've been doing this type of work for a long time. I do what I promise!"

"I sure hope so." Sandra quickly got up from her seat, turned, and left the office.

Forsythe sat fidgeting in his car as he didn't like the feeling he got from this neighborhood. He couldn't follow Sandra any further without being seen. He was worried and realized how much he really cared for her. Why else would he be worrying and following her if he didn't care?

He looked around, thought about their conversation, and wondered if they shared the same values. He had strong feelings for her, but wondered if their relationship really would work in the end. Was he being blinded by his heart? Was his head saying something else? He had lost touch with his gut instincts and was feeling overwhelmed and confused.

Forsythe saw Sandra exit the building and watched her small red car pull away from the curb. He didn't follow.

Chapter Sixteen

Kelly O'Brian drove into the parking lot at the *Westview Centre* to visit with her father. She told Simon that she needed a few hours to visit and to deliver some mail to him. The envelope had a return address of a law firm in the city and Kelly wondered why it had been sent to their old Marpole apartment.

Patrick O'Brian had just finished his breakfast and was sitting on the patio in the backyard. The receptionist to the area where many of the residents liked to enjoy the early morning summer day directed Kelly.

"Hi, Dad! How are you doing this morning?" Kelly smiled and took a seat next to her father.

He turned toward his visitor. "Hi, young lady. Good morning," he replied from a wooden deck chair where a blanket draped across his knees.

"You got some mail, Dad." Kelly showed her father the large envelope. "Let's see what's in it!"

Kelly tore open the end of the envelope and found a single-page letter and another sealed envelope inside. "Hmm ...." Kelly pulled out the single sheet of paper and read the letter out loud to her father.

Dear Mr. Patrick O'Brian:

I'm the acting solicitor for Mr. Charles Whitford. He has instructed me to execute his Last Will and Testament following his death. Mr. Whitford's wishes are very clear and his attached letter explains his rationale for the instructions that he has directed me to execute. Please contact my office at your earliest convenience.

"Dad, do you remember that Mr. Charles Whitford worked for your company *DigiCast*?" Kelly looked up from the short note with a frown on her face. "Charles Whitford," she uttered barely audible.

Patrick O'Brian didn't understand and Kelly knew that her father had no memory of any of those events. She sat dumbfounded at the lawyer's letter and pulled out the white envelope, placing the large one on the ground. Kelly opened the envelope that had been manually addressed to Patrick O'Brian.

She unfolded the letter and read it to her father.

Dear Patrick,

You must be receiving this letter as a result of my death. I trust you are in good health.

I don't know where to start, except that I am ashamed of what Mark Rawlings and I did to you and DigiCast. We were both very selfish and never considered the consequences of our actions. I have spent my entire life taking from others and breaching their trust. I can't change the past, but can try to do the right thing now. You are a trusting man and have always thought about others before yourself.

I'm sad to say that I don't know what happened to the funds that Mark and I took from DigiCast. Only Mark knew. I doubt they will ever be found. I tried to force Mark to tell me where he had hidden the money. Of course, I wanted it for myself. We had an argument at his house on Galiano Island and I shot him by accident in the heat of the argument.

I have instructed my attorney to leave you all my assets. It doesn't excuse my actions but may help you now. I have listed at the back of this letter all my bank accounts in Canada and the Grand Cayman Islands. The legal documentation held by my attorney shall be sufficient authority to gain access to those accounts

In closing, I can't apologize enough.

Regretfully,

Charles Whitford

Kelly sat stunned and silent with her father. Patrick had turned away from his daughter and stared at the peaceful backyard. "That was a sad letter!" Her dad said nothing else.

She hadn't fully processed what she had read and she sat with her father for a while. Both were silent. The letter had been shocking and filled her with sorrow.

Kelly decided not to tell Simon of the strange turn in events until she had talked to Whitford's lawyer.

♓

Vancouver detectives from the downtown precinct wanted to talk to Jako Palma and they wanted to see if they could flush him out in connection with the Zoric murder. Kelly and Simon were invited to come along; after all, they had provided the lead.

The four RCMP plain-clothes detectives showed their badges to the receptionist at the *West Coast Casino*, who called Security to escort the visitors to Jako's office on the nineteenth floor.

Peter Dobson, representing "Security," exited the elevator and approached the receptionist's counter.

Simon turned around, recognized Dobson and pulled his service Glock. "Freeze, Dobson!"

The other detectives turned and witnessed Dobson stop at the command.

"What's this about?" Peter asked.

"We've an APB on you. You're wanted for the murder of Marcel Bessier. Turn around!" Simon yelled, watching his suspect carefully.

Kelly pulled her handcuffs from the back of her belt, grabbed each of Peter's hands and yanked them behind the muscular tall blond man. She cuffed him and took his concealed weapon. She found a switchblade in his back pocket and took that weapon, too. Simon put his gun away and pulled his cell to call for a squad car to pick up Dobson.

"Looks like our lucky day, Simon!"

Deciding they no longer needed an escort, the two downtown detectives got the security code from Peter Dobson and took the elevator to the nineteenth floor.

Kelly looked at Simon. "They'll keep us in the loop and we can join them later. This guy's ours."

The West Vancouver squad car appeared outside the lobby; Simon and Kelly walked Dobson to the car and two uniformed officers placed him into the squad car's back seat.

"Book that guy for the murder of Marcel Bessier. We'll be back to the precinct shortly," Simon said and called Hollingsworth. "Hey, Captain. We caught a break. A car's bringing Dobson to West Van. We'll be there shortly and we've Dobson's weapon. The ballistics should prove to be interesting."

The pair of downtown detectives returned from their visit with Jako Palma and met Simon and Kelly outside.

"Jako's a pretty cool character! He wasn't very happy about Dobson's arrest, though. You could see it in his face. We'll keep a watch on him and see what move he makes now that we've pushed a few of his buttons. We'll keep in touch with you."

Everyone shook their heads, understanding the plan, and left the casino.

♓

Sandra Vaughn didn't feel very comfortable with her agreement. She liked the judge and he had been very good to her and she wondered how Forsythe would react if he knew what she was going to do. She definitely wanted to get out, and she definitely wanted Forsythe. How and when, were the questions that nagged her thoughts.

She hadn't gone out rowing yesterday and she still wasn't in the right frame of mind for it today either. She had gotten a sense that Forsythe might be questioning their relationship and she couldn't blame him if he was.

Sandra sat on the park bench outside her condo. Her father said that he would always be there for her, and she wondered what he would say if he knew that she wasn't the girl that he thought he had raised! She hated the mess that now had her trapped. If the investigation of Judge DeWit took any bad turn she certainly would be looking for a new job or worse yet, facing criminal charges. She hoped that Forsythe would be there in the crunch, but it was starting to look like an unrealistic expectation, at best.

♓

Simon and Kelly signed in. They registered their visit to the West Vancouver cell block. Peter Dobson sat in the first interrogation room; his lawyer was scheduled to arrive in less than ten minutes.

The pair of detectives joined Peter in the room and they sat down.

"We know your lawyer is being sent by Jako Palma and that he will be here soon. We want to offer you an opportunity to cooperate with us without interruption."

"What kind of cooperation?"

"We've got you cold on the Marcel Bessier murder. We know that you just followed Jako Palma's orders. Confirm that's how it went down and that'll likely help you when sentencing's delivered. It could be a good call by you but you've got very little time before your lawyer's here."

Peter Dobson sat and thought about the offer. "My lawyer may be my best opportunity."

"Murder One with undisputed evidence is tough to fight no matter how good your legal help is, Dobson," Simon said and pulled his cell phone from his pocket. "You likely have less than five minutes to decide," he checked the time display on the cell.

Peter looked at the two detectives. "Okay, okay. I've never been sloppy before, but I got careless and left some evidence behind this time. I work for Jako Palma and he called the shots and told me to waste Bessier. Bessier was into Jako for a large gambling debt and Palma got pissed when Bessier couldn't make his payment, so Palma had him eliminated. Bessier was jerking Jako around and stalling; Jako cuts a guy some slack only so long. It was just business!" Dobson growled.

"If someone else does the dirty work he can stay at arm's length! Now you've got the legal problem; I'm sure he'll be able to reach you in the slammer, too, so you'll have to give us more to nail him or you won't feel safe for a long time."

Peter's lawyer appeared in the room. "Don't say anything more, Mr. Dobson." The lawyer closed the door to the interrogation room. "You've rights and I'm here to help you."

"Ah, thank Mr. Jako. It's okay, I don't need you." Peter looked up at the man who stood at the doorway.

"Are you very sure, Mr. Dobson? Mr. Jako's very concerned about you!"

Dobson waved the man out of the room. "Tell Jako thanks, but no thanks."

"Give Mr. Palma our best!" Simon told the lawyer as he departed the interrogation room.

"Ah … you guys will find out anyway. The switch blade you took from me likely has the blood of Raj Jattan. Jako wanted RJ terminated and you'll find his body at a house on Bowen Island. Charles Whitford's place," Peter sighed. "Zoric was Jattan's guy and Jattan was buggin' Jako about some CD disk that he wanted Jako to find for him."

"A CD disk! What was so important about a CD disk?" Kelly exclaimed and glanced over at Simon.

"Buggered if I know, but Jattan was pushing Jako too hard and that really pissed Jako!"

"Do you have any proof that Jako contracted you to do that hit?"

"Proof!" Peter laughed. "Ya got to be kiddin'! There's no proof!"

"Any other hit that you know about that there may be some evidence around that ties Jako?"

"Hmm … well there was a meeting with Jako, Raj Jattan, Lothar Zoric and myself. One of Jako's girls, uh Sandra, was in the meeting and she called Bessier to meet with Jako and me to work out his gambling debt."

"Did Sandra hear anything concerning the order that he gave you to take Bessier out?"

"Nope. You might be able to get my cell phone calls to Jako and use those?"

"That's very thin but we'll still follow that up."

"Any connection with Palma and Lothar Zoric's murder concerning the bombing of the *Island Airways* plane destined for Galiano Island?" Kelly asked, knowing that there was.

Dobson sat quiet and thought about his response. "That was Jako. He thought that Zoric was a loose cannon and that he had to be eliminated. I just executed Jako's need to get the kid out of the picture; uh, Jako paid for the materials I used, though. You might get him through those purchases and make your connection that way!"

"Okay, we'll pass your info onto the DA and maybe you'll be cut some slack," Simon peered at the tall man. "Anything else?"

Peter Dobson only sat and said nothing more.

"Okay, then," Simon said and the two detectives left the interrogation room.

"We had him by the shorts and he knew it!" Simon smiled at Kelly. "We'd better look into the Jattan murder at Whitford's place. Hmm … I'll bet the CD we found was the one that Raj Jattan was looking for!"

The detectives reached their desk on the second floor and Kelly looked at Simon as he sat in his chair. "Simon, I haven't told you about my crazy morning with Dad," she said, feeling that she had to tell someone her astonishing news.

"Crazy?" He looked at her face as she continued to stand. "What crazy?"

"You're not going to believe this!" She took a breath and sat down in her office chair. "Dad received a letter that was sent to our old house in Marpole. I can't believe those people still had my forwarding address." She slowly exhaled. "Anyway, the letter was sent by Charles Whitford's lawyer. The letter inside said that Charles had instructed the lawyer to leave everything he had to Dad! He said that he was sorry for the things that he had done to Dad and *DigiCast*."

"You've got to be kidding!" Simon stared in disbelief, "Charles Whitford left everything to your dad?"

"No, I'm not kidding! The letter instructed Dad to call the lawyer who is looking after Charles' estate and to meet with him." Kelly shook her head. "There were bank account numbers on the back of Charles' letter and the lawyer said that the Will is very specific!"

Simon chuckled and rubbed his forehead as Kelly blurted out the thought that had been running through her head since she left *Westview*, "I guess the Whitford property on Bowen will belong to my dad! We can sell it and pay for his care. I don't know the extent of the estate but what a surprise, eh?"

"Surprise! I'm in shock! Do you want to go to Bowen with the team to check out the Raj Jattan story?"

"Maybe tomorrow once the ME has done his thing. I think we need to deal with Jako. Let's see the Captain," she said and took another breath to calm herself down. "I need to see that lawyer, too."

The pair gave Hollingsworth an edited version of the Dobson confession and Kelly told her boss about the Whitford letter.

"Is there a conflict of interest now, Captain?" Kelly inquired, worried that she'd have to remove herself from the Whitford case.

"I don't see any here, Kelly. Carry on, but I need to be kept current just in case. If there's any question in your mind about some conflict, pass the issue to Simon to deal with."

"Simon, why don't you check with the downtown boys and see what the best course of action with Jako Palma would be, based on Dobson's confession. Maybe it's their case, especially if the bomb materials can be connected to Jako."

"I'll talk to them, Captain." Simon pulled his cell from his pocket.

Kelly's cell rang as they sat in Hollingsworth office. "Hello, Detective O'Brian." She stepped from the office to take the call.

"Hey, Detective, it's Officer Hastings in Galiano."

"Ah yes, Officer Hastings."

"I've a couple of updates. You wanted to stay in the loop, right?"

"Yes, that's right. Thanks for the courtesy," she replied and listened intensely.

"We've recovered the Bessier Bayliner at the marina at Whaler Bay on Galiano. We also have an RCMP detail from Saltspring Island watching the house on Cain Road. Nothing there yet to report. The Saltspring head office has also told us that there was a shooting at Arthur Fleming's house in Thieves Bay on Pender. Apparently you're looking into Mr. Fleming's affairs."

"What's the story on the shooting?"

"Mr. Fleming shot an intruder who had threatened his life, according to Fleming."

"Who was the victim?"

"A Mr. Terence Weiss, a guy that Fleming said he had put into the can fifteen years ago. Fleming claims self-defense."

"Ah. We suspected that Terence Weiss was still twisted about his incarceration caused by Fleming. Too bad it came to that! Where's Fleming now?"

"We had no reason to detain him. We assume he's still in Thieves Bay, Detective."

"Okay thanks. Keep me updated if something breaks at the Cain place," she said and returned to the Captain's office.

Simon hung up his cell phone as Kelly took her seat. "Downtown wants to stay with the Jako investigation. It's their program. They're going to arrest Jako today for the *Island Airways* bombing. They're confident that they can connect him to the plane bombing."

"Okay with me! We've our hands full already," Kelly said. "Officer Hastings from Galiano Island just called. Terence Weiss was killed by Arthur Fleming yesterday at Fleming's place. Fleming claimed self-defense."

"Weiss was a big man and very angry. Fleming's very lucky to have survived," Simon added.

"Okay, I've still got to follow up on that Whitford letter. Let's get back to our paperwork for now," Kelly remarked as she got out of her seat.

♓

The casino was buzzing with the news that Peter Dobson and Jako Palma had been arrested by the RCMP. Everyone was concerned that the situation would cause them to lose their jobs.

Sandra had been told by the business manager, Shaun Bourgeous, that everything would be worked out and that business was as usual. Her shift was about to begin and her poker table was filled by regulars. The events hadn't impacted the gambling, at least not yet.

The talk did send Sandra a message. Maybe her opportunity to get out was coming. "If Jako Palma remains in custody I could get out!" she was thinking as she saw Judge DeWit smiling at her from across the table. She smiled back. "Just do this Logan thing. Focus on that, because the Palma thing is a long shot!"

♓

The summer sun had disappeared behind the mountains on the north shore a number of hours before. The four RCMP officers remained buried in the bushes surrounding the Cain Road property and they had left their unmarked vehicles scattered far down the road. They had been watching Jordan Fisk pace around inside the house all day, obviously waiting for someone.

A Nordic Tug slowly slipped into the dock. Jordan had turned on the outside house and dock lights and ran toward the dock to help Arthur Fleming tie up the trawler.

"Hey Jordan, have ya been okay today?" Arthur said as the boat drifted toward the dock.

"No problem, Mr. Fleming. All quiet here."

"Our buyers should be here shortly. Let's go inside, wait, and grab a drink," Arthur suggested as he threw a line to Jordan.

The RCMP watched through their field glasses for another half an hour. The buzzing of the hand-held phones wasn't heard through the underbrush, but the sound of the approaching motor vessel alerted everyone. "Okay guys, something's going down. Stay focused." The comment was muffled by the dense vegetation.

A few minutes later, the large aluminum hull of a boat appeared with the pilot's station placed at the stern, leaving a large open deck; the metal hull reflected the dock lights in the night. The sky was clear but the darkness left most things in shadow.

Four men jumped from the low hull as the boat maneuvered into position in front of the trawler.

Arthur heard the scraping sound as the boat slipped along the edge of the dock and he left the house to meet the men as they tied up. Jordan watched from the picture window in the sitting room as Arthur spoke with one of the large figures on the dimly lit dock. The conversation was brief and the five people entered the sitting room.

"Okay Jordan, business has been concluded. Let's help these men load their cargo!"

Jordan eyed each visitor, who all had large black tattoos of widow spiders on their arms. They all wore armless tee shirts and were dressed in black. "Ah … yea, sure," Jordan said and led the men to the basement.

"Here it is. Let's get it loaded. We can't be here all night!" a gruff voice growled.

The parade of six men carried the wooden crates from the basement to the dock, stacking them beside the aluminum-hulled boat.

The RCMP spotted another boat slip toward the dock just as the men left the dock to grab another load of crates. Its engine had been shut off and the boat drifted alongside the aluminum-hulled boat in the darkness. None of the six men had heard the second boat arrive at the dock.

Four men slipped over the side of their boat and onto the aluminum boat, keeping very low as they worked their way across the open deck toward the wooden dock. They heard the returning six men grunting under the weight of the crates as the line of the six men appeared from the back door of the house. The air was still. The RCMP watched.

The second load of three crates was placed on the deck on top of the first three.

"Thanks boys, for your good work. We'll take that shipment now!" a man who had been sprawled out on the aluminum deck yelled as he stood up with a 9mm semi-automatic machine gun pointed at the group of six men on the wooden dock.

"The fuck ya will!" one of the Black Widows yelled loudly on the dock, drew his weapon and shot the man with the semi-automatic and then ducked behind the pile of wooden crates.

The atmosphere exploded, filled with the sound of firing automatic and handguns spraying bullets everywhere as men darted for cover in the darkness of the night. Some victims fell into the water from the boats and dock and others lay silent on the ground and in the nearby bushes. The initial barrage of firing guns subsided and the occasional individual burst of a weapon came from surviving targets seeking a vantage point or improved cover. Everyone was trapped outside. The backlight of the house made for easy targets of those on the dock and in the nearby bushes. The night became silent again.

The RCMP moved into covered vantage points while the two groups pinned to their positions by the dock and house lights watched each other. One of the RCMP officers grabbed a microphone.

"This is the RCMP! Drop your weapons. You can't escape. We've the area well surrounded. Drop your weapons now!" The night went quiet again. "You've one minute or we'll pick you off one at a time. Drop your weapons now!" the microphone voice blared into the darkness.

"Fuck you!" a voice screamed back from the aluminum boat with a gunshot aimed toward the microphone.

A barrage of RCMP bullets responded, spraying the area where the shot had been made.

"Okay," came a single voice from the aluminum boat. The sound of a weapon hitting the deck could be heard through the silence. A large man's hands rose from behind the pilot house and the beam of a flashlight lit his face.

"Okay, okay." Another voice came from the dock area. Two more sets of hands appeared over the cargo boxes that sat on the dock.

"We see three of you only. Anymore?" the RCMP microphone blared out.

"Just me!" The voice came from the man standing on the aluminum boat.

"Just us two here!" The voice came from a man standing behind the wooden crates.

"All of you stand absolutely still and don't move!" an officer with the bullhorn warned and two other officers appeared with their weapons trained on the three men standing with their hands up. The RCMP officers slowly entered the bloody battle zone, their eyes darting around for any others who might still be waiting in the dark. Each body was checked for a pulse. The weapons were removed and placed into a stack away from the captives.

"I've got one here with a pulse. He's the only one. Call for an ambulance!" one of the officers called out.

Three men lay dead on the dock and three had landed in the water but their bodies were not visible in the darkness. One of the officers climbed on the trawler and turned on the searchlight mounted on the top deck. The search revealed the three bodies floating on the water surface, slowly moving with the outgoing tide.

Young Jordan Fisk was being handcuffed. "I'm just a helper. I never had a gun! I worked for that man over there. Mr. Fleming told me what to do." Jordan pointed to one of the dead bodies lying beside a crate on the dock.

"We'll get everyone's statement later, kid," the officer said as the squad cars were brought into the driveway and the three uninjured captured men, including Jordan, were placed inside.

The injured fourth man died at the scene before the ambulance arrived.

♓

It was eleven and Sandra's relief had arrived to take over the next poker hand. The poker players knew that it was break time and half the players left the table.

Sandra checked with the desk and was told that Room E04 had her party waiting. She nervously checked her purse as the elevator travelled to the eighteenth floor. She was greeted with a large smile as the door to E04 opened.

"Come in, Sandra. I've already poured your wine."

Sandra entered the room, found a light blue $2,000 chip and a purple $500 chip on the dresser and she quickly scooped them into her purse. She placed the purse by the bed as she smiled at the judge.

"You look a little stressed tonight. I've been watching you," the thin man with an English accent remarked. "I know your tells!" he grinned.

"It's nothing," Sandra replied as her heart beat quickly. Motioning to the dress zipper, she asked, "You'll help me with that won't you?"

She turned to take the wine glass from the bedside table and she felt her dress zipper slide down her back. She pushed her unzipped dress off her shoulder and turned around to undo his pants. "Hmm … taking no time for a drink first tonight, huh?" she muttered as she kicked off her shoes and started to unbutton his dress shirt. They both were in their undergarments in no time.

"I'd like to do something different tonight, Anthony," she said seductively taking off her sexy bra and then took a sip from her wine as her bare breasts teased him.

He looked at her, wondering what she was going to suggest. "A plan to relieve that stress of yours maybe?" he asked as he ran his finger around her nipple.

"Ah … yea, that's right. Why don't you finish undressing in the bathroom and jump into the shower. I thought that a quick wet massage may heat things up first." She grinned and took another glassful of wine.

"Hmm … sounds devilish! What a great idea." He walked into the large bathroom and started the shower. Sandra heard him slide the glass door open. "I'm ready."

"I'll be there in a moment!" Sandra searched the man's pants, found the iPhone® and grabbed the special download device from her purse. She plugged it in as she had been instructed and the red light began flashing. "I'm just slipping out of these panties and I'll be with you in a sec!" she called out as she pulled down her black thong and peeked seductively around the bathroom door, flipping them into the shower. "I'm just giving you a moment to get things activated, ya know!"

She noticed the flashing light had turned green. She moved her nude body quickly, unplugged the device and ensured it was placed into the bottom of her purse. She grabbed the iPhone® and returned it to the pants pocket where she had found it. She reappeared naked by the bathroom door. "Ready for a wet one, Anthony?" She joined him in the shower.

Chapter Seventeen

It took a few days for Elizabeth Richardson to accept the fact that she was finally free from Marcel Bessier. She had to read the newspaper article numerous times to convince herself that it was true.

She was still afraid to return to her old self and her real identity as she had become comfortable in her new life. There was only one major reason that she would expose the truth of her faked drowning after all these years; it certainly wasn't Marcel's money or her celebrity as Joy Bessier, the artist.

Elizabeth had stayed up the night before and wrapped the painting that she had taken from the West Vancouver waterfront house. After all, it was her painting. It did have the Joy Bessier signature and that was part of who she was. Elizabeth had included a small note, which she had placed inside the frame.

She had addressed the painting to Kelly O'Brian, RCMP headquarters, West Vancouver, and she had looked up the address on Marine Drive and ensured the artwork was ready to be delivered.

Elizabeth had arranged for a courier to pick up the parcel from her work place at the *Chocolate Boutique* café. She was excited and nervous about the events that she knew would result from her gift.

♓

Kelly contacted Charles Whitford's solicitor and explained on the phone to the lawyer why it had taken a few days for her to learn about Charles' directive. She also discussed her father's condition and that she had the power of attorney to act on his behalf. They made an appointment for the following week to complete the necessary documentation so Charles' wishes could be carried out.

Simon was itching to return to Victor Catroppa's antique shop and waited for Kelly to return from making her phone call. "So … is Charles Whitford's letter legit?"

"Yep! I guess I've a few things to think about and the lawyer says the Will's being executed immediately and everything's in order," she replied, shaking her head in amazement.

"I've got the key that we found in the Cain Road house and I've got my notes on the combination numbers, too. Let's go and see what Mr. Catroppa's got for us."

"I'm coming!" Kelly was also excited and curious. "I sure hope Catroppa has been able to find Mark Rawlings' stuff!"

It was Friday morning and the traffic was always lighter downtown on Fridays. Many people take the day off in the summer and take an extended weekend. Kelly found a parking space on Dunbar Street.

The little doorbell announced the detectives' arrival. The elderly Italian man came from the back room and greeted them, "Ah, Detectives, good morning. I've got good news. I've gathered Mark Rawlings' things together for you. They're over here!"

The man walked around the cluttered antique shop and stopped in the back of the shop. "After Mark's death I moved his things to this back corner. They were his things and I had no right to sell them, even though I'm sure I could've."

The three stood by an old floor safe covered in dust. There was a small cardboard box sitting on top.

"It took a while to find the box; it was in the back on a shelf, buried behind things I'd bought to sell long ago," Victor said, grabbing the box and handing it to Simon. There wasn't very much inside, mainly old photographs.

"Hmm … there's not much in here! Is that all there was, just these photos?" Simon asked and handed the box to Kelly.

"Oh … I'm not sure. It's been a very long time. There's this safe of course."

"Mr. Catroppa, what do you know about this safe?" Kelly looked up from poking around in the small box.

"I've always kept it here for him. In the few years before his murder, he would periodically come and place things inside. I never knew what he put in there though. It wasn't any of my business so I left him alone when he visited. You know you need a key and the combination to open this thing and I don't have either, I'm afraid!"

"We think we have both, Mr. Catroppa." Simon pulled the silver-colored key from his wallet.

"I've always been curious as to what Mark had put inside. I guess I'll finally find out," Victor said as his eyes light up in anticipation.

"Let's hope so!" Kelly exclaimed anxiously.

"Kelly, this is yours. Here's the key." Simon handed over the key that was in the bag.

"Yours, young lady? Were you related to Mark?" Victor asked surprised.

"I believe so. It's a long story. I hope that this safe has some answers to the mystery though."

Simon pulled his notebook from his pocket and Kelly took the key from the plastic bag.

"Here goes!" Kelly knelt down on the old concrete floor of the shop, inserted the key and twisted it. "It turned!" she yelled out, her eyes wide with anticipation as she glanced up at Simon.

"Okay, ready?" Simon looked at his partner. "The first number is twenty-six. Turn the dial completely around at least twice to the right and stop at twenty-six."

"Okay, twenty-six." Kelly turned the dial. It was stiff and took some effort to rotate. "Okay," she said as the number appeared beside the marker above the dial.

"Now turn the dial left, once all the way around, then on the second time stop on thirteen."

Kelly was careful to turn the dial slowly. "Okay, thirteen."

"Now turn right and stop at sixty-nine."

Kelly turned the dial halfway around and stopped. She took a deep breath. "Okay, sixty-nine!"

Everyone looked at each other as the dial rested with the number sixty-nine at the marker.

"Push the chrome lever down," Simon instructed.

The lever moved! The safe door opened a crack.

"Oh my God! It worked!" she screamed and pulled the heavy safe door fully open. The three curious heads looked inside.

The large old banker's safe had three shelves. They were full.

The first shelf was stacked with bills of cash. The second shelf had a pile of papers. Kelly pulled them out and placed them on the floor. "Simon, these are bearer bonds. This must be the embezzled money from *DigiCast*!" she exclaimed and quickly thumbed though the pile of certificates.

"Humph!" she muttered and turned her attention to the third shelf that contained an assortment of loose papers. She pulled the first paper out and unfolded the document. "This is the deed to the Cain Point Road house on Galiano Island. It's in the name of Marriam Tremblay." She handed it up to Simon.

"We already figured that. Maybe there's a clue in there as to why Mark had that certificate," he said and placed it on top of the open safe.

Kelly pulled an envelope from the third shelf and extracted the documents that were inside.

"It's an adoption document!" Kelly couldn't believe what she had read. She sat shocked and passed the paper up to Simon.

"It's the adoption of a Marriam Tremblay by," Simon turned to Kelly, "… Patrick and Rosalyn O'Brian." The room was silent. "The document's signed by the parents, Mark Rawlings and Joy Tremblay."

Kelly sat beside the safe. She didn't say a word, just silently began to cry; tears formed and dribbled down her cheek. "I always suspected that Rosalyn wasn't my real mother." Kelly trembled and sniffled. "I always thought my dad was Patrick, though." Tears flowed as she hung her head. "I don't get why all the secrets! Why not just tell me?" She stopped crying and wiped the tears from her face. "It looks like I'll never know the whole story!"

"Patrick's your father, KO! He raised you and a piece of paper will never change that," Simon tried to comfort her.

"Mr. Catroppa, can you get us a bag so we can gather all this up and take it to the office? You can work with me to log everything if you don't mind," Simon asked as he lifted Kelly from the floor. He took her to the back room and found a chair. "Sit here until I get everything taken care of out there. Okay?"

Kelly nodded her head and sat silently as Simon returned to log the contents of the safe with Victor.

♓

Sandra met Edgar Logan as agreed at noon in his office. She slid the iPhone® copy device on his desktop. "Here you go, as agreed! Got my cash?" she asked stiffly.

Edgar grinned. "Good work, Sandra. I knew that you could do it!" He plugged the device into his computer and verified that the information was there. "I just had to check that this wasn't empty!" He opened his drawer and gave her an envelope. "I always keep my promises."

Sandra checked that the agreed twelve grand was all there. "This is the one and only time, Mr. Logan! Remember to forget everything else, too." She paused, "Never talk to me again!" She turned and left the office.

♓

Simon's cell rang as the pair of detectives drove back to the precinct from the antique shop. Simon picked up the call and listened. "Okay, thanks!"

He turned to face Kelly as she sat silently driving back to the office. "The medical examiner's finished his report from the Whitford place. They did find Raj Jattan murdered and have finished processing the scene. We'll have the report when we get back."

Kelly hadn't said anything since they left the antique shop. The drive was unusually quiet the rest of the trip back to the office, where the detectives returned to their desks and Simon placed the safe contents on his desk. "I'll take this to the evidence locker and I'll be right back," Simon said as he turned to leave.

"Hey, Detective O'Brian, there's a package here for you." Captain Hollingsworth motioned her into his office. "It arrived by courier while you were out. It's addressed to you—I signed for it." He handed her the brown paper-wrapped parcel.

She sighed, her face still red from crying. "Thanks Cap." She took it from him and placed it on her desk.

"Get a gift? It must be your lucky day!" Simon joined her at their desks.

"Lucky day! Humph … I don't know about that!" she grumbled with a sad voice and found her seat. "There's no name indicating who sent this," Kelly said checking the package. "Strange, but what else is new?"

She pulled away the brown paper from the parcel. "It's a painting!" she exclaimed with a frown.

Simon picked up the note that had fallen onto the floor. "KO, you missed this note. It says, 'See me any day after two p.m. Elizabeth Richardson.'" Looking up at Kelly, he added, "It has an address on Bowen Island."

"Simon, the painting's signed Joy Bessier!" Kelly said looking confused.

"Joy Bessier! Now that's interesting. Let's go tomorrow and take Hunter. We can make a day of the trip." Simon thought that it would be best to accompany Kelly. Anything might happen and she might need a friend.

♓

Edgar Logan and his assistant Janice headed toward Judge Anthony DeWit's private chambers. Edgar wore an *InCourt IT Services* jacket and his assistant carried a small black bag with the same name stenciled on the exterior in white. It was noon, and Edgar knew the office routine and the Judge's habits: he usually took his secretary for lunch on Fridays. The office would be vacant for over an hour.

Janice watched the entrance to the office as Edgar picked the lock. They entered and closed the door. They posed as computer systems repair personnel for the Courts Building so they didn't look out of place. Edgar had transferred all the information from the Judge's iPhone® onto a small thumb drive. He inserted the small device into the office computer that sat under the judge's desk. The screensaver password was presented. Edgar had retrieved the password from the iPhone® and he entered it into the computer screen. The password message cleared and Edgar quickly searched the private files after entering another file password. He quickly copied all the files onto the small USB drive, withdrew the device and returned the machine to its initial state.

He and Janice were finished within one minute and vacated the office. No one had noticed them and they left the Courts Building and headed back to Edgar's office in the East End. He hoped that the files contained what his client was looking for.

"Okay Janice, let's see what we got," Edgar said as they entered his office. He plugged the flash drive into his computer and tried to open a file.

Each file was encrypted and Edgar used a specialized software routine that simulated the encryption and presented the information in a readable format. Detailed records concerning funds transfers and tampered judgments confirmed the allegations that Edgar's client had expected.

Edgar smiled and picked up his phone. "Hey it's me. I got what you wanted. I have it all! Where do you want to meet to conclude our arrangement?" Edgar scribbled down the address and time. "Okay, see you then." He smiled at Janice. "It looks like bonus time! Let's get a late lunch."

♓

Kelly O'Brian's cell phone rang.

"Detective O'Brian, it's Officer Hastings calling," the caller announced.

"Yes, Officer. How's Galiano today?"

"Perfect day." The caller paused. "We had a major event at your Cain Road house last night."

"A major event. What kind of event?"

"There was a gun transfer taking place and a shooting war broke out between the *Los Chinche* and *Black Widow* gangs. They've been at war for years. Anyway, it appears as though

Arthur Fleming was running guns and selling them to the *Black Widows.* The *Los Chinche* must've gotten tipped off and tried to seize the guns for themselves."

"Ah … I knew that something was going on at that house!" Kelly remarked.

"It's good we had four officers there! It was a blood bath. We captured three and seven died, including Fleming."

"Are any of the three talking?"

"We got the basic information I've told you from the single *Los Chinche* survivor. The *Black Widow* soldier hasn't said anything. The kid with Fleming, a Jordan Fisk, says that he was hired only to help with handling the shipment. He says that he didn't know what was in the crates. We recovered the entire shipment of weapons—lots of big stuff."

"Thanks, Officer. Send me a copy of the full reports when you have them prepared, please." Kelly requested and looked up from her desk. "Simon, Fleming's dead. Some gun war at the Cain house."

"That explains what Fleming was doing with the house! He was using it as a transfer station. Perfect cover." He paused and smiled. "Great idea to have that place watched, KO!"

♓

Forsythe Harrison received a message on his answering machine to meet Sandra at the casino for her eleven o'clock break. He was still struggling with his emotions concerning Sandra, and wasn't sure that he was ready to talk to her. He decided to hear what she had to say. It might help him work through his confused state.

He arrived early at the casino and sat at the bar drinking a beer. He saw her working at the poker table across the room. She was beautiful.

Her relief appeared and took over the poker table and half the players took the break. That was common and Forsythe had seen that happen before. He didn't blame the men for wanting to spend their time while Sandra served the cards. He'd do the same thing.

Sandra joined Forsythe, took the bar stool beside him and ordered a cold white wine. "Hey I'm really happy that you showed. I wasn't sure that you would." She placed her hand on his that was resting on the bar.

The feel of her hand on his felt good. He smiled. "Of course I came."

"I couldn't wait any longer to tell you that I'm in love with you, Forsythe Harrison. I know that our relationship's the most important thing to me."

Forsythe turned and took her hand.

She continued, "I know some of my work here is disturbing and I don't want it to get in the way. I want to be with only you!" Her eyes searched for an acceptance in his face but she couldn't tell what he was thinking. "My boss, Jako Palma, was arrested yesterday afternoon," Sandra spoke very softly, almost a whisper. "I'm going to quit. Tonight will be my last night here. I wanted you to know."

Forsythe was about to respond and she placed her finger on his lips.

"Don't say anything. Think about what I have told you and I'll see you at the sailing club tomorrow." She smiled, "I've got to get ready to start my next shift soon. Please go now."

Sandra got off the bar stool and walked toward the washrooms.

Chapter Eighteen

Sandra Vaughn had been awake all night. She couldn't get Forsythe from her thoughts and she hoped that she hadn't lost him. She knew that it was shocking for him to know that she had been with men for money. She knew that even her heritage may be a concern as she thought about their relationship going forward.

She was still stressed about Jako Palma, too. She knew that the cops would likely not be able to hold him for very long. He was a wealthy and powerful man and he likely had very effective lawyers. She didn't know if her role in the murder of Marcel was anything to worry about either.

Sandra was exhausted from thinking about everything. She couldn't tell her father—there was too much to say and now wasn't the time. She was alone and had to work through things by herself.

She sat in her scull, reviewing all that had kept her awake all night, and allowed the boat to simply drift in Coal Harbour. It was early and the large cruise ships would soon begin to return from their Alaskan visit. There was a silence that took place only at this time of morning. She inhaled the fresh salty air and tried to calm her racing mind, hoping that things would work out.

♓

Kelly O'Brian had taken Hunter for an early run in Vanier Park. She had been up all night, tossing and turning. She had mixed feelings about her discoveries. She had finally discovered who she was, but the answer wasn't anything that she had expected. Her mother, Joy Tremblay, had drowned many years ago and her biological father was Mark Rawlings, an unethical man who had robbed her father, Patrick O'Brian. The discovery was devastating and she had cried frequently the night before while trying to come to terms with the revelations.

She thought about her father, Patrick, and couldn't understand why he hadn't told her of the adoption. The mysterious clues to her identity and the missing *DigiCast* money nagged her. Her mind struggled with the bazaar realization that her biological father, Mark Rawlings, had destroyed the life of her adopting father, Patrick O'Brian.

Then who was Elizabeth Richardson and how did she fit into all this?

♓

It was Saturday morning and Forsythe Harrison often took his cycle out for a workout. His mind was jumbled with trying to separate his emotions from the facts about Sandra. His lawyer personality was the practical, logical, and calculating side of himself. His mind told him that a long-term relationship with Sandra wouldn't work, but his heart didn't agree.

He worried about her safety. He worried about other things that she may have not told him. He worried that it was just a physical attraction that couldn't last. He worried that he may not really know who she truly was. He also worried that he could lose her.

He suspected that Sandra would be at Coal Harbour; he rode his bicycle in the opposite direction.

Sandra needed to remind herself how things might have been. She needed to remind herself about her struggle. She needed a reality check.

She appeared at the food bank early and watched as the line of the less fortunate grew. Here everything was black and white. People did what they had to do to survive. It wasn't pleasant, and she had, in the past, been there many times herself. She had found the strength to move on and make a better life. It was time for her to move on once again.

She went inside to stand on the other side of the long lines.

♓

Kelly put on a nice summer dress. She didn't want to visit Elizabeth Richardson as a detective. The delivered painting was personal, and most of this case had turned out to be personal. She wanted to be Kelly O'Brian today, at least in appearance;

she selected a large handbag and placed her badge and service pistol inside.

Hunter looked at her. "Okay, okay. I'm still a cop! Let's go. I promised Simon that I'd pick him up at the transit station by eleven."

"Good morning, all." Simon jumped into his familiar spot in the gray Taurus. "Are you feeling okay?"

"I'm a bit trashed to be honest. Didn't sleep well, but Hunter and I had a good long walk this morning. I think we both feel better," she said taking a quick glance at the dog in the back seat.

"You sure look stunning in that summer dress. You didn't have to dress up for me, you know!" Simon grinned, hoping to get Kelly to smile.

"I thought we could get to the island a little early, catch something to eat, and walk Hunter before we drive to uh, Smugglers Cove Road and meet this Elizabeth Richardson," Kelly said stiffly.

"Yea, make a day of it. Sounds great." Simon looked over at the driver. "You're going to have a lot to handle in the next while, with the properties and the *DigiCast* stuff. If you need help, you just let me know, okay?"

"Thanks Simon. I still can't believe that the place on Galiano Island is really mine! I really wonder why Mark Rawlings did that!"

"Huh, I'm blown away at the Charles Whitford confession and turning over everything to your dad! This is sure a case full of surprises! You know—you just never know what people live with."

The Richardson house was in a quiet part of north Bowen Island. Kelly hadn't said much during lunch. Snug Cove had been busy and the activity distracted Kelly from the nervousness she felt in her gut. She didn't want to admit it to Simon, but the past few days had been overwhelming. Her emotions had swung from excitement to sadness and disappointment. She was disappointed that Patrick O'Brian wasn't her biological father, even though he was truly her dad in every other way.

She was secretly glad that Simon volunteered to come along; she trusted him and with all the surprises, he was the one stable factor in her life.

They found the address; the small quaint home was inviting. All three climbed out of the car and Kelly rung the doorbell. A striking woman in her late forties came to the door wearing an artist smock. "Good afternoon, you must be Kelly O'Brian. I'm so excited to finally meet you," the woman said with a smile, but was inwardly feeling very stressed.

"This is my partner, Simon Chung, and Hunter, my companion."

"Please, come in. I thought that we could talk on the back patio. I've made some fresh lemonade." Elizabeth smiled and escorted her visitors through the kitchen and past the art studio. She had an unfinished oil painting on an easel.

Everyone took a seat. Hunter sat beside Kelly on the stone patio.

"I don't quite know where to start," Elizabeth said nervously. "It has taken me a long time to be able to have the strength to tell my story. I guess that I've many regrets in my life and I've experienced great joys, too. I hope that you'll understand." The woman looked directly at Kelly.

The air was silent. Simon sat still and studied his partner.

"The story begins before you were born. Your father, Patrick, and I were secret lovers," the woman said softly.

Kelly's eyes widened. She sat forward in her chair. "My father and you?"

"Yes, my dear, I'm really Joy Tremblay," the woman blurted out, almost in tears. "I was your father's office secretary at *DigiCast*. We had an affair and had our first romantic night together at Georgina Point. I became pregnant with you and your father didn't want anyone to know, especially Rosalyn."

"You're my mother! You were reported to have drowned seven years ago!"

"I'll get to that." The woman took a drink of her lemonade.

"I wanted to keep the baby, hoping that someday your father would leave Rosalyn. We concocted a story and Mark Rawlings agreed to help us. When you were born Mark agreed to register himself as the father. You became our daughter, Marriam Tremblay, and I became a single mother. Mark and I had nothing in common. Your father's society friends never knew."

"Rosalyn knew. When I was a child, I heard her say that I wasn't hers."

"Yes Kelly. Patrick didn't want me to be burdened with being a single mother and convinced Rosalyn to go along with your adoption, as he wanted so much to be your father. Patrick told Rosalyn that having you would bring joy to her life, as she hadn't been able to conceive. This way you would be brought up in a good home and be with your real father."

"Did Rosalyn know that I was his daughter?"

"Patrick never admitted it to her as far as I know. He didn't want to have a social scandal for Rosalyn to handle, but I believe that she really suspected the truth. It may've been one of the reasons for their divorce in the end. I suspect losing the business, the failed company and loss of everything, was the last straw for Rosalyn."

"The painting of the lighthouse was originally a gift from you to my father then?"

"Yes. It was intended to be a reminder of our first night together, and the beginning of your life. I did that painting after the failure of *DigiCast*. Mark and I remained friends, though in retrospect I believe that we remained friends so he could keep tabs on Patrick through me. I figured out about the embezzlement of the company's capital, but was afraid of Charles Whitford and kept everything to myself."

"Do you know why Rawlings transferred the Galiano house to me?"

"Mark became concerned that if the company failed, he would be liable as an owner and director to repay the banks and creditors. Putting the house in your name eliminated the risk that they would take the house. He still got the use of it though, which seemed good enough to him at the time. The ownership didn't matter as he had *DigiCast's* money, and no one knew where it was, not even Charles." She paused, "Well, except for me, of course."

"You obviously knew all about Rawlings' safe."

"He told me about the safe, the combination and where he hid the key. He wanted to keep the information from Charles Whitford. Charles started the entire scam, and Mark felt that he got manipulated. He wanted to stop, but Charles insisted that they both were in too far and it was too late to stop."

"I had intended for your father, Patrick, to figure out the clues I left on the painting. I never figured that he wouldn't have been curious. It seems that he just appreciated the painting for what it was."

"So what's your disappearance all about?"

"When your father got divorced and the company had failed, his only focus was looking after you; time had passed and restarting a relationship with me was not on his mind! I married Marcel a year later. I wanted a life, I wanted someone to love me, and I wanted to put the whole deception of your father and you behind me."

"So what was the problem? Marcel was a wealthy man and you must've loved him."

"Yes, for a short while. He gambled heavily. I had done well with my art and earned a good income. He wanted my money to pay his gambling debts and became very abusive when I refused to continue to fund his habit." She took a drink of her lemonade and then continued, "I got desperate to leave, but I was very frightened of Marcel. I had to turn to the only man I knew who I thought could help me."

"That must've been Charles Whitford!"

"That's right. Charles was a devious man, and he had connections. He promised to help me for a fee—Charles was all about money. We worked for months planning my escape and he got me my new identity as Elizabeth Richardson. I had time to create bank accounts and purchase this house as Elizabeth before we staged my death."

"Did Marcel ever figure out that you were still alive?"

"No, I don't think so, not until early this week. He was just happy to receive the life insurance money. I'm sure it fixed a lot of gambling debts back then. He was in no panic to miss that opportunity. I became really scared when Charles Whitford was murdered. Charles had insisted on keeping my ID when he exchanged it for my new ones as he said it was insurance for him. I knew where he had hidden it, so I returned to find it after his death. I didn't want Marcel to find out about Elizabeth! When I got into Charles' place all my ID was gone. I panicked, knowing someone had it and it proved that I wasn't dead. I hated the thought that Marcel would find out."

"How did that lead to Marcel finally realizing that you didn't drown?"

"I went back to our place in West Vancouver. I thought that he had no reason to change the house security codes, and I knew he kept a revolver and shells in our safe. I went to get the gun to protect myself, because I was sure that he would eventually show up."

"But he didn't show."

"No. He had no clue as to my new identity."

"How did you stage your death?"

"Oh … I had Charles teach me how to operate his boat and how to navigate in the dark. We practiced on days when Marcel was going to be at work all-day and go to the casino at night. Anyway, one night Marcel and I went to a party and I pretended to get intoxicated. I knew Marcel was in one of his moods so I picked a fight with him and took our Bayliner that was moored at our dock at the house. I was in full evening dress at the time."

"That took courage."

"I was scared to death and I took the boat to Charles' place. We drained most of the fuel from the yacht. He followed me in his boat and we went out into Collingwood Channel. No one else was there. We left the yacht's engine running; I climbed aboard his boat and we returned to Bowen Bay. The yacht eventually ran out of fuel, drifted around until someone spotted it in the morning."

She continued, "I'm sorry, Kelly. I couldn't expose my identity until I felt that I was safe from Marcel, no matter how long that took. I hope you can forgive me. You were my child and I let you go with someone else. That has been my biggest regret." The woman paused. "How's your father these days, Kelly?"

"He's in a care facility for Alzheimer's patients and he no longer has a memory of anything. I couldn't ask him for help in explaining your clues or his past with *DigiCast*. I had no idea of his struggle back then when all the troubles were taking place. Teenagers are far too self-focused," Kelly replied with tears in her eyes.

"We all are sometimes my dear, in different ways and at different times." Elizabeth smiled. "Would you take me to see him?"

"Yes, of course. Okay, tomorrow. I'd like that."

"Can you all stay for a while longer? I would like to hear all about you. I have so much to catch up on! I'll get more lemonade."

♓

Forsythe Harrison had been pacing around his apartment since he returned from his cycling workout. He finally came to grips with his struggle about Sandra and he decided what he was going to do. He wasn't sure how Sandra would handle his decision though.

He knew that Sandra made it a point to be early on sailing days. He wanted to be at the Kitsilano Club before she arrived. He didn't change for racing; it was not a day for racing and having fun. He took a deep breath and tried to relieve the tension.

The beach was crammed with Sabots. It was another perfect day for sailing. Forsythe knew Sandra had a passion for sailing and would be very upset that they weren't going to do it together today, but his mind wasn't on sailing. Sandra occupied his entire focus and he had to deal with only that.

He sat in the front lobby waiting for her to appear. She was late and he began to worry.

The Sabot races were about to begin. Sandra had said that she would be coming. The lobby was empty, as everyone was on the beach side watching the races. Forsythe sat alone. This wasn't how he expected the evening to begin. He thought about calling her, but decided to wait. He would know soon enough if she was coming. He could hear everyone yelling and screaming as the races started. He sat in silence waiting.

He turned and saw her in the distance, walking on the beach toward the club house. He was relieved that she had come. His heart started to pound as she approached.

"Hey, missing a partner are ya?" She smiled and looked steadily into his eyes as she stood directly in front of him.

"Anytime I'm with you, I'm not missing a partner. Interesting outfit for sailing!" He grinned, looking back directly at her.

"We'd make a pair the way we're dressed, eh? Walk with me." Sandra took his hand and they went down the beach away from the club.

"I've been thinking about us all day, Forsythe. I've searched my soul and checked with my heart." She took a deep breath and exhaled slowly. She took his other hand and faced him.

"I know I come from a background that is nothing like you know. I know I've done things that could never be understood let alone accepted by people close to you. All I know is that I want to be with you. That's all that matters for me. But it must matter to you, too!" she blurted out, almost blinded with the tears forming in her eyes.

Forsythe smiled, caressed her and kissed her. "I'm sure of only one thing. I love you and we can work through anything, together. We're a team." He pulled his hand from hers and reached into his pocket, staring into her eyes. "I want to be with you always. Be my partner always. Marry me, Sandra

Vaughn. Save me from not having you in my life." He opened the box, pulled a ring from the clasp, and placed it on her finger. "It matters to me. Only you matter to me."

Sandra looked at the diamond ring. "Yes, you're all I want, too. Yes, I'll marry you; forever we'll be partners and lovers." She kissed him as they stood on the beach.

They turned, taking each other's hands and walked in silence along the edge of English Bay.

The End

The Myth of Kukulkan

The next book in the Kelly O'Brian Series

This fictional detective mystery is set in Mexico City and Vancouver Canada, where Detective Kelly O'Brian gets involved in the unraveling of a 450-year-old Mayan puzzle.

A set of thirteen tokens, believed to have been made by King Kukulkan, the last King of the Mayan empire, were thought to contain clues to a mythical secret hiding place of the King.

Detective O'Brian and Detective Mendoza of the Mexican police force get involved in murder, deception and romance, as they work together to protect the ancient artifacts from organized crime and self interest groups.

See www.rushingtidemedia.com for more information about this novel or other Kelly O'Brian detective stories.

CPSIA information can be obtained at www.ICGtesting.com
Printed in the USA
LVOW11s1252040314

375882LV00001B/6/P